From INCIDENT AT EXETER:

"You could see clear as a bell. And it was right up above us, right over the car. The red light was very bright—like the color of a fire engine light that flashed. And it tilted. You couldn't see wings or anything. That's why I was sure it wasn't an airplane. It seemed to creep along. And when it left, it zoomed right off. It wasn't ten seconds in getting out of sight. And another funny thing happened that night . . . The field up on Shaw Hill. It seemed to light up. You know what a landing strip at an air base looks like? The colored lights that outline the runways and taxi strips on the field? Well, I saw a group of lights on this field that looked a little like that . . ."

Here is an extraordinary account of sixty respectable Americans who saw with their own eyes flying saucers over the United States.

Mad-Con May 9, 1987

INCIDENT
AT EXETER

JOHN G. FULLER

Unidentified
Flying Objects
Over America
Now

A BERKLEY MEDALLION BOOK
Published by G. P. Putnam's Sons
Distributed by Berkley Publishing Corporation

Preface

It was in mid-September of 1965 I learned of the incident at Exeter, a report which was interesting because it was on the official records of the police department, and verified by two officers of the department whose character, reliability and composure in crisis have been certified firmly by their superior officers. Further, the incident was observed by at least five people, at a distance and over a time period that allowed for clear and unmistakable observation.

Exeter lies in a surpassingly beautiful slice of southern New Hampshire, where the Atlantic, tall pine forests, and pre-Revolutionary homes have joined to create the background for a mystery—a mystery as fantastic and sweeping as the legend of Sleepy Hollow, mixed with the most vivid trappings of science fiction. A dozen miles to the northeast is Portsmouth, home of the naval base since 1800, and now host to the Pease Air Force Base. B-52 and B-47 jet bombers rumble out from the runways here on a constant 24-hour schedule. Off the coast nearby are the ghostly Isles of Shoals, neighbors to the shattered hull of the sunken atomic submarine, the *Thresher*.

Autumn here is brilliant; it hurts the eyes. You approach the town from the east through a colonnade of burnt orange and russet maples, past the Old Harrison House on Water Street, a historical relic of the eighteenth century, and continue on to the center of town. Here, where Front and Water streets merge is a stone bandstand, where the townspeople still gather on a summer evening for a brassy concert. Not far up the hill on Front Street is Phillips Exeter Academy, spawning ground for

Ivy League hopefuls. Just past the Academy is the Exeter Inn, a sleepy and docile hostelry, and haven for elderly gentility as well as for well-heeled parents when they come to visit their sons at school.

A dozen parking meters down from the stone bandstand on Water Street, the Exeter Police Department occupies a dwarf-size suite of rooms in a hulking brick monstrosity bearing the architectural scars of the industrial revolution.

There's a friendly informality about the police station, perhaps because its size creates an intimacy all its own. On the daytime shift, the desk is monitored by Mrs. Evelyn Oliver, a congenial and efficient lady who mans the radio microphone, dispatches patrol cars, and handles the office detail briskly and without fuss. Chief Richard Irvine, a handsome and somewhat laconic man, joins her in making the most of the cramped quarters and both have been puzzled and confused by the mystery plaguing the area. For the most part, the desk handles the usual type of routine that any New England town of 6,500 residents might face: high school pranks, an occasional drunk, a tavern brawl, a family fight, an unlocked warehouse, a prowler here and there, and a continuous dribble of automobile accident cases. The townspeople are either of sturdy Yankee yeoman stock, varied racial groups who settled in Exeter during the industrial revolution, or the academic cluster at the Phillips Academy.

It was nearly a month before I could clear my schedule after I learned of the case, and I arrived in New Hampshire on Wednesday, October 20, for an appointment with the officers involved, patrolmen Eugene Bertrand and David Hunt, of the Exeter Police Force. It was the beginning of a search which was to continue for many weeks, sometimes on the basis of an 18- or 20-hour day. The point of the search was to find the most logical possible explanation for a dramatic and unusual circumstance involving an Unidentified Flying Object, or UFO as the Air Force likes to call them.

If it had not been for the transistor tape recorder I carried, I would have had serious misgivings about completing the project. The reports that I recorded seemed so improbable, so other-worldly, that written notes alone might not have been enough to convince both the editors of *Look* Magazine and the publishers that over 60 people testified to what they saw with intensity and conviction.

But anyone listening to the many hours of taped interviews cannot doubt the sincerity or honesty of the people involved. Nor was there opportunity or desire for collusion, for many of those who testified were widely separated from each other. Several who experienced low-level encounters suffered genuine shock. They recalled it during the interviews with unself-conscious conviction which it would have been almost impossible to feign.

While the interviews in cold type cannot convey all this conviction, it is important to remember that it is there, underlining the fact that these conservative New England people are stating what they believe to be the whole truth.

All the dialogue in the book recounting these experiences is taken verbatim from the tapes.

This book was no sooner completed, when UFO reports began to break out in unprecedented numbers all over the country. After my research in Exeter, I was convinced that this would happen, surprised that it had not happened sooner. For the first time, the general press began treating the subject with respect.

I knew that Exeter was only a microcosm, a reflection of a story (the biggest newsbreak in history?) that was taking place, or bound to take place in increasing frequency all over the world. Since one reporter cannot hopscotch everywhere to track down an effective story, I decided to use Exeter because of a well-documented case there involving the police. It could have been any number of other places with similar reports.

When the now-famous Michigan cases broke in March, 1966, House Republican leader Gerald R. Ford formally requested a Congressional Investigation, and the wire services furnished front-page stories for the nationwide press. But when an Air Force investigation indicated that some of the sightings might be attributed to methane, or marsh gas, the press again backtracked and seized on this as a blanket explanation for the UFO phenomenon.

This distortion was deplored by Dr. J. Allen Hyneck, head of the Astronomy Department of Northwestern University, who himself had advanced the marsh gas theory.

In a letter to me on March 29, 1966, he wrote:

I am enclosing the actual press release I gave out at Detroit because I wanted you to have the full story. The release was not handled in the papers as released, which of course it rarely is.

You will note my insistance that the swamp sightings and their highly likely explanation does not constitute a blanket explanation for the UFO phenomenon. I'm afraid this point was missed, too.

In the official release so badly distorted by the press, Dr. Hyneck states:

The Air Force has asked me to make a statement of my findings to date. This I am happy to do, provided it is clearly understood that my statement will refer to two principal events as reported to me. . . . It does not cover the hundreds of unexplained reports. . . . I have not investigated those. . . . I have recommended in my capacity as Scientific Consultant (to the Air Force) that competent scientists quietly study such cases when evidence from responsible people appears to warrant such study. There may be much of potential value to science in such events. We know a very great deal more about the physical world in 1966 than we did in 1866—but, by the same token, the people in the year 2066 may regard us as very incomplete in our scientific knowledge. . . .

JOHN G. FULLER

Westport, Conn.
April, 1966

CHAPTER I

At 2:24 A.M. on September 3, 1965, Norman Muscarello, three weeks away from joining the Navy, plunged into the Exeter police station in a state of near shock. He was white, and shaking. Patrolman Reginald "Scratch" Toland, on duty at the desk, helped him light a cigarette before he calmed down enough to talk.

His story came out in bursts. He had been hitchhiking on Route 150 from Amesbury, Massachusetts, to his home in Exeter, a distance of twelve miles. The traffic was sparse, and he was forced to walk most of the way. By two that morning he reached Kensington, a few miles short of his home. Near an open field between two houses, the Thing, as he called it, came out of the sky directly toward him. It was as big as or bigger than a house. It appeared to be 80 to 90 feet in diameter, with brilliant, pulsating red lights around an apparent rim. It wobbled, yawed, and floated toward him. It made no noise whatever. When it seemed as if it was going to hit him, he dove down on the shallow shoulder of the road. Then the object appeared to back off slowly, and hovered directly over the roof of one of the houses. Finally, it backed off far enough for Muscarello to make a run for the house. He pounded on the door, screaming. No one answered.

At that moment, a car came by, moving in the direction of Exeter. He ran to the middle of the road and waved his arms frantically. A middle-aged couple drove him into Exeter and dropped him off at the police station.

The kid had calmed down a little now, although he kept lighting one cigarette after another.

"Look," said Muscarello. "I know you don't believe

9

me. I don't blame you. *But you got to send somebody back out there with me!"*

The kid persisted. Officer Toland, puzzled at first, was impressed by his sincerity. He kicked on the police radio and called in Cruiser #21.

Within five minutes, Patrolman Eugene Bertrand pulled into the station. Bertrand, an Air Force veteran during the Korean War, with air-to-air refueling experience on KC-97 tankers, reported an odd coincidence. An hour or so before, cruising near the overpass on Route 101, about two miles out of Exeter, he had come across a car parked on the bypass, a lone woman at the wheel. Trying to keep her composure, she had said that a huge, silent, airborne object had trailed her from the town of Epping, twelve miles away, only a few feet from her car. It had brilliant, flashing red lights. When she had reached the overpass, it suddenly took off at tremendous speed and disappeared among the stars.

"I thought she was a kook," Bertrand told Toland. "So I didn't even bother to radio in."

Toland turned to the kid with a little more interest. "This sound like the thing you saw?"

"Sounds exactly like it," said Muscarello.

It was nearly 3 A.M. when Patrolman Bertrand, still trying to calm Muscarello down, arrived back at the field along Route 150. The night was clear, moonless, and warm. Visibility was unlimited. There was no wind, and the stars were brilliant. Bertrand parked his cruiser near Tel. & Tel. Pole #668. He picked up the radio mike to call to Toland that he saw nothing at all, but that the youngster was still so tense about the situation he was going to walk out on the field with him to investigate further. "I'll be out of the cruiser for a few minutes," he said, "so if you don't get an answer on the radio, don't worry about it."

Bertrand and Muscarello walked down the sloping field in the dark, Bertrand probing the trees in the distance with his flashlight. About 100 yards away from the roadside was a corral, where the horses of the Carl Dining farm were kept. When they reached the fence, and still saw nothing, Bertrand tried to reassure the kid, explaining that it must have been a helicopter. Muscarello refused to be placated. He insisted that he was familiar with all types of conventional aircraft.

Then, as Bertrand turned his back to the corral to shine his light toward the tree line to the north, the horses at the Dining farm began to kick and whinny and bat at the sides of the barn and fence. Dogs in the nearby houses began howling. Muscarello let out a yell.

"I see it! I see it!" he screamed.

Bertrand reeled and looked toward the trees beyond the corral.

It was rising slowly from behind two tall pines: a brilliant, roundish object, without a sound. It came toward them like a leaf fluttering from a tree, wobbling and yawing as it moved. The entire area was bathed in brilliant red light. The white sides of Carl Dining's pre-Revolutionary saltbox house turned blood-red. The Russell house, a hundred yards away, turned the same color. Bertrand reached for his .38, then thought better of it and shoved it back in its holster. Muscarello froze in his tracks. Bertrand, afraid of infrared rays or radiation, grabbed the youngster, yanked him toward the cruiser.

Back at the Exeter police station, Scratch Toland was nearly blasted out of his chair by Bertrand's radio call. *"My God. I see the damn thing myself!"*

Under the half-protection of the cruiser roof, Bertrand and Muscarello watched the object hover. It was about 100 feet above them, about a football field's distance away. It was rocking back and forth on its axis, still absolutely silent. The pulsating red lights seemed to dim from left to right, then from right to left, in a 5-4-3-2-1, then 1-2-3-4-5 pattern, covering about two seconds for each cycle. It was hard to make out a definite shape because of the brilliance of the lights. "Like trying to describe a car with its headlights coming at you," is the way Bertrand puts it.

It hovered there, 100 feet above the field, for several minutes. Still no noise, except for the horses and dogs. Then, slowly, it began to move away, eastward, toward Hampton. Its movement was erratic, defying all conventional aerodynamic patterns. "It darted," says Bertrand. "It could turn on a dime. Then it would slow down."

At that moment Patrolman David Hunt, in Cruiser #20, pulled up by the pole. He had heard the radio

11

conversations between Bertrand and Toland at the desk, and had scrambled out to the scene. Bertrand jumped out to join Hunt at the edge of the field.

"I could see that fluttering movement," Hunt says. "It was going from left to right, between the tops of two big trees. I could see those pulsating lights. I could hear those horses kicking out in the barn there. Those dogs were really howling. Then it started moving, slow-like, across the tops of the trees, just above the trees. It was rocking when it did this. A creepy type of look. Airplanes don't do this. After it moved out of sight, toward Hampton, toward the ocean, we waited awhile. A B-47 came over. You could tell the difference. There was no comparison."

Within moments after the object slid over the trees and out of sight of Bertrand, Hunt and Muscarello, Scratch Toland took a call at the desk from an Exeter night operator.

"She was all excited," says Toland. "Some man had just called her, and she traced the call to one of them outside booths in Hampton, and he was so hysterical he could hardly talk straight. He told her that a flying saucer came right at him, but before he could finish, he was cut off. I got on the phone and called the Hampton police, and they notified the Pease Air Force Base."

The blotter of the Hampton Police Department covers the story tartly:

Sept. 3, 1965: 3 A.M. Exeter Police Dept. reports unidentified flying object in that area. Units 2, 4 and Pease Air Force alerted. At 3:17 A.M., received a call from Exeter operator and Officer Toland. Advised that a male subject called and asked for police department, further stating that call was in re: a large, unidentified flying object, but call was cut off. Call received from a Hampton pay phone, location unknown.

At 4:30 A.M. that morning, Mrs. Dolores Gazda, 205½ Front Street, Exeter, and mother of Norman Muscarello from a previous marriage, was in her own words "pretty shook up." Without a phone, she had had no word from her son since early the previous evening. Nervous and wakeful, she watched the police cruiser pull up outside her second-floor flat, where she keeps a spotlessly clean apartment in the face of a restricted budget. She ran to the outside wooden stairs, and watched officers Bertrand and Hunt escort her son up.

"You know what a shock this could be to a mother," she says. "And of course I could hardly believe this fantastic story. It wasn't until I talked to the two police officers that I knew what they went through. When he came in with the police, he was white. White as a ghost. I knew he couldn't be putting me on. Thank God the police saw it with him. People might never believe him."

By 8 A.M. that morning, Patrolman Bertrand returned to his modest clapboard home on, oddly enough, Pick-pocket Road. His attractive young wife, Dorothy, was dressing the children and straightening up the house.

"When Gene came in the door," she says, "I knew right away that something unusual had happened. He said that I wouldn't believe what he saw during the night, and then he told me about it. And I still didn't believe him. Until after all the reports came in."

For days afterward, whenever he went to bed Bertrand would think about it. "It's a startling thing," he says, "and you think about it because you wonder what it is. Your mind imagines the impossible. The world is going so fast that it could be something from outer space. It makes you wonder, it really does. Dave and I talk about it often. I get the feeling from him that he doesn't think it belongs to the Air Force. I want to keep my mind open. Look for a reasonable explanation. But then, as I look back in my mind again, I wonder. When I first heard the kid tell about it, I thought it must have been a plane. But the more he talked, I knew it couldn't be one. Then I was sure he was talking about a helicopter. I did ask him on that four-mile ride out to the place, did you feel any wind? I know from a helicopter, he's bound to feel some wind from it. But he said he didn't. I thought he might have got scared, and was mistaken. When we watched it, Dave and I and the kid tried to listen, to hear a motor. We did everything to check it out. We weren't believing our eyes. Your mind is telling you this can't be true, and yet you're seeing it. So you check out your eyes to make sure you're seeing what you're really seeing. We just couldn't come up with an answer. I kept telling Dave, what is that, Dave? What do you think? He'd say, I don't know. I had never seen an aircraft like that before, and I know damn well they haven't changed that much since I was in the service."

Lt. Warren Cottrell was on the desk at 8 o'clock that morning. He read Bertrand's report, a rough piece of yellow manuscript paper hunt-and-pecked as a supplement to the regular blotter. It read:

> At 2:27 A.M., Officer Toland on duty at the desk called me into the station. Norman J. Muscarello, 205½ Front Street, was in the station and he was upset.
> He had told Officer Toland that on the way home from Amesbury, Mass., in Kensington, N.H., while walking along Rt. 150 an unidentified flying object came out of the sky with red lights on it.
> He got down on the road so that it would not get him. Officer Toland sent me to this place where Muscarello had seen this thing.
> The place was a field near Tel. and Tel. Pole #668 on Rt. 150. I did not see anything.
> I got out of the cruiser and went into the field and all of a sudden this thing came at me at about 100 feet off the ground with red lights going back and forth. Officer Hunt got there and also saw this thing. It had no motor and came through the air like a leaf falling from the tree. By the time Hunt got to this field, the UFO had gone over the trees, but he saw it.
>
> (Signed) PTL. E. BERTRAND

Cottrell called the Pease Air Force Base to reconfirm the incident, and by one in the afternoon, Major Thomas Griffin and Lt. Alan Brandt arrived. They went to the scene of the sighting, interviewed Bertrand, Hunt and Muscarello at length, and returned to the base with little comment. They were interested and serious.

By nightfall that evening, a long series of phone calls began coming into the police station, many from people who had distrusted their own senses in previous sightings before the police report.

Nightfall also marked the beginning of a three-week nightly vigil by Muscarello, his mother, and several friends. In the short time left before he was to go to the Great Lakes Naval Training Station, he was determined to see it again. He did.

CHAPTER II

On the morning of September 14, 1965, some eleven days after officers Bertrand and Hunt had filed their report, I was faced with a deadline for the regular column I write for the *Saturday Review*. At this time, I knew nothing about the incident at Exeter and little, if anything, about Unidentified Flying Objects. At one time several years before, I had helped produce a CBS-TV show which had, as guests, some technicians who had sighted UFOs—but that was the extent of my knowledge. As usual, I began the slow, painful search through the mass of undecipherable notes and clippings, kept in the deep, lower-right desk drawer, in the search for column material.

The material was not very promising: a stack of routine, boiler-plate releases on forthcoming books, a few notes scrawled on the backs of envelopes and match covers, notes on an interview with two authors which had turned out to be insufferably dull, and a pile of news clippings marked for follow-up. Clippings often provide the source material for good copy, solely because news stories come and go fleetingly, and are never heard from again. Yet some of them are tantalizing, whetting the curiosity without satisfying it. Additional investigation often reveals a better story than the original.

One of the clippings in the file was an AP dispatch from *The New York Times* of August 3, 1965, over a month old. The dateline was Oklahoma City:

Authorities in Texas, New Mexico, Oklahoma and Kansas were deluged last night and early today by reports of unidentified objects seen flying in the sky.

The Sedgwick County sheriff's office at Wichita, Kansas, said the Weather Bureau had tracked "several of them at altitudes of 6,000 to 9,000 feet."

The Oklahoma Highway Patrol said that Tinker Air Force Base here had tracked four of the unidentified flying objects on its radar screen at one time, estimating their altitude at about 22,000 feet. A Tinker spokesman refused to confirm or deny the reports of radar observations.

Reports poured in from Pecos, Monahans, Odessa, Midland, Fort Worth, Canyon and Dalhard, Tex.; Hobbs, Carlsbad and Artesia, N. Mex.; Chickasha, Shawnee, Cushing, Guymon and Chandler, Okla.; and Oxford, Belle Plaine, Winfield, Caldwell, Mulvane and Wichita, Kan.

The Oklahoma Highway Patrol said police officers in three different patrol cars had reported watching the objects fly in a diamond-shaped formation for about 30 minutes in the Shawnee area. The patrol said the officers had described the objects as changing in color from red to white to blue-green.

At 3:40 A.M., the Weather Bureau at Wichita said it had tracked one of the objects south and west of Wellington. The bureau said the object had first appeared on its radar at an altitude of about 22,000 feet and had then descended to 4,000 feet.

Descriptions telephoned to the police and other authorities included these:

"I was a disbeliever, but I saw something up there tonight, and so did other observers at the Weather Bureau."

"They were red and exploded in a shower of sparks and at other times, floated like a leaf."

"You could see it with the naked eye. It looked like it was on the ground or hovering just above the ground. It was red, greenish, blue and yellowish white, about 100 yards long and egg-shaped."

Spokesmen at Tinker and McConnell Air Force bases are referring all queries to the Air Force in Washington. In the past, the Air Force has said the sightings have turned out to be such things as balloons, birds, searchlights, jet exhaust, kites, meteors, missiles.

As of last July 20, the Air Force had checked out 9,127 such sightings since 1947 with 667 still unidentified.

I had clipped the item, first because it had appeared in *The New York Times*, which is very reluctant to print stories of Unidentified Flying Objects. Second, the sightings seemed to be much more heavily documented than the usual report of this sort of thing: three different pa-

16

trol cars, weather observers, Air Force base and Weather Bureau radar. All this would seem to rule out hysteria, illusion, or incompetence in observation. Fourth, I was curious about what the follow-up would be. Certainly with such complete documentation as this, there would be extensive discussion and comment, even in the pages of the august *Times*.

Little or nothing appeared after the original story, however. It was some weeks later that I decided it might make an interesting column to take a single isolated case of a UFO sighting and track it down to prove it out as either an illusion, a mistaken identity, or something which had to remain a mystery. It would, if nothing else, be an interesting space-age ghost story, and it was on this premise that I put in a long-distance call to the National Investigations Committee on Aerial Phenomena in Washington.

NICAP—as the organization is referred to in alphabetical shorthand—was set up in 1956 under the direction of Major Donald E. Keyhoe, USMC (Ret.). It is known for its conservative and technical approach to the subject. Among its Board of Governors and panel of special advisers are former Air Force officers, commercial airline pilots, engineers, technicians, clergymen, astronomers, retired naval officers, and NASA technicians. In the spring of 1964, it issued a scholarly and well-documented book titled *The UFO Evidence* which analyzes 746 reports from among 5,000 signed statements it has in its files. I had received a press copy of this volume when it was first published, well over a year before, but had never bothered to look at it. It was helpful now in locating the organization by phone, but I decided not to study it at this time to avoid developing any preconceived ideas. I wanted the column to be an objective report, uninfluenced by other opinions. I had often found in the past that it is better to come into a story with "intelligent ignorance," if you could call it that, plus a fair measure of friendly skepticism.

On the phone, Richard Hall, the Assistant Director of NICAP, was cooperative and helpful. "We've got a tremendous number of reports on these Southwest sightings," he said, "but the newspapers dropped them fast. The main case—the one involving the Tinker Air Force

Base—was at first reported as a confirmed radar-and-visual sighting. Now the Air Force has come along and singled that case out to say that their radar did *not* confirm the visual sightings of the Oklahoma Highway Patrol. But we're used to this."

I asked Hall why.

"The Air Force is constantly trying to knock down all UFO reports," he said. "They've clamped down the lid, and issued denials of reliable reports repeatedly. This is our big battle. For instance, we've got information to contradict the Air Force denial here. It's a nine-page report of the Oklahoma Department of Public Safety, outlining a sighting by the police, and confirmed by the Carswell Air Force Base radar. And the reports are still going on. Reports from all over."

"Could you give me some examples?" I asked.

"Well," he said, "on September third—just a week or so ago—there were two extreme low-level sightings reported to us. One in Exeter, New Hampshire; the other southeast of Houston, Texas. Both of them are police reports, so we can count on them at least being fairly reliable. In the Texas story, two policemen from Angleton started to investigate a large object which had landed in a field. When it moved toward them, they jumped back in their car and drove off fast."

"What about the Exeter case?" I asked.

He gave me a brief summary of officers Bertrand and Hunt and their story. I made a note to contact their New England subcommittee member, a Mr. Raymond Fowler, who was a technician with Sylvania Electric's Minute Man Program.

"What else have you run into lately?" I asked.

"About a month ago," Hall said, "as a matter of fact, on August fifteenth, two coastguardsmen in Virginia reported an elliptical object hovering near a radio antenna. It was a more-or-less featureless egg-shaped object, according to them, and it took off rapidly after a few moments."

I decided to confine myself to recent reports from competent observers, preferably at low level. This would at least help to rule out mistaken identity as far as high-flying planes, meteors, planets or reflections were concerned. According to Hall, a rash of sightings began in July in Antarctica. Technical and scientific teams from Argentina, Chile, and Great Britain had reported a perfect disk hovering about their stations on July 3. Similar sightings were reported in the Azores. During August, a former Air Force flight instructor, a Costa Rica control tower operator, and a weather observer saw such an object at close range. In the same month, a missile engineering analyst, Francis C. Jennings of Seattle, Washington, filed a detailed report, as well as a U.S. Forest Service officer in a lookout tower in Idaho. On August 3, five police officers in Cocoa, Florida, observed four objects in diamond-shaped formation. And on August 19, in Cherry Creek, New York, near Buffalo, New York State Police thoroughly investigated a landing of a UFO, reliably reported, which left a bluish substance staining the ground.

Hall was obviously intelligent, analytical, and serious. But to adjust from ordinary journalism to the other-worldliness of this subject is not easy. Adjustment is not even desirable, because it would tend to diminish objectivity.

"Tell me something," I asked Hall. "What is NICAP's position on all this?"

"You mean what are our conclusions?"

"Yes."

"Well," he said, "we have carefully considered all the evidence we have, and we support the hypothesis that UFOs are under intelligent control—and that some of them might be of extraterrestrial origin."

I reached Raymond Fowler, the New England sub-committee member, on the phone later in the day. He had, he told me, returned from Exeter, New Hampshire, a few days before, and had just filed an 18-page report to Washington which had probably not arrived there yet. He had obtained signed statements from both policemen involved, surveyed the area, and confirmed as much detail as possible about the sighting.

"I can't seem to find any holes in it," he said. "Both the officers are intelligent, capable, and seem to know what they're talking about. The sighting was near, and it was low. Bertrand's experience in Air Force refueling

19

makes him capable of discriminating between a UFO and anything else in the air, commercial or military."

We talked for nearly an hour as he read me portions of his report and I took down copious notes. For the amount of space in my column—only 1,000 words—I didn't plan to make a trip to Exeter. But I did intend to check out every possible fact by phone to make sure I was reporting material direct from the source, rather than hearsay. The call to Fowler was the first of seven. But the incident still had to be confirmed direct from the source, and it wasn't until after nearly three hours of long distance conversation that I was satisfied that I could report at least the available facts.

After confirming with the Exeter police desk that the story was officially on the blotter of September 3, 1965, I talked with Lt. Warren Cottrell, who told me that both Bertrand and Hunt were level-headed and calm, and not at all inclined to exaggerate. What's more, the station had been getting too many reports from too many reliable people to question the fact that *something* was being seen, and being seen regularly. "They're still coming in from all over," the lieutenant said. "And either you believe these people or call them nuts. Well, I know a lot of them, and they definitely are not nuts. They're good, quiet respectable people who wouldn't be inclined to go around making up yarns like this. Now take Bertrand, for instance. He's one of the toughest boys on the force. We send him out on all the rough jobs. Not afraid of anything. But boy, he was scared *this* time. I will say this—if only *one* of these boys saw this thing, I might have taken the live ammunition out of his gun. Or if I had any reason to doubt him and Hunt, I'd put 'em in the back room and give 'em some blocks to play with. And I'll tell you this much—if I had seen this thing, the way they describe it, and I was *alone*—nobody else would've ever heard about it."

A call to the Hampton, New Hampshire, police confirmed their side of the story: the hysterical, unidentified man in the phone booth, the report into the Pease Air Force Base. In addition, the officer on duty at the desk added: "We've been getting an awful lot of calls lately, and they seem to be responsible people. I don't really know what the heck is going on, but something is." Another call to the Manchester *Union Leader*, which covers a large area of New Hampshire, brought me in touch with James Bucknam, managing editor. He said that dozens of people in a wide area around Manchester (some 20 miles west of Exeter) had told him about UFO sightings, most of the reports being corroborated by more than one person. He read me the paper's coverage of the Bertrand-Hunt story, as written by their reporter who arrived in the Exeter police station shortly after the sighting. The details checked in substance with Fowler's more technical account, as did the story from the Exeter *News-Letter*.

I was unable to reach Patrolman David Hunt, but finally got through a call to Patrolman Eugene Bertrand, who patiently went through his story in detail. "I was sure this was a helicopter that the kid was describing. But when it come up from behind the trees, I knew right away that it wasn't a helicopter or any kind of craft I ever ran into. Then when it started coming at us, I kept wondering why we didn't feel any breeze from the blades, and *no sound*. No sound at all, that's what got me. No tail, no wings, no sound. All I can tell you is that it was definitely a craft, a big one, with the lights so bright that you couldn't make out the shape at all. And it was low. Not much over the treetops. . . ."

Muscarello, I learned, did not have a phone, and there was no other way to reach him in time for the deadline on the column. I sat back and went over my notes, scrawled on a dozen pages of yellow foolscap. The elements of the story were so sensational that it was important to document only those facts which had been confirmed first hand. I had talked to the NICAP representatives in both Washington and New England, two newspaper editors, the police lieutenant at Exeter, the Hampton police desk, and Bertrand himself. There was no doubt that these people took this thing seriously, and all seemed of better than average intelligence. Even though I had been warned that I would get little or no information from the Pease Air Force Base in Portsmouth, a dozen or so miles away from Exeter, I put in a call to the Public Information Office there and spoke with Sgt. Robert Szarvas. "About the only thing I can do," he said, "is to confirm the fact that there have been a large number of sightings reported to us. Some of them come from important and influential people, there's no doubt about that. Matter of fact, a wire service reporter for the UPI who's always been ribbing us about UFOs, told me, 'I hate to bring this up, but I saw one myself.'

"The Air Force has a set procedure, and our hands are tied for releasing any specific information. When we get a report on a UFO, we take down the information, send out a rated officer who gathers as much information as possible. This is sent along to Wright-Patterson Air Force Base in Dayton, where they have a team of scientists who evaluate all the reports that come in. They're supposed to come up with the answers, but any release of information is made directly from the Pentagon."

"How much information does the Pentagon release?" I asked him.

"Well," Sergeant Szarvas said, "I don't think it's so much censorship as it is that the local bases aren't able to supply as much competent information on the subject as the Wright-Patterson air base can supply."

As Richard Hall of NICAP had suggested, it looked as if the Air Force position was a one-way street.

CHAPTER III

I wrote the column with extreme care, giving the exact words of the persons involved in the incident at Exeter who had talked with me on the phone. I pointed out that State Police in Oklahoma, Texas, Kansas and New Mexico had risked their jobs and reputations for sanity in documenting a wide number of observations, as well as the two policemen in Exeter, New Hampshire.

The police aspect seemed significant. It is one thing to start an irresponsible rumor, or to report a fleeting glimpse of some kind of light or object in the sky which may be puzzling. But police officials in widely separated geographical areas are not likely to radio their superiors with detailed descriptions of their observations unless the evidence is almost overwhelming. Nor are weather observers and radar men. The very essence of their jobs depends on reliability for accurate observation. It was only because of the reliability of the witnesses and the extent of their observations that I could even consider writing about them.

In the face of this, it was hard to understand the attitude of the Government and the Air Force, as well as the scientific fraternity in general. Such authorities must maintain a very reserved and conservative approach to the subject. This is fully understandable. But indications seemed to be that the subject was totally ignored, tossed aside with a laugh, or downgraded to the status of mass illusion. And yet if there were even partial demonstrable truth to the reports, and to the theory that the earth was host to extraterrestrial visitors, it would become the biggest newsbreak in history.

Many of the letters from *Saturday Review* readers who read the column reflected puzzlement. A Mr. Ralph Newman, from Darien, Connecticut, wrote:

> Nobody is more bewildered than I am about this flying saucer matter. From the start of reading about strange objects over Sweden in 1946 and off and on in the press, including *The New York Times*, which is generally a believable paper, I keep thinking there must be some kind of *answer!*
>
> I am forever hearing of our government investigation departments on this matter as saying it's all so much mistaken identification (balloons, bright stars, etc.), or just so much hysteria, or plain falsehoods or fiction or hallucinations . . . or malarky.
>
> Your account of "following through to a conclusion" (you didn't seem to come to any conclusion in the column) was interesting. Who can doubt these policemen? And have you heard any more from these police, or sighting of odd objects in the sky from that area since you wrote the article?
>
> It certainly seems to me that if UFOs are hysteria, imaginary, and unreal objects, then why cannot a logical scientific authority *prove* this is so from a completely accepted viewpoint? After almost 20 years, I am unhappily having

the growing notion that UFOs are forever going to be in the same category as ghosts, haunted houses: We'll always hear of such vivid accounts, sightings . . . but never get the proof.

But golly, modern-day cops report such things! And so have other cops in recent times, airline pilots, too, sticking their necks out to report seeing the seemingly inexplicable. Though *True* Magazine is not my idea of sober writing, there is an interesting book condensation by Jacques Valée, a French mathematician connected with NASA, in the October issue. He writes so sincerely, as sincerely as your UFO item reads, but dammit, I just don't know what to believe.

All I can say is I urge you to print more, if you learn more on this UFO matter, in *Trade Winds*. Maybe you'll come up with the truth in the matter. . . .

His mood was reflected by many other readers. From North Texas State University, James Davidson wrote:

I was most interested—and depressed—with your article (*Saturday Review*, October 2, 1965). Clearly evident is the public attitude, fostered in part by the Air Force and a host of "scientific" writers, that has long plagued investigation of this interesting and very important subject.

You say the "skepticism is a healthy thing." True. But scientific bigotry is not. Far from being healthily skeptical, we are profoundly convinced that there just is no such thing as a UFO. And starting from this grand, self-evident proposition, we wisely deduce that anyone who does see one is either malicious, foolish, or innocently misguided— and probably feebleminded.

No one wants to be like that. Consequently, those who have seen UFOs often remain silent. Exceptions only confirm the wisdom of their decision: I recently saw a young man, who knew no better than to admit that he had seen a UFO, made the fool of the week on a television interview.

Of course national hysteria is a poor alternative. But is it not just possible that we are mature enough to listen to facts for a change?

Another letter, from P. S. Hensel in Cleveland, expressed similar feelings:

For the past 16 years, especially, thousands of sane humans, just as sane as the many police officers and airplane pilots and scientists around the world, have been seeing these things. But to the Air Force, they are hallucinations, flying stars, and planets. Dozens have seen UFOs of one type or another; many have faith in their fellow-men so that they do not deem them liars, fools.

I was impressed with the quality of the letters, none of them hysterical or crackpot. Madeline Moschenross, writing from Elizabeth, New Jersey, recounted an experience which she, as an obviously intelligent and levelheaded person, had gone through:

I feel much better now that I've read your column on UFOs. For back in 1950 or so, I called a top New Jersey newspaper to report what seemed more than a phenomenon, more than what even were called "flying saucers."

I was looking out a bedroom window in front of my home, after midnight, when my attention was drawn to a perfect circle the size of an extra-large child's balloon. It remained stationary for quite awhile, then moved as though propelled, then stopped again. I went to another bedroom to wake up a member of my family, but changed my mind. Supposing this thing wasn't there? An illusion? Returning to my own room, I noticed The Thing had progressed a little nearer, and possibly slightly lower. It remained a long time. I decided to go to bed after reading a bit. Sometime later, I moved on to the bathroom in the back of the house, looked out of the window and saw an amazing sight. A great circle of bright red (like a mammoth setting sun) was behind the leafless branches of some trees. How near the area in which I lived, I could not gauge. Again I hurried to waken the member of my family, but he didn't want to be roused. I don't know how long I watched the thing. I began to conjecture: the earth's movements are so mysterious, maybe this is some axis-turning sight only the few—the awake and the curious—are privileged to see. Like another world's setting. I went to bed—and as mentioned before, next morning informed the Newark *Evening News*. And of course, I was probably considered a nut.

From Alfred Rathmann, in Manitowoc, Wisconsin, came these questions:

From a strictly pragmatic point of view, I can't seem to see why scientists doubt the reports on sightings. Our own space program is rather impressive considering the short span of time that Homo sapiens has come out of the caves into the light of a sophisticated world.

I wonder if governments in general are keeping back facts on the total question of flying saucers? Could the fear of mass riots be the reason for the secrecy behind our own Air Force reports on UFOs? Reported radar sightings of UFOs are numerous. Reported sightings by qualified airline pilots, Air Force personnel, etc., are to be found in respected journals. I feel that a great deal of research on the subject would bring out a more logical ground to view all these sightings. Wouldn't you agree?

Frankly, at this point, I didn't know whether to agree or not. I knew that the only research which would satisfy me would be that taken direct from the source, without benefit of hearsay. The checking and rechecking on the incident at Exeter made it seem likely that something definite was to be learned there. But thorough as my inquiry was, it had been done entirely by phone. The mystery was challenging, as challenging as the conquest of Everest.

Early in October, I received a call from a Gordon Evans, an analyst and writer for a leading industrial institution. He had read the column, and was interested because it was a fresh, new case at low-level altitude supported by police testimony. He had spent a good many years analyzing the UFO subject, and offered further information. His call intrigued me because his approach to UFOs seemed literate, informed, and conservative. We arranged to have lunch on October 5.

Evans had some interesting theories. He contended that the Government knew all about UFOs, that they did exist, that they were interplanetary, and that an analysis of the evidence and action of the Government would lead logically to this conclusion.

"During the 1960's our final bill for space exploration could run over seventy billion dollars, and that's a conservative estimate," Evans said. "And when you stop to think about the reasons the Government tries to give for this massive outlay, they just don't add up. The so-called explanation is that it's part military, part economic, part scientific. 'Deep space' is practically useless as a military operation. They'd get much more military advantage from 'near space.' But most of the funds are going to be spent on lunar and planetary projects. Economic value? Another WPA or an increased war on poverty would do a much better job. Scientific? We've got enough problems here on earth to solve before we should take off for deep space—at least at this stepped-up pace, and with these budgets. Yet Congress is voting the funds, and the Government is spending them. And when you look at Russia's gross national product—much less than ours, and with a lot more economic planning—and then figure out how much *they're* spending on deep-space projects, it makes even *less* sense.

"Nobody's trying to say the people running the Government are idiots, or madmen. They're well aware how weak all this reasoning is. But they don't dare say anything else officially. The fact is that the earth is not the first in space by a long shot. And what the situation amounts to is that we're facing a half-voluntary censorship. As soon as any reliable expert begins to catch on, he's squashed on the basis that it's good for the people to be kept in the dark. The whole thing works out pretty neatly. This is what accounts for the paradox—a practically conclusive case for alien spacecraft hovering over the earth, and a seeming—only *seeming,* don't forget—lack of reputable scientific interest in the subject."

Evans also had a hunch—and he labeled it clearly as such—that the C.I.A. was making sure that any real news break-through would be very subtly sidetracked in a variety of ways. "There are a lot of really crackpot flying saucer groups in the country, as you know. Absolutely wild and irresponsible. And they put out these ridiculous newsletters which are so absurd you cannot understand how any human being would print them, and still stay out of the Laughing Academy. There are some people who have the sneaking suspicion that the C.I.A. actually creates some of these groups, makes them up out of whole cloth, so that the entire UFO situation becomes a laughing matter. So that a sensible person who gets involved in the subject is forced into sort of a guilt by association with these nuts."

Evans' theories were fascinating, but I had no way of evaluating them. Official silence would, in any case, block any chance of exploring them. If they were worthless, there seemed to be no way of proving that, either.

Evans mentioned that Carl Jung once said that the

best way to dispel fear of an unknown is to dispel its mystery. "Jung was interested in the possibility of alien spacecraft coming to the earth, with governments trying to overprotect the population from reality. If a society were not ready for it emotionally, much more alarm might be caused. A grand plan for guarding the public from panic could lead to a greater panic, a greater social dislocation. If they suppress knowledge by state power, by official deception, it becomes an unnatural thing, and it's bound to fail eventually."

He went into the report from the Brookings Institution which suggested that grave social consequences might follow from contact with highly evolved life beyond the earth. The report had given considerable attention to this possibility. "Anthropological files contain many examples of societies," it said, "sure of their place in the Universe, which have disintegrated when they came to associate with previously unfamiliar societies espousing different ideas and different ways of life. . . . It has been speculated that, of all groups, scientists and engineers might be the most devastated by the discovery of relatively superior creatures, since these professions are most clearly associated with mastery of nature. . . ."

Evans contended that the Brookings Institution took the human spirit for too fragile a structure. "The human spirit is tougher than they think," he said. "A little realistic humility does no harm. How much does civilization owe to cultural borrowing? Of course, if it's proved that man isn't alone in the solar system, the loss of what Harlow Shapley calls our 'cosmic loneliness' will certainly have a profound effect on our consciousness. But do they have to be so negative? Where there's been social collapse in the past, it's usually been the result of greed or brutality. Any UFOs which have been encountered haven't shown any such tendencies yet. They've avoided us, in a sense, in that they haven't shown any attempt to communicate with us directly. Suppose it turns out that socialism is the prevailing principle of these advanced civilizations? How is capitalism going to feel about that? Or suppose they're theologically minded? The Marxist materialists aren't going to be very happy about that. If a change is to come, I think we'd be a lot better off if it came naturally, without lying to the public."

If a civilization were *really* advanced, Evans reasoned, the chances were it wouldn't be destructive. And in spite of the thousands of reports on UFOs, there had been no indication at all of any hostile motives.

But reason and logic seem strangely inadequate for this situation. With detailed documentation of sightings coming from hundreds of technical and expert sources, it would be reasonable and logical to believe without question that UFOs existed. With denials coming from leading scientists, Air Force and government authorities it would be equally logical and believable to deny the existence of the phenomena. Each of the two factions is automatically put in the position of calling the other either a liar or an incompetent. It is of course ridiculous to suggest that a leading scientist is incompetent. It is almost equally ridiculous to assume that hundreds of policemen, airline pilots, technicians and reliable people are liars or incompetent observers. The question could be posed: Are the scientists lying—for the assumed protection of society, and are the observers not lying, but mistaken in their observations? And was it worth time, money and effort to try to find out?

The answer to the last question was important. Aside from the strong lure of an unsolved mystery, the possibility of the existence of interplanetary visitors is of vital importance. The warlike nations of the world might become suddenly more amenable to working out their differences amicably. The suicidal collision course of the Great Powers might be shifted in the interest of overall world welfare. The petty quarrels of man might be submerged in the interest of the wider Universe. The fear of alien visitors would obviously cause a disruption in the pattern of normal life. But what greater fear is there than the potential incineration of the earth by hydrogen bombs? And how could any super-civilized visitors match or exceed man's inhumanity to man? The choice between even total dislocation of civilization (if UFOs were proven real and interplanetary) and total incineration (Atomic War) would be easy to make. The former is curable, the latter is not.

CHAPTER IV

Before the widespread reports from the Southwest during August of 1965, interest of the press in UFOs had been reasonably dormant for several years. Scattered items had appeared, but for the general public the subject was almost forgotten in contrast to the years following World War II, the early 50's, and especially 1957 when for two weeks headlines across the country reported UFO cases involving electromagnetic effects on automobile ignitions, radios, and lights. In Hammond, Indiana, for instance, police chased an elongated object when a loud, beeping sound interfered with their cruiser radio. A few days before this, James W. Stokes, a high-altitude research engineer at White Sands, saw an elliptical UFO sweep across the highway twice, as his car engine and radio failed. About the same time, a group of electronic technicians and ham radio operators north of Ottawa, Canada, reported seeing a huge brightly lighted sphere, projecting beams of light, hovering above a hill. Two radios failed, except for a rapidly modulated strong single tone picked up on one frequency. The UFO finally disappeared into the clouds.

Most interesting, however, were the recent cases. After my column on the incident at Exeter appeared in the *Saturday Review*, NICAP sent me several interesting reports from Washington noting an increase not only in recent cases, but in extreme low-level, and even landing reports. In chronological order, the cases covered a time period between April, 1964 through August of 1965.

The material seemed sober and well-documented. On April 24, 1964, a New Mexico police officer saw an egg-shaped craft the size of a car blast off from a desert gully. The Air Force, instead of labeling the UFO a delusion or hoax, finally admitted he had seen an "unknown vehicle."

On November 8, 1964, at Montreal, Canada, a Mr. Nelson Lebel sighted a round, luminous craft hovering above the trees some 2,000 feet from his house. Later, the area was searched by a retired Canadian army officer, Lebel, and representatives of a Montreal newspaper. A circular depression was found, with grass and foliage scorched around it. Above the site, investigators found branches of trees broken and blackened.

On November 30, 1964, at Terryville, Connecticut, a medical official saw an unknown flying object with a blinding white light descend toward a nearby woods. When he drove into a clearing where the UFO had landed, the craft took off, rushing over the top of his car. It disappeared at "faster than jet speed," leaving a burned area and definite landing marks.

On December 21, 1964, at Staunton, Virginia, a gunshop owner saw a huge UFO, shaped like an inverted top, land briefly near Route 250. Later, Geiger counter checks by two Dupont Company engineers showed the landing spot to be highly radioactive.

On January 12, 1965, at Custer, Washington, a round, illuminated craft landed on a farm near the Blaine Air Force Base. Apparently, it was the same 30-foot flying disk which was tracked by Air Force radar as it swooped down to buzz the car of a federal law enforcement officer. Snow melted and the ground was scorched in a circular area where the UFO had landed. One of the witnesses said that the Air Force instructed him not to discuss the case.

On January 25, 1965, at Williamsburg, Virginia, a UFO descending rapidly from the sky caused engine failure in the car of a Richmond real estate executive. The strange craft, aluminum-colored, with an inverted-top shape, hovered just off the ground for 25 seconds. Then it shot straight up, with a swish of air, and disappeared with tremendous speed. On the same night, several miles away, a top-shaped UFO came toward the ground near the car of another Richmond businessman. An electromagnetic effect stopped his car as the UFO touched down.

On January 27, 1965, two NASA engineers, one a

former Air Force pilot, saw a UFO with flashing lights descend near Hampton, Virginia. Engineer A. C. Grimmins told NICAP that the flying disk zigzagged to a brief landing, then rapidly climbed out of sight.

On May 24, 1965, an American engineer by the name of Paul Norman, along with J. W. Tilse, a commercial pilot with 11,500 flying hours, watched a brightly glowing object approach them at Eton Range, Australia, 42 miles from Mackay. Two other men were with them. "It was about three hundred yards from the hotel where we were staying," reported Pilot Tilse. "It had a bank of spotlights, twenty or thirty of them, below a circular platform. It was solid, metallic-looking, thirty feet or more in diameter."

As the machine settled on a sparsely timbered ridge, illuminating the trees, the orange glow of the lights diminished. But it was still too bright to tell whether the glow came from inside, through ports, or from lights encircling the craft.

Finally, the craft lifted. As it did, the men saw a massive, tripod-type landing gear which the glow had concealed. Each of the three legs had a bright, pulsating light. But after a few moments, they were no longer visible. As the UFO reached 300 feet, it accelerated rapidly, but no exhaust, no trails, could be seen.

"I had always scoffed at these reports," said Tilse. "But I saw it. We all saw it. It was under intelligent control, and it certainly was no known aircraft."

The next day, Tilse photographed a circular impression on the ground where the UFO had landed or hovered. As confirmed by local police, it was a perfect circle, its inside diameter, 20 feet. The Regional Director of Civil Aviation has accepted the report as genuine.

NICAP, in assembling these reports, required detailed investigation by their subcommittee members, and signed statements wherever they could be obtained. Wherever possible, their representative would try to punch holes in the story. It was especially true of the case reported by the New York State Police on August 19, 1965, at Cherry Creek, New York, a town tucked in the western corner of the state, some 50 miles south of Niagara Falls.

On Friday, August 20, 1965, Jeffrey Gow, a member of

NICAP, went to the Fredonia State Police Barracks to investigate the sighting by Mrs. William Butcher and her three sons, William, Jr., seventeen, Harold, sixteen, and Robert, fourteen. Trooper E. J. Haas had been dispatched to the Butcher farm the previous evening at 9:15 P.M. to check the event, and was impressed with the fact that the Butchers seemed to be a reliable and honest family, not the sort that might be likely to try to create a hoax. Trooper Haas had, in fact, run a background check on the family, and reported that the neighbors confirmed this.

Gow ran down the details of the police report with the trooper, and then visited the farm the next morning. Here he carefully pieced together the story, making maps and sketches as he did so.

He found that Harold Butcher, the sixteen-year-old, was milking the cows in the main barn, near the east window, at about 8:30 Thursday evening, August 19. The boy was listening to Radio Station WKBW, and the 8:15 news had just ended, giving Harold accurate knowledge of the time. At just about this moment the boy heard the three-year-old bull, which was tethered in the field to a metal pipe, let out a noise he describes as "like I have never heard come from an animal before."

Harold looked out the east window, as Gow reports it, and saw that the bull out in the field was in the process of bending the metal pipe, even though the bull was tethered through the nose. Then the boy saw a football-shaped object hovering just above tree level, about 450 feet from the barn.

It was a silver-chromelike object, some 50 feet in length, and approximately 20 feet thick. It seemed to have two vertical seams, with apparent rivets along the edges. When the craft moved vertically, a red vapor was emitted along the bottom. When it moved horizontally, a yellowish tail appeared from one of the points of the "football."

The object went down just behind a large maple tree, and Gow reports that the boy was unable to tell whether or not it touched down, because there was a slight elevation between the object and the barn that partially obstructed the view. As it descended slowly, the red vapor seemed to come "from the edges, not the middle."

There was no wind, but the object emitted a *beep-beep* or a *bizz-bizz* noise.

He noted that the radio was making "a heck of a noise like a loud static," even though WKBW has a strong, clear radio signal in the area. Gow gathered that the boy then ran outside toward the object, and just before he reached the place where the bull was tethered, the object shot upward and into the clouds "as fast as the snap of my fingers," as Harold put it. When it rose, the band of red vapor, about 50 inches wide, shot from the edges toward the ground, then bounced back into the ship as it hovered momentarily about 10 feet in the air. As it shot higher, the pitch of the *bizz-bizz* sound increased. Harold claims he heard a sonic boom at the moment the craft disappeared into the clouds, but others in the vicinity were not aware of it. Inside the farmhouse, Mrs. Butcher did notice a definite interference on her radio.

The object pushed into the clouds, leaving a luminous green glow. Harold ran to the farmhouse, yelling about what he had seen, and darted out again with his brother Robert. The two of them saw the UFO hovering over a pine grove, but Robert saw it only long enough to notice the red vapor as it went up behind the clouds. As the two boys returned to the house, the family, including Mrs. Butcher and Kathleen Brougham, a sixteen-year-old friend, rushed out, but not in time to see either the craft or the luminous cloud. Mrs. Butcher called the Fredonia State Police Barracks and Trooper Haas was ordered to the scene. Mr. Butcher was away from home at the time.

Shortly after the phone call, Kathleen Brougham ran into the house, knocking over the young Butcher daughter as she did so. "It's here again!" she screamed, and ran out as the others followed her. Only Mrs. Butcher remained inside to soothe the youngster who had been knocked down. The four young people, William, Jr., Harold, Robert and Kathleen watched the object across a field about 700 feet away, as it moved in a southeasterly direction "with a glowing yellow vapor trail." To Harold, the object seemed the same as before, possibly because he was filling in details from his previous experience. The others, in the increasing darkness, could make out the

34

yellow vapor, a greenish glow in the clouds above, and a faint outline of the object. After watching it for about a minute, they reported that it moved off in the direction of Jamestown, disappearing over a hill.

Trooper Haas, accompanied by Trooper Neilson, arrived shortly afterward. Together with the youngsters, they walked toward the spot where Harold had first seen the object, several hundred feet from the barn, and beyond the post in the field where the bull was tethered.

For the first time, Gow reports, a distinct, pungent odor was detected, and later Mrs. Butcher noted that Harold and her younger daughter both complained of upset stomachs. It was fully dark by this time, and the troopers, using flashlights, did not find anything unusual at the site. The cows at the Butcher farm, however, reacted sharply. Instead of their normal two and a half cans of milk, they barely filled one.

The following afternoon, Captain James A. Dorsey and five other officials of the Niagara Falls Air Force Base came to the Butcher farm to investigate. Harold had found a purple liquid substance which he said "smelled like 3-in-1 oil." Mr. Butcher dug up a sample of this and put it in a shoe box, giving it to the State Police who in turn gave it to the Air Force for analysis. Although no Air Force report on the substance is available under the regulations, the base did indicate to the Buffalo *Evening News* that the four youths definitely "did see something."

With the Cherry Creek report, NICAP also sent more detailed information on the Texas and Oklahoma sightings during August of 1965, which had pushed their way through the reticence of the editorial staff of *The New York Times,* and which, in fact, had influenced me in doing the column in the *Saturday Review.* In the light of the details, I was a little surprised that the *Times* had apparently not followed up on the story.

Considerable interest was aroused in the darkness of the early morning of July 31, 1965, when a police officer by the name of Louis Sikes, from Wynnewood, Oklahoma, reported a 45-minute UFO sighting and both Tinker and Carswell Air Force bases came up with a fix on their radar. The night of August 1 was jammed with reports throughout the night. Three different Shawnee, Oklahoma, police cars reported diamond-shaped formations of UFOs for 30 to 40 minutes, shortly after 9 P.M. They were said to be moving in a northerly direction and changing colors from red to white to blue-green, and moved from side to side at times. In Chickasha, first news of the sightings came from radio station KWCO, with James Cline, police dispatcher, confirming that he had a report from Patrolman C. V. Barnhill verifying them. In Oklahoma City, police dispatcher Lt. Homer Briscoe said police headquarters received over 35 calls between 8 P.M. and 10 P.M., with most of the estimates indicating that the objects were at an altitude of 15,000 to 20,000 feet.

"People are upset," Briscoe said. "They want to know what they are, and we can't tell them."

Meanwhile, the Oklahoma Highway Patrol headquarters was trying to keep its teletype clear, and sorting out the reports from all over the state:

SINCE 8 A.M. THE TOWER HAS RECEIVED IN THE NEIGHBORHOOD OF 25 TO 50 VISUAL SIGHTINGS, MANY BY POLICE OFFICERS AND HIGHWAY PATROL TROOPERS, OF VARIOUS UNIDENTIFIED FLYING OBJECTS FROM THE PURCELL AREA NORTH THROUGH THE NORMAN AREA TO CHANDLER AND BACK THROUGH MEEKER AND SHAWNEE.

THREE SHAWNEE OFFICERS HAVE FOUR OF THE OBJECTS IN SIGHT AT THIS TIME, ALSO ANOTHER HAS CROPPED UP FROM THE SOUTH OF TECUMSEH AND IS APPARENTLY GOING TO FLY DIRECTLY OVER SHAWNEE.

THE SIGHTINGS VARY FROM ONE TO FOUR OF THE OBJECTS AT VARIOUS TIMES, STARTING IN A REDDISH COLOR AND VARYING TO A WHITE AND BLUE LUSTER.

SHAWNEE REPORTS THE OBJECTS SEEM TO BE FLYING FOUR TO A FORMATION IN A DIAMOND-TYPE FORMATION. CUSHING HAS REPORTED FOUR OF THE OBJECTS.

OKLAHOMA HIGHWAY PATROL UNITS 30 AND 40 HAVE ALSO MADE VISUAL SIGHTINGS. TINKER AIR FORCE BASE HAS HAD FROM ONE TO FOUR OF THEM ON RADAR AT A TIME AND THEY ADVISE THEY ARE FLYING VERY HIGH AT APPROXIMATELY 22,000 FEET, WHICH SEEMS TO COINCIDE WITH THE VISUAL SIGHTINGS, ALL OF WHICH ARE "VERY HIGH FLYING OBJECTS."

On the following day, Wright-Patterson Air Force Base issued a statement which said: "There has been no confirmation that any of the sightings were tracked on radar." It went on to ascribe the sightings to the planet Jupiter and other stars.

And again the same questions were posed: Were dozens of patrolmen and troopers throughout most of the state of Oklahoma, as well as the entire Oklahoma State Highway Patrol, liars and incompetents? Or was the official Air Force spokesman a liar and an incompetent?

Many people in the Southwest on those fiery evenings in early August took exception to the Air Force proclamations that they were looking at stars or planets. A twenty-three-year-old Sioux City, Iowa, high school English teacher said he tracked one of the objects for a considerable length of time. "Anyone who would say this was a star or planet would be out of his mind," he said. He described the object he saw as he was driving with his wife as "bright, yellowish, and zig-zagged slightly. This was replaced with a red light surrounded by three white lights, the red light being the brightest." He got out of his car, turned off the ignition to see if he could hear the sound of an airplane motor. There was none.

An Air Force weather observer in Oklahoma City also took exception to the casual explanation by the Air Force Public Information Office. "I have repeatedly seen unusual objects in the sky," he said, "and they are no mirage. One of them looked like it had a flat top and flat bottom, and it was not a true sphere. There seemed to be two rings around it, and the rings were part of the main body."

Major Hector Quintanilla, chief of the Air Force "Project Blue Book," which analyzes and ostensibly explains sightings as they are reported from over the entire country, actually withdrew his own initial report of a sighting by two Texas sheriffs on the night of September 3, 1965—the same night that Officer Bertrand and Norman Muscarello crouched under the silent object in Exeter, New Hampshire.

Chief Deputy Sheriff Billy E. McCoy and Deputy Sheriff Robert W. Goode were patrolling an area in Texas about forty miles below Houston. In the distance, about five miles away, they noticed a bright purple light, moments later noting a smaller blue light near it. The lights suddenly moved swiftly toward their cruiser.

In a report to the Air Force, the two officers said:

The object came up to the pasture next to the highway, about 150 feet off the highway and about 100 feet high. The bulk of the object was plainly visible and appeared to be triangular-shaped, with a bright purple light on the left and the smaller, less bright, blue light on the right end. The bulk of the object appeared to be dark gray in color with no other distinguishing features. It appeared to be enormous—about 200 feet wide and 40–50 feet thick in the middle, tapering off toward both ends. There was no noise or any trail.

The bright purple light illuminated the ground directly underneath it and the area in front of it, including the highway and the interior of the patrol car. The tall grass under the object did not appear to be disturbed.

There was a bright moon out [the moon had gone down by the time the Exeter officers made their observation in New Hampshire, over 1,600 miles away] and it cast a shadow of the object on the ground immediately below it in the grass. Deputy Sheriff Goode was in the driver's seat with his left arm laying in the open window. Although he was wearing a long-sleeved shirt and a coat, he later said that he felt the heat apparently emanating from the object.

The two men, shocked by the approach of the craft, drove away at 110 miles an hour. Then, although frankly scared by the sighting, decided to drive back to see if it was still there. It was, and they again drove away to avoid another close encounter.

The report of the local Air Force investigating officer reads:

After talking with both officers involved in the sighting, there is no doubt in my mind that they definitely saw some unusual object or phenomenon . . . Both officers appeared to be intelligent, mature, level-headed persons capable of sound judgment and reasoning. Chief Deputy Sheriff McCoy holds a responsible position in the department requiring the supervision of over 42 personnel. Both officers have been subjected to considerable friendly ridicule from their contemporaries and the local townspeople; but have continued to profess the facts of their sighting.

After a phone call to Deputy Sheriff McCoy, Major Quintanilla withdrew his report that the sighting had been a star or a planet, and stamped the sighting UNEXPLAINED.

The press across the country, stirred from its apathy, began to react as the reports increased during August, 1965. In Houghton, Michigan, personnel at the U.S. Air Force Radar Base in the Keweenaw Peninsula slipped for a moment from behind the Air Force UFO curtain to report to the UPI "solid radar contact" with up to ten unidentified flying objects, moving in a V-formation over Lake Superior. The objects were moving out of the southwest and were heading north-northeast at about "9,000 miles per hour," the base reported. They were 5,200 to 17,000 feet high. Seven other objects were spotted over Duluth and jet interceptors gave chase, according to the UPI report, but could not maintain the speed of the UFOs and were easily outdistanced.

Other UPI releases marked the augmented pace of the sightings. UFOs were reported hovering and bobbing over the northern and western Minneapolis suburbs, with Captain Robert Riley of the State Highway Patrol and three patrolmen observing the phenomenon in seven different communities nearby. A total of 50 police and sheriff squad cars radioed in reports between 12:20 A.M. and 2:30 A.M. on August 3, 1965. About 50 miles west of Paris, France, Alexander Ananoff, one of France's leading space experts, reported watching a "flying saucer" at sunset. Ananoff, 1950 winner of the international Astronautics Prize, described the object as "disk- or lens-like in shape." It moved a considerable distance while he watched it and finally disappeared above a cirrus cloud, which, as he stated, "exists only above 21,000 feet." At the Canberra Airport, Australia, Air Traffic Control officers and other expert aircraft observers spotted a mysterious, glowing object which hung suspended at about 5,000 feet for 40 minutes, according to the Associated Press. At Lisbon, Portugal, according to the same source, glowing objects zipped across the sky and interfered with the operation of radios and electromagnetic clocks. These descriptions of the object seemed to tally with those given in an official Chilean Air Force report of sightings a little earlier over the Antarctic.

As the news of such observations increased during the summer of 1965, so did editorial comment. The cautious and accurate *Christian Science Monitor* said:

Flying saucers sighted early this month over Texas may give scientists something to think about for a long time.

They were among many reported sightings around the world lately. But they give the clearest evidence of all that something strange was actually in the sky.

Many Texans definitely saw something that even experienced investigators now admit defies explanation.

The Texas saucer appeared as a bright light in the sky, with lesser lights clustered around it. It was visible to some for several hours.

There was no temperature inversion strong enough to produce such an effect.

It wasn't a scientific balloon, since none had been launched.

It makes the clearest case yet for a thorough look at the saucer mystery.

The Fort Worth *Star-Telegram* ran these comments on its editorial page:

They can stop kidding us now about there being no such things as "flying saucers."

Too many people of obviously sound mind saw and reported them independently from too many separate localities. Their descriptions of what they saw were too similar to one another, and too unlike any familiar object.

And it's going to take more than a statistical report on how many reported "saucers" have turned out to be jets and weather balloons to convince us otherwise.

The *Times-Star* of Alameda, California, ran a strong editorial. It noted especially the UPI story from Houghton, Michigan, in which the solid radar contact had been admitted by the Air Force:

What distinguishes this story from many others involving Air Force personnel is that it was not accompanied by a paragraph or two explaining that the objects had finally been identified as a flight of ducks, comets, balloons, or something else, equally commonplace.

Why wasn't it?

The most likely reason is that the Air Force spokesmen, whose job it is to explain away the seemingly improbable in terms of the commonplace, have been getting such a workout lately that either they are starting to break down or their superiors are finally coming to the conclusion that they are making the Air Force appear ridiculous.

Of the two, the latter seems more likely. The business of attempting to protect the public from panic—the obvious reason for the Air Force's traditional policy of identifying unidentified flying objects as weather balloons, etc.—is something that cannot be indefinitely sustained, particularly when the source of the presumed potential panic is a mass of peculiar things that persist in flying around where large numbers of persons can see them. To do that is no more possible than it is for panic to be sustained by individuals for more than a few hours at most. It's too exhausting. One can flee a horde of little green men from outer space only so long. Presently one gets tired and decides to do something else, even if it is no more than sitting down.

But whatever the reason may be why the Air Force spokesmen are becoming less vocal, the time is long overdue for the Government to disclose to the public all it knows about the UFOs.

In other words, it would surprise almost no one today to learn that some UFOs are spacecraft from elsewhere in the solar system or beyond. In fact, it would be even more surprising to learn that they were not. Hence, the only way in which the public interest can be served in the matter is for the Government to disclose what it knows about these phenomena.

The recent sightings, the extreme low-level sightings by responsible officials which couldn't possibly be mistaken for planes or stars or balloons, were impressive, as were the 600 older cases documented by NICAP so painstakingly in its book *The UFO Evidence*. Together, the old and new cases covered the entire globe. As a single reporter, I could not possibly track down enough direct interviews over such an area and contribute anything new in clarifying the mystery.

But I could, I felt, take one single microcosmic area where a recent, low-level sighting had been made, and

41

explore it to absolute rock bottom. In a small way, I had done this over the phone with the Exeter experience. With groundwork laid, there would be many advantages in following this up. What's more, although NICAP had done a thorough job in documenting cases throughout the world, they had not completed a crash program in a single area.

To accomplish this, I made plans to go to Exeter to explore in person the incident there, and gather whatever other information might be forthcoming.

CHAPTER V

Just before I left New York for Exeter, a reader of the *Saturday Review* sent me a clipping and news photograph of the now-famous sighting made near the Santa Ana, California, Marine Corps Air Base. The picture was taken on a Polaroid by Rex Heflin, a county highway department investigator, on August 3, during the height of the summer sightings. Heflin reported that he was working near the air base when he caught a glimpse of a silver object which he estimated to be 30 feet in diameter and 8 feet deep. It made no sound, but a beam of white light seemed to rotate underneath the object. During the time the UFO was near, he had tried to communicate with his supervisor over a two-way radio in his vehicle, but the radio was inoperative. After the object disappeared, the radio worked perfectly.

The picture was amazingly clear: Flat, metallic, looking almost like a squashed German helmet, the UFO was slightly tilted in the air, and barely higher than the telephone poles along the road. Heflin told reporters that he was willing to take a lie-detector test to prove that the picture was not faked. Further, he had used a Polaroid camera, which precludes tampering with a negative.

From NICAP, I also received a reproduction of a dramatically clear picture of a glowing UFO object taken by a youthful amateur astronomer in Beaver County, Pennsylvania, just north of Pittsburgh. James Lucci, seventeen, had been taking a time exposure of the moon when the UFO moved into camera range. Three professional photographers had examined the picture, and declared it to be genuine. It looked like a glowing upside-down dinner plate, dwarfing the full moon in the background and revealing a line of trees on the horizon.

A third picture was a tight close-up of the Wichita Weather Bureau radarscope, showing four unidentified blips which were recorded at the height of the August 1 sightings in the state of Kansas. They were confirmed as unidentified by John Shockley, Wichita weather observer.

Among the summer's reports was one from the Secretary of the Argentina Navy who issued an official public statement:

On July 3, 1965, a giant, lens-shaped flying object was seen, tracked and photographed at the Argentina scientific base, Deception Island, in the Antarctic. Lt. Danial Perisse, Commanding Officer, confirmed by radio that the large UFO alternately hovered, then accelerated and maneuvered at tremendous speeds. While being tracked by theodolite and watched through binoculars, the unknown object caused strong interference with variometers used to measure the earth's magnetic field, and also registered on magnetograph tapes. Color pictures were taken through a theodolite by a member of a visiting group from the Chilean scientific base.

The Chilean Minister of Defense supplemented this by reporting that a similar UFO had been seen by all personnel at its Antarctic base, and had caused such strong radio interference that it temporarily blocked an attempt to relay news of the sighting to the English and Argentine bases.

A further official Argentine Navy statement indicated that a large UFO had caused severe electromagnetic disturbances on the compasses of its Navy transport ship *Punta Medanos*. The compass needles "suddenly and simultaneously" swung off course, pointing toward the UFO. "The power which caused this electromagnetic interference is indicated by the distance involved," the report said. "The UFO was 2,000 meters (over a mile) away from the ship."

In contrast to this persuasive evidence, I received a letter from Raymond Fowler, the New England subcommittee member of NICAP, indicating that several newspapers around the Boston and Exeter area were ascribing the sighting at Exeter, made by Muscarello and patrolmen Bertrand and Hunt, to a flying billboard owned by the Sky-Lite Aerial Advertising Agency of Boston, and piloted by Daniel Vale, of Londonderry, New Hampshire.

The Amesbury, Massachusetts, *News* began its article with an almost audible breath of relief:

"The unidentified flying object spotted in this area by many residents, has finally been identified!" it began.

Fowler enclosed the clipping with his letter, and went on to say:

This is a misleading news-story being carried by some newspapers in this area identifying the New Hampshire UFO sightings as an advertising plane. It so happens that our subcommittee makes routine checks with the Sky-Lite Advertising Agency before investigating UFO reports. Many times this plane has been reported as a UFO. However, during the period of the New Hampshire UFO sightings, including the morning of September 3, this aircraft was never flown. I went over the plane's flight paths, and it never left the ground between August 21 and September 10.

Joseph Budina, the owner of the company, also informed me that his aircraft rarely flies into southern New Hampshire and when it does it is usually in the Salem and Manchester area, miles away from the Exeter area. He told me that he told the Amesbury *News* that perhaps some UFOs reported in New Hampshire could have been his aircraft. Unfortunately, this newspaper used his statement to explain the sightings in the Exeter case.

The Sky-Lite aircraft does not carry red flashing lights. It carries a rectangular sign carrying white flashing lights. It was not airborne during the S. E. New Hampshire UFO flap. I have notified the Amesbury *News* of the true facts and have asked them to set the record straight.

RAYMOND E. FOWLER
Chairman, NICAP MASS SUBCOM

It now seemed logical, however, that some mistaken

44

UFO reports *would* have come in as a result of the use of this advertising plane. But it did *not* seem logical that it could cause an ex-Air Force veteran and now a police officer to file an official report of a low-altitude, silent object hovering just over the treetops, in the company of two other witnesses. Since nothing could be taken for granted, I put in a long-distance call to Joseph Budina in Boston, and arranged to have lunch with him and his pilot there before going up to Exeter. He repeated over the phone that his craft was not airborne at all between August 21 and September 10, and said he was convinced that his craft could only account for a fraction of the many sightings reported in the southern New Hampshire and Massachusetts areas.

One more news item appeared just before I left for Boston, an AP release of October 17th, with the head-line:

MEXICANS UP IN THE AIR OVER FLYING SAUCERS

The summer of 1965 could go down in Mexican history as the summer of the flying saucers. Sightings began late in July after reports of similar phenomena from South America. Then, suddenly, all Mexico seemed to be seeing luminous disks, hovering lights and high-velocity balls of light.

Scarcely a day passed without the Mexican press reporting that "unidentified flying objects" had terrorized a peasant family by day or a whole town by night.

Sometimes a string of OVNI [*objects voladores no identificados*] had converged on a cigar-shaped "mother ship."

As the saucer-sighting fever gripped the Mexican capital, staid businessmen could be seen climbing to the roofs of their office buildings clutching field glasses.

However, the stirring of Latin blood has always been assumed to be much easier than to stir that of staid New Englanders with their reputation for laconic taciturnity. If the New Hampshire, Down-East Yankees would talk of their experiences, there would be a better chance of making some kind of journalistic—and realistic—appraisal of the mystery.

I met with Joseph Budina and Daniel Vale, owner

and pilot respectively of the Sky-Lite Advertising Company, on October 19, at the new Boston Sheraton Hotel. They had with them a letter which I had asked them to write me, indicating that their plane could not be involved with the incident at Exeter.

"Dear Mr. Fuller," it read. "Regarding the newspaper reports that our airplane was the source of the recent UFO sightings in Exeter, N.H., late at night and early in the morning of September 2nd and 3rd, 1965: Please be advised that our airplanes and equipment were not operating at any time immediately before, during or after the above-mentioned dates." It was signed by Vale, as chief pilot and manager of operations. I had figured, and rightly so as I was to discover later, that many people would be reticent to discuss their sightings if skeptics could accuse them of being unable to tell the difference between an advertising sign and a UFO. NICAP was aware that many people are extremely reluctant to discuss their sightings because of possible ridicule.

Both Budina and Vale were helpful in filling me in on the background of the area and the area UFO stories. It was pilot Vale's theory that newspapers throughout New England had received so many phone calls from people sighting strange objects, that they seized happily on the advertising plane as a quick explanation of the phenomenon. "The reporters that I've talked to," said Vale, "said they received an awful lot of calls, at any time of the day or night. And this thing got to the point where it was never-ending. Of course they really couldn't explain anything. They were left up in the air as to what to say about the things. So as soon as they found out about our airplane, about our equipment, what it did, they immediately got hold of Joe and myself.

"One reporter called me up at home, and was pushing very hard about the story on the Exeter police. Well, when I found out that this took place sometime after midnight, I told him that this couldn't possibly be our plane, because we were never airborne any time after eleven, at the latest. Well, he was all excited about this idea because he thought that he had come up with a real explanation for all the UFO reports. But even though I explained again that the Exeter thing couldn't possibly

46

be our equipment, he said that he thought this would make a good explanation, and he was going to write it up."

Neither Budina nor Vale would relax with a drink at lunch because they were going to be flying that afternoon. But we all ordered cherrystone clams, and went on with the conversation.

"Anyway," Vale continued, "anybody who gets a close look at the sign couldn't possibly be scared, the way a lot of these people who have been reporting UFOs have been. Maybe from a distance, it looks puzzling. But anybody can tell what it is the minute it gets in clear view."

The discussion with Budina and Vale failed to reveal anything new and significant, but did furnish a clear warning: Any testimony about UFOs seen in the neighborhood of Exeter should be checked out carefully against the possibility of people mistaking the advertising aircraft for a UFO. The plane, Joe Budina told me, would of course make conventional aircraft noise. It was a Piper Tri-Pacer, especially equipped to carry the advertising sign.

Budina revealed one other thing of interest: At about 9 P.M. two evenings before he had received a call from the police in a southern Maine town, asking if his craft was in the air. A mysterious object was sighted and tracked on radar nearby and both the police and a Federal Aviation Authority tower wanted to know more about it. Budina's equipment was on the ground at the time, and he never heard more about it.

I planned that day to visit Ray Fowler, the NICAP representative, at his home in Wenham, Massachusetts, and also to check further news items in Boston. The UPI office had little information to offer: They kept no special file on UFOs, although they had of course written up the sightings around Exeter and Portsmouth. The AP also had little new to offer. Both news services were wary of the crackpot element involved in some sightings, as I was, and our conversations underlined the importance of being extremely conservative in reaching any conclusions.

I dropped by the city room of the Boston *Globe*, and talked for awhile with Russell Burbank, a young reporter who had been assigned to several UFO stories, but he was as puzzled as anyone else about the phenomenon. He had done one of the stories on the Sky Lite Advertising plane, but had not checked out the plane's log against the Exeter sightings. He had been inclined, he said, to close the file on the subject for awhile. In the morgue of the *Globe* were many clippings, some old and some new, but none of them offered more than the usual clues: sightings sworn to by many observers, but no direct and tangible physical evidence available. Dozens of sightings had been reported within a hundred-mile radius of Boston for many years before Joe Budina had launched his Sky-Lite Advertising plane. There was an impressive increase in recent sightings of low-level UFOs—anywhere from 10 to 100 feet from the ground.

Typical of these observations on file in the morgue of the *Globe* was a story from Amesbury, Massachusetts, of a UFO which was seen by at least ten people, not more than 15 to 20 feet above the ground. As Diane Drew and Robert Dore left the home of Dore's grandparents in Amesbury, they noticed that the animals at the house were unusually nervous and restless. They began driving up Hunt Road, when a round, illuminated disk suddenly appeared and began to glide toward them very slowly. They quickly turned and called out Mr. and Mrs. Linwood Dore, the grandparents, and neighbors. The witnesses agreed completely on the behavior of the object: It was shaped like a large dinner plate, close in appearance to an artificial moon. It changed color when it altered direction, moved from side to side as well as up and down. As it changed motion, the colors seemed to change from red to green. When members of the group tried to go near the hovering object, it took off at a tremendous rate of speed, shooting up over the treetops.

Later, the residents all along Hunt Road heard and saw planes flying overhead after the object had left, one of them circling the area for an hour.

With some time to fill before visiting Fowler, I drove to Amesbury, 45 minutes north of Boston, and dropped by the branch office there of the Haverhill, Massachusetts, *Gazette* to talk to Jean Miller, of that paper, and Ken Lord, editor of the Amesbury *News*. It was a typical building of the New England dusty-brick era, when mill towns sprang up at the drop of a waterfall. Sitting in the dingy office, both Lord, a barrel-chested Yankee editor, and Miss Miller, a fragile and intelligent young lady, admitted their puzzlement about the whole UFO situation. They felt, in fact, that they were damned if they did believe in the phenomenon and damned if they didn't. The advertising plane, they admitted, couldn't possibly explain the continuous sightings that kept plaguing them, especially the low-level reports of silent objects which hovered, remained stationary, and then took off at incredible speeds. They each had several stories which they hadn't even bothered to print because of the volume of sightings. The Air Force base at Portsmouth, they reported, was obviously hamstrung for giving any local information, and lamely and continuously referred everybody to the Pentagon, which never made any reports of value in exploring the mystery.

I arrived at Raymond Fowler's house in Wenham that evening, tired and puzzled. It was a modest, cheerful home in which his English wife marshaled his three scrubbed and polished young children at dinner with easy British grace. Fowler, a level-headed, serious college graduate with training as a minister, worked as a reports administrator on Sylvania's Minute Man Project in nearby Waltham. He also works for NICAP, without pay, as all subcommittee members do, taking in enough money from donations at lectures to cover phone calls and investigating expenses.

In his small upstairs office, jammed with books and papers, he revealed his concern about Air Force policy, which he thought was based on the erroneous belief that it would prevent possible panic throughout the country. He felt that since even the Air Force admitted that UFOs seemed to pose no threat to national security, the investigation and dissemination of information about the phenomena should be turned over to scientific agencies.

He was also concerned about far-out and irresponsible UFO groups who publicized anything and everything related by overemotional people, and whose flagrant exaggeration damaged carefully documented cases.

He was impressed by an interview he had with Patrolman Bertrand at Exeter several weeks earlier. "Bertrand told me," Fowler said, "that he didn't want to make any guesses at all. He said, 'I'll tell you exactly what I saw,

49

and no more. I could guess that the object was egg-shaped, because I saw no protrusions, nothing. It seemed to be compressed.' And he said, 'Maybe it wasn't egg-shaped. It could have been another shape. It's only the impression I got.' "

Fowler had several suggestions for my research up in Exeter on the case. "You might check out the major and the lieutenant and the colonel who investigated the case for the Air Force. There's a report that they went up from time to time to the field where Bertrand and Hunt saw the object, and waited for this thing. Another thing is that you might look into some of the other farmhouses in that vicinity. They might have seen something, especially when the dogs were barking; they might have got out of bed and looked out. Maybe they'd be willing to talk. You never can tell in these cases."

Fowler went on to discuss several other cases he had run into, painting a general picture of his extensive activity for NICAP. Oddly enough, in nineteen years of study, he had never seen a UFO himself. But he was impressed by the documentation of the hundreds of cases he had explored, and the apparent validity of the witnesses. "Take a case I investigated in 1963," he said. "The people reported a Saturn-shaped UFO over the power lines in back of their house. It woke the whole neighborhood up. The husband knew nothing about UFOs, and I had a picture from a previous case which he had never seen and knew nothing about. I asked him to sketch what he had seen—and he drew his own picture, which was practically identical to the picture I had. There were the man and his wife, and the neighbors all around who woke up. There were other people in the area who reported it, but I didn't get a chance to check them out."

"What about more recent ones? This year, for instance?"

"Well," Fowler said, "take the case of Dr. Woodruff, Dr. Richard Woodruff. He's the Chief Medical Examiner of the College of Medicine, University of Vermont. Just after the first of the year. I've got signed statements by both Woodruff and a state trooper who was with him. They were both traveling back home after testifying on a case before a grand jury in Brattleboro. Here's the report, as verified by both Dr. Woodruff and the trooper."

Fowler took out the typewritten report, three pages of documentation. The date was the 4th of January, 1965, the time, 5:15 P.M., EST. The place was between Bethel and Randolph, Vermont, on Highway 12. The report began:

Dr. Woodruff, Vermont State Pathologist, a staff member of the University of Vermont College of Medicine and respected scientist, was traveling back to Burlington with Vermont State Trooper ——— [Name withheld on request], after testifying before a grand jury in Brattleboro, Vermont. As they were driving along Highway 12, suddenly, just above distant treetop to their left, a sharply defined object glowing an orangish-red with an intensity somewhat less than an automobile headlight came rapidly in sight and crossed the highway in front of them. Its apparent size was that of a football held at arm's length. It appeared to be round but the exact shape could not be ascertained because of its great speed. Trooper ——— exclaimed, "My God, did you see that?" No sooner had he spoken when a second similar object came into view followed shortly after by a third object. All followed the same flight course climbing slightly and moving west to east to their right and above the valley where they appeared to fade into the distance.

Duration of the sighting was 30 seconds. The objects were viewed through the automobile windshield. They appeared to be solid. No sound was heard. Speed was faster than a jet aircraft. Estimated distance of the objects from the observers—½ to 1 mile. The weather was clear, stars were visible and there was no moon. Dr. Woodruff reported the incident to the Burlington *Free Press* and to Mr. Edward Knapp, head of the Vermont State Aeronautics Board. Several Vermont and New Hampshire papers carried a full account of this sighting. In his statement to the press Dr. Woodruff said: "I have hesitated to call. I know everything I say will be open to misinterpretation. But remember, two of us saw the same thing at the same time. I was not seeing things, and I am not too overly imaginative and neither is the trooper."

"Quite a report," I said to Fowler.

"The interesting thing," he said, "is the Air Force

evaluation on the second page. They attribute it to 'probable observation of meteors—specifically of Quadrantids.' This is from Major Jacks, the Pentagon Public Information Officer who handles their statements. And here's an excerpt from Dr. Woodruff's comment on the Air Force report."

Fowler pointed to a paragraph on the second page, from Dr. Woodruff's letter of February 9, 1965:

> I am amazed that the major could not come up with a better solution than this. If I had thought that there was a possibility that the three objects we saw were meteors, I never would have mentioned the matter. . . . While I make no speculation as to what the objects we saw might be, I do feel most definitely that they were not meteors.

Following the quote from the doctor's letter were reports of additional witnesses to the sighting: four people in one car in the same area and a statement from Hugh E. Wheatley, Chairman of the Board of Selectmen of Randolph, Vermont. Both descriptions were almost identical to the one filed by Dr. Woodruff and the state trooper.

"Of course," Fowler went on, "you get a variety of shapes and designs reported on UFOs, which leads to the conclusion that there are several types. They all seem to more or less fall into classified patterns, though. We often get reports of the disklike or pancake shapes, with diameters about 10 times their width. And you get various sizes reported—from ten feet or so, up to one hundred feet in diameter. This is probably the most common report. Then the second most common is the cigar, or cylindrical, shape. The third is the brightly defined lights at night. Or lights in formation, which move with purpose. Then you have the Saturn shape, not too many of those, and the round globe and cone shape sightings. But the disk shape is the most common. Sound patterns vary; most are silent; some report a humming or whirring sound. The lighting patterns, of course, change with different speeds, movements and altitudes. That's why you're likely to get variations in descriptions of the objects when they're seen."

We skimmed through some of the dozens of reports on Fowler's desk. They were detailed and well-documented, with frequent references to possibilities which would rule out the sighting as a valid UFO. There was an airline stewardess in Watertown, Massachusetts, who had been awakened at 4 o'clock in the morning. She had watched a bright, white-silver disk as it moved slowly across the sky over a period of ten minutes before it disappeared. Fowler's report took nothing for granted:

The moon was 20 days old—the day before the last quarter. It was not visible from the bedroom window that the observer viewed the object from. This agrees with her account. Vega and Altair would be the brightest stars in the western sky. Size, brightness and movement negate stars. These two stars were probably among the few that the witness stated she observed while watching the object. Balloon possibility: Favorable. The sunrise for 7/19/65 was 5:23 EDT. At 4 A.M. EDT the sun would have been approximately 20° below the easterly horizon. Thus any object with an elevation of 20° or more above the western horizon would begin to reflect sunlight. Speed, as balloon possibility: Favorable. The object moved very slowly. Information obtained from the U.S. Weather Bureau shows wind velocity to have been 8 mph (Logan Airport, Boston). Direction, as balloon possibility: Unfavorable. The object moved south to north. Information obtained from the U.S. Weather Bureau shows the wind was west-southwest (Logan Airport, Boston). A balloon would have moved into the northeast, instead of northwest. I telephoned the witness after our interview in regard to the balloon answer. She is familiar with balloons, and was bewildered to think that I suspected she had seen one. The object falls into the class of "Unidentified," and was reported during the beginning of the upsurge of UFO sightings in Massachusetts.

There was no question about it: Fowler was a thorough and painstaking investigator.

One particularly vivid report among the many concerned two sisters in Turner, Maine, in 1959. It was a clear summer's evening, with a bright moon. Emily Deneault, a microelectronics operator, was in her driveway when she heard a humming or whirring sound. She glanced across the road and saw strange lights flying low over a field about 1,000 feet away. At first she thought it was an airplane about to crash, but no motor was heard, and the lights appeared to stop and remain motionless over the field. She sent her son Robert to alert the others in the house. Her stepfather, Alex Blanchard, joined her, while her sister Rita got on the phone just inside the door and told the telephone operator what they were witnessing. The operator contacted the Civil Defense headquarters at nearby Auburn.

The object, after moving back and forth across the field, "floated" down to earth and the lights went out. Then another object crossed the field and hovered over the landed one. They were identical and were described as being like two saucers, one inverted over the other, joined by a dark rim which looked as if it were made of dark glass. Behind this seemingly transparent rim were bright blue lights which revolved around the rim. They were as intense as a welder's torch and made Emily's eyes water as she looked at them through the binoculars. The objects themselves seemed a dull silver-gray in color, definitely solid, and moved about in a strange floating manner. Then the object on the ground floated upward, slightly to the left, and joined the other one. Both took off at a "terrific speed." Later, two jet aircraft flew over an adjoining field. It was not known whether they were attempting to intercept the objects.

The next morning Emily and her father went out to the field where the objects had been. They found a small area of singed grass which smelled as if it had recently been burned.

Fowler checked the characters of all these observers and found them to be unimpeachable. They had withheld the information for several years because of the fear of unwanted publicity.

Fowler's attitude toward the Air Force policies stemmed from his conviction that they were not only withholding information but attempting to block any kind of Congressional inquiry into the UFO mystery, even imposing a form of censorship. He admitted that perhaps 80 percent of the sightings could be explained as relating to airplanes, weather balloons, or birds, stars, or meteors. But 20 percent couldn't possibly be ascribed to these mistakes.

According to the Newark *Ledger,* one group of 50 pilots got together to protest the Air Force policy of pooh-poohing the serious reports dozens of qualified pilots had turned in at the risk of their jobs and reputations. They were later joined in their protest by several hundred other pilots. The cavalier dismissal of such technically qualified personnel was not only irritating, it was damaging.

While the Air Force continues an offhand dismissal of qualified reports, its own "inside" regulations to its personnel are serious and detailed. The official regulation #200-2, as of July 20, 1962, is far from a joking matter. It covers seven full pages of instruction packed into tightly spaced 8-point type.

It describes UFOs as "any aerial phenomena, airborne object or objects which are unknown or appear out of the ordinary to the observer because of performance, aerodynamic characteristics, or unusual features."

It goes on to describe the objectives of the Air Force UFO program: "Air Force interest in UFOs is threefold. First, as a possible threat to the security of the United States and its forces; second, to determine the technical or scientific characteristics of any such UFOs; third, to explain or identify all UFO sightings. . . ."

The official regulation admits that "there is need for further scientific knowledge in such fields as geophysics, astronomy, and physics of the upper atmosphere which the study and analysis of UFOs and similar aerial phenomena may provide."

The responsibilities of reporting incidents, according to Air Force regulation 200-2, rests on Base commanders, who "will report all information and evidence of UFO sightings received from other services, government agencies, and civilian sources. Investigators are authorized to make telephone calls from the investigation area direct to the Foreign Technology Division (FTD) of the Air Force Systems Command, Wright-Patterson Air Force Base, Ohio. The purpose of the calls is to report high-priority sightings."

The Commander of the Air Force base nearest the location of a UFO sighting is instructed to "conduct all investigative action necessary to submit a complete initial report of a UFO sighting. The initial investigation will include every effort to resolve the sighting."

The job of interpreting the data is left up to the Air Force Systems Command Foreign Technology Division at the Wright-Patterson Base. From here the report goes to the Headquarters of the U.S. Air Force, and no information can be released except from the Office of Information of the Office of the Secretary of the Air Force. Up to the present, this has been a stone wall for any meaningful information.

But further evidence of the seriousness with which the Air Force considers the UFO problem is indicated in Paragraph #5, which states: "Both the Assistant Chief of Staff, Intelligence, Headquarters, USAF, and the Air Defense Command have a direct and immediate interest in the facts pertaining to UFOs reported within the United States."

The releasing of information to the public is definitely a sacred cow. According to Paragraph #7, only the Office of Information, Office of the Secretary of the Air Force, can do this "regardless of the origin and nature" of the UFO.

There is only one exception—and that is significant. The base commander may "release information to the press or the general public *only after positive identification of the sighting as a familiar or known sighting.*" (The italics are mine.) If the sighting is unexplainable, the only statement that the local base can release "is the fact that the sighting is under investigative action and information regarding it will be available at a later date. After completion of investigative action, the commander may release the fact that the Air Force Systems Command (Foreign Technology Division) will review and analyze the results of the investigation. He will then refer any further inquiries to the local Office of Information."

In analyzing regulation 200-2, NICAP has pointed out that several specific paragraphs amount to direct contradictions of official denials of censorship on the part of the Air Force.

In regulation 200-2 is the statement: "Air Force activities must reduce the percentage of unidentifieds to a minimum. . . ." NICAP claims that this shows an obvious intention to explain away UFO reports, not to investigate them scientifically and admit that many cases cannot be explained.

Another statement in the regulation is considered by

NICAP as direct censorship: "Air Force personnel . . . will not contact private individuals on UFO cases nor will they discuss their operations and function with unauthorized persons unless so directed, and then only on a 'need to know' basis."

There are other provisions to which NICAP takes exception, and the battle between it and the Air Force continues without letup.

CHAPTER VI

I checked in at the desk of the Exeter Inn on the morning of October 20, 1965, in the somber, paneled lobby, waited over ten minutes for a somnambulistic bellhop to take me to the room. Two tape recorders, a Polaroid camera and a suitcase took up most of the space, but the room was cheerful and I would be spending little enough time in it.

I was there only a few minutes when the phone rang. It was Russell Burbank, the *Globe* reporter who had been helpful to me in assembling the clippings in the paper's morgue. He had just discovered that a United Press International stringer reporter, who lived near Exeter, had herself made a clear sighting of a UFO very recently and he thought I might like to interview her. He gave me her name, a Mrs. Virginia Hale, in nearby Hampton, and I immediately called her.

She told me that she had kept her sighting quiet, had not even reported it on the wire, because she was afraid she might be accused of being "just another nut." She had kept the UFO in view for nearly twenty minutes, ample time for her to study it in considerable detail. I made an appointment to see her at her home the following day, and then went about the job of unpacking.

I met officers Bertrand and Hunt for lunch in the sprawling, tea-roomish dining room of the Inn. Only a few hushed patrons were lunching at the time, and Hunt's bulk as he came through the door of the dining room dominated the room. He looked twice the size of Bertrand in every dimension. He had a quiet, wry New Hampshire accent and a salty sense of humor.

Bertrand was wearing zylonite glasses, was soft-spoken and serious-looking. Although he appeared slight and scholarly, I recalled that his lieutenant had told me over the phone that he was invariably assigned to the tough cases. Over a porterhouse steak I learned more about what had happened and—I was surprised to learn —was *still* happening in Exeter following Muscarello's UFO sighting.

"For quite a stretch there," Hunt said, "three or four phone calls a night would come into the station. Most of them were pretty sensible people, and a lot of them came pretty close to the description of the things we saw."

"I think you'll find," Bertrand said, "that a lot of people are really afraid to report seeing these things. I know I was damn glad when Dave pulled up in his cruiser that night, if nothing else than to check me out. Some people might be making mistakes, but I'm convinced a lot of them aren't. When I was in the Air Force, I used to work right on the ramp with the planes. I could tell what kind of plane might be around, just by the sound of it. Right after this thing went away on September third, an Air Force jet came over. Dave and I both saw it. It was very clear what it was. No comparison at all between it and the object, in either lighting or configuration or sound, or anything else. And of course, the B-47 was high, and the object was low. Right down over the trees. It was impossible to make a mistake in comparing the two. And on the way out to the place with Muscarello, I thought the kid for sure had seen a helicopter. But it wasn't. Not by a long shot."

"He's a pretty cool kid, Muscarello," Hunt said. "It would take a lot to shake him up. And he was shaken up, there's no doubt about that."

Hunt went on to say that Muscarello was now at the Great Lakes Naval Training Station, but suggested I could get some details from his mother.

After lunch, Bertrand and Hunt got in my car, a small-ish Volvo sedan which sagged a little under Hunt's weight. We drove out Route 108, then turned left on Route 150 southerly toward Kensington and Amesbury. Hunt pointed toward another road slanting up a hill ahead of us.

"Up this road another kid, Ron Smith, saw the thing too."

"When did that happen?" I asked.

"About three weeks after we saw it. Said it passed over his car twice."

"Anybody with him?"

"Yes, his mother and aunt. They were all scared to death when they pulled into the police station."

"What kind of kid is he?" I asked.

"Pretty decent, from what I know," Hunt said. "Works in the grocery store after school, right across from the police station. You might be able to find him this afternoon."

I made a mental note to interview Smith, just as we approached the Kensington line and Tel. and Tel. Pole #668. We pulled up near it and got out of the car. Stretched across the field was a heavy wire with a metal sign on it, reading KEEP OUT.

"The owner had to put this wire and sign up right after it happened," Hunt said. "Dozens of cars out here every night for weeks afterward. People dropping beer cans and cigarette butts all over the place. Some of 'em used to wait here all night to see if it was coming back."

We looked out over a wide, sweeping field of some ten acres, rimmed by tall evergreens. To the left was the tidy neo-Colonial residence of Clyde Russell. To the right, about a hundred yards away, was the rambling, ancient saltbox farmhouse, its timbers tidily restored by Carl Dining, a gentleman farmer who kept several horses and other livestock. Behind the Dining house was a split-rail fence forming a corral, where the horses were romping. The ground sloped down toward the evergreens, and in the far distance we could see the Atlantic shore at Hampton, a half a dozen miles to the east.

I asked Bertrand to reenact the scene in as much detail as possible.

"Well," he said, "I pulled up in the cruiser right by this pole here. I know it's #668 because I checked it that night. Muscarello was with me. We got out of the

59

car, and looked around. Nothing was in sight. Nothing at all. But the kid insisted that we look around. He was still upset, still tense. I had him describe to me, just as I'm describing to you, exactly what happened. Except that it was dark then, about three in the morning. He told me that he was walking right by the pole here, when the thing came at him from his right—right over the field here. It hovered right over the roof of the Russell house there, he said, and was about twice as big as the house. Then it looked like it was really going to make a dive at him, he said, so he lay down on the ground in the shoulder of the road. Right about there—" And Bertrand pointed toward a gravel gully next to pole #668.

"We got back in the cruiser and waited for about ten minutes. Still nothing showed up. Then I called back the station and told Officer Toland—he was on duty at the desk—I told him, I don't see a thing. But the kid said, Let's go all the way out on the field. Maybe we'll see it then. So I called back on the cruiser radio and said I was going out on the field. Just in case they wanted to reach me for something."

Bertrand pantomimed the motions in detail, reliving the incident.

"Well, we both got out of the cruiser, walked down the field, down the slope, down to over by that fence there."

He pointed to the split rails of the corral, about 75 yards down the slope. "I was shining my light all around to see if I could spot anything. Especially over toward those woods."

He pointed toward the woods several hundred feet away, in the direction of Hampton.

"When he yelled 'I see it! I see it!' I turned fast and looked up. He pointed near the trees over there—the big ones. The leaves are off it now, but they weren't then. It was coming up behind them. It hovered, looked like it banked, came forward toward us. He seemed to freeze, and that's when I grabbed him and ran back to the cruiser. We got in the cruiser and I called in saying I was seeing it. Dave came. Dave came, and it was moving down toward the end of the field, across the tops of the trees."

60

"Just to the right of the big trees," Hunt said. "That's when I saw that fluttering movement. And the pulsating lights."

"You both were right where we're standing now?" I asked. We were still at the edge of the road looking down the field, next to the KEEP OUT sign.

"We were standing where we are now," Hunt said.

"Dave was right by the car, and I jumped out to join him here. We decided to take off, but we waited a few minutes, and then we saw it go off across the horizon. Toward Hampton."

Bertrand pointed back toward the two big trees. "These trees must have been blocking the light when we first got here," he said. "It was somewhere, but I didn't see it. Then it came up from behind the trees, it's thick there, thick enough to hide it. It came up and it looked like a big red ball when it was still behind the trees."

"Was it rising up slowly?" I asked.

Bertrand moved his hand slowly in an undulating motion, rocking it from side to side. "It was rising like this," he said; "looked like it was waving back and forth. And no noise. That's what got me. No noise. Except for the horses out in the barn and in the corral. I could hear them kicking, kicking hard. Soon as it was gone, they stopped. And before it came up over the trees they were quiet. Same with the dogs. You could hear several dogs howling when it came in sight, then they stopped when it left."

"When the thing was leaving this area," Hunt said, "it moved across the tops of those trees. And it stopped still twice. When it stopped the second time, there's a house barely out there, you can barely see it, I mean. It went from left to right across the horizon, and then dropped out of sight."

I turned back to Bertrand. "Where were you when you grabbed the kid?"

"Right down by the fence. By the corral. There's a little birdbath there. You can see it."

"What was the closest point it got to you?"

Bertrand pointed toward the Russell house. "Right about over that house."

"When you ran back to the cruiser with Muscarello, how did it maneuver?"

"I was yelling on the cruiser radio, and I had my back to it," Bertrand said. "But the kid was watching. And the whole field turned red. That house was red. Everything was red—the inside of the cruiser. Everything was lit up."

"All the way to the trees?"

Hunt said, "Seemed to me to be all the way to the trees."

"And the field?"

"The whole field," Bertrand said. "I was afraid we were going to get burned."

I looked over toward the Russell house. "Is this the house Muscarello ran to?" I asked.

"That one. Yes. The people thought he must have been a drunk. Can't blame 'em."

"When you got back in your cruiser and radioed the station, did Dave come right away?"

"He was already on his way," Bertrand said. "I had just got through calling, and I saw his headlights coming down the road."

Although the story was already familiar to me, through my earlier phone calls, the newspaper accounts, and Ray Fowler's detailed report for NICAP, I wanted to explore every detail fully, even if it was repetitious. What interested me most was the consistency of the stories. Except for very minor variations, the different versions agreed. Occasionally, as I went back over the details, a few new ones would emerge, details half forgotten in the initial excitement.

"About how far above the trees did the thing seem to be?" I asked.

"Well," said Bertrand, "I figure those trees to be about seventy feet high. And it was about thirty feet above them. That's how I figured the altitude of the thing was about one hundred feet."

"A little lower," Hunt said, "and it would have looked like it was skimming the trees. And it was rocking over them. An airplane couldn't do this if it tried."

"And here's another interesting thing," Bertrand said. "Right after the thing disappeared toward Hampton, we waited, and that's when we saw the B-47 going over—a conventional jet we see all the time around here. Everybody knows them—and the B-52s and the Coast Guard helicopters. Kids in their knee pants know them here. Grandmothers know them. Anyway, when we got back to the station and Scratch Toland told us about the hysterical man calling from the Hampton phone booth, Dave and I back-timed what happened and figured that the man made this call just about the time the craft had moved from us to Hampton."

"And then I saw it later," Hunt said. "About an hour later, down on the 101 bypass. But it was too far away then, and I didn't make any big fuss about it."

"You couldn't identify it for sure?"

"Not positively," Hunt said. "But I could pretty well say it was the same thing. And it was still over Hampton."

We got back in the car, and Bertrand directed me toward Drinkwater Road, and then over Shaw Hill, where Ron Smith and his mother and aunt had reported their sighting several weeks later.

"They were scared, there's no doubt about that. Shaking. Really white. The second time he saw it, Smith said it backed up over his car. Like it went into reverse gear. Said it was round with bright lights over the top of it. On the bottom, some different colored lights. Said it looked like it was spinning, like a top."

The rolling hills of southern New Hampshire spread out before us from the top of Shaw Hill. The pre-Revolutionary farmhouses, most of them spanking white and freshly painted, sat placidly with their big squat center chimneys, a far cry from the Space Age, and especially an outer-Space Age.

Next to the tiny room housing the police desk is a small courtroom to handle those cases requiring immediate attention. It is spotlessly clean, with shiny brown woodwork out of respect for the serious business of the dispensation of justice.

It was in this solemn room that I interviewed young Ron Smith, a pleasant-looking seventeen-year-old whom I had found in the grocer's across the street, unpacking a carton of chicken soup. His boss at the store, skeptical of the UFO situation, had let him off for a few minutes, on the assurance that I wouldn't let him take a ride in a flying saucer. "He's too good a worker to lose," he said.

Young Smith was used to this gentle ribbing, he said, ever since he and his mother and aunt were driving that night first on Drinkwater Road, then on Shaw Hill, not more than a half a mile from where Bertrand, Hunt and Muscarello encountered their inexplicable craft. "They can kid me all they want," he said. "I know what I saw. They don't. Nobody can tell me I didn't see it. Nobody. That's all there is to it."

Smith, a senior at Exeter High, was planning to go into the Air Force after he graduated. His marks in school were fair to good, averaging around a gentleman's C. His boss at the store, in spite of the ribbings he liked to tender Smith, thought he was a top worker. Mrs. Oliver, at the police desk, knew the boy, described his character as exceptionally good.

Sitting at the attorney's desk in the tiny courtroom, I asked him to describe his experience in as much detail as possible.

"Well," he said, "I was riding around with my mother and aunt. It was a warm night, I guess around eleven-thirty P.M., and this was just about two or three weeks after the officers here saw this object. All of a sudden, my aunt said, 'Look up at the sky!' I thought she was kidding, but I looked up, and then stopped the car. I saw a red light on top and the bottom was white and glowed. It appeared to be spinning. It passed over the car once and when it passed over and got in front, it stopped all of a sudden in midair. Then it went back over the car again."

"Stopped in midair?"

"Stopped in midair, went back over a second time, stopped again. Then it headed over the car a third time and took off. It scared me, it really did. And I started to come back into Exeter to report it to the police. I got partway back—all the way to Front Street—when I came to my senses. I wanted to go back to make *sure* it was there. To take another look to make sure I wasn't seeing things. We did go back. And sure enough, it was in the same spot again. It passed over the car once, and that was the last time I saw it."

"Did it take off fast, or slow?" I asked him.

"Well, it didn't rush. It just sort of eased its way along. Then it took off fast."

"How about sound? What kind of sound did it make?"

"It didn't make any real sound. Just sort of a humming noise, like a cat when it purrs. And incidentally, I got up again that morning, about four A.M., to see if I could see it again. But I didn't see it."

"What did your aunt and mother say at the time you first saw it?" I asked.

"Well," Smith said, "my aunt first thought it was a plane. And then she saw that it was oval, and didn't have any wings on it. We could see that it wasn't a plane and we watched it for the first time about fifteen minutes. When it was passing over the car, I could see it best. It was oval, it didn't seem to be completely round, it was oval. It moved along slowly, sort of a bright light, a glare, like an ordinary light bulb, shiny."

"Any color at all?"

"There was a red light around the edge, but the center was white."

"You say it went right over the car?"

"Yes, it was right over the car. It was a very clear night. . . . It was kind of flat, but it wasn't completely flat. Sort of like an upside-down plate."

"What about its surface? Could you tell anything about that?"

"No, you couldn't distinguish it that well. But it was big."

"You say you're familiar with the Air Force planes, like the B-52s. How did it compare in size to one of them?"

"It was bigger. It was huge. You couldn't get it mixed up with a B-52. Or a B-47. This was down low enough so you could distinguish it pretty clearly. Not more than half a mile up at the most. Not much over two thousand feet or so."

"How about a meteor? Did you stop to think it might be one of those?"

"No, not a chance. This was a machine. I've seen a lot of meteors."

"Or a helicopter?"

"Helicopters make an awful racket. All this did was hum. And you could see it clearly enough to see that it *wasn't* a helicopter. A helicopter wouldn't scare me, or my aunt or my mother. This did, and I mean scared us."

"The weather was good, you say?"

"You could see clear as a bell. And it was right up above us, right over the car. The red light was very bright—like the color of a fire engine light that flashes. It was real bright. And it tilted. It tilted and you couldn't see any wings or anything. That's why I was sure it wasn't an airplane. It didn't move like any aircraft. It seemed to creep along. And when it left, it zoomed right off. It wasn't ten seconds in getting out of sight. And another funny thing happened that night."

"What was that?"

"The field up on Shaw Hill. It seemed to light up, not from the craft in the air, but from something else. You know what a landing strip at an air base looks like? The colored lights that outline the runways and taxi strips on the field? Well, I saw a group of lights on this field that looked a little like that. I thought if I drove around to the other side of the hill, there would be something there. So I did, but by the time I got there, I could see nothing. Just as dark as anything. So then I drove around back to where I was before, and there were the lights again. I couldn't understand it."

After Smith left to go back to the store, I looked over the story he had given the police that night. There were no discrepancies, and Mrs. Oliver noted that from all reports from the night-duty officers, Smith was as scared as he said he was.

I went to a phone booth, though, and called his mother. She confirmed the account in detail, but was a little reluctant to talk about it. This was a pattern I was to find repeated many times. In addition to Yankee reticence and taciturnity, the subject matter here was so strange, so bizarre, that those involved with it had a constant underlying fear of ridicule. Yet when they did summon the courage to speak, they did so with impressive energy and conviction. As the police lieutenant had said in my first inquiry over the phone, "If I had seen this thing, and I was alone, nobody else would have ever heard about it!"

Shortly after the interview with Ron Smith, I learned that Bob Kimball, a newsreel cameraman and stringer in

New England for all three of the major television networks, lived in Exeter and had been very interested in the Muscarello-Bertrand-Hunt incident. I had worked with Kimball before on several documentary films I had produced, and knew him to be a hardy and pleasantly cynical man, traits which often characterize the newsreel cameraman in any area. At dinner that night at the Exeter Inn, I welcomed the chance to get his opinion, which I knew would be well-weighed and considered.

Kimball frankly admitted that he was puzzled and baffled. He had a long-standing habit of spending a great deal of time at the Exeter police station, especially late at night when he found it hard to sleep. Used to the irregular hours his profession demanded, Kimball was essentially a night person. His habit was to drop by the police desk about midnight, chat with Officer Scratch Toland at the desk, follow up on any interesting cases which came over the radio. Along about three in the morning, he would join Rusty Davis, owner of the local taxi company and another one of the night people, and the two would drive over to a bakery in Hampton, in the rear of a small restaurant and bakery called "Sugar 'n Spice," for coffee and hot doughnuts, just out of the oven. This was a ritual for both of them.

"Unfortunately, I wasn't around the night of the Muscarello case. I was sleeping, which is something I don't usually do, and don't approve of. I would have given my left arm and an Arriflex camera to have caught a picture of that thing. Gene Bertrand finally did wake me up—about four-thirty A.M., I guess it was—but by the time we got out there, nothing was in sight, and I was still half asleep. And Gene was still shaken, which is very unusual for Gene. He's a tough cookie. So is Hunt. They're not the kind to go around making up any story."

I asked him what he made of it all.

"I just don't know," he said. "I can't figure it out, and I find it hard to even guess at it. Something was there, and something is continuing to happen. That much I'm sure of. Too many people all around the area are reporting this seriously, and a lot of them aren't dummies by a long shot. I kept thinking if I could only get a picture, a good picture, a close-up, then we'd have something to work on. I carry a loaded camera in the car with me all the time, but still no luck."

"If so many people are reporting sightings, why wouldn't the chances be in favor of your catching one?" I asked him.

"Well," Kimball said, "there are a lot of things to consider. In the first place, you can never predict where a report is going to come from. It might come from Manchester, from Portsmouth, from Derry, from Kensington —it's just not predictable. You'd have to have a dozen photographers stationed in as many separate localities as possible, sitting all night long and waiting. This is impractical. And some of them have been reported so high, you'd need a special lens. You can never tell what time a report is going to come in. And then it might be a false alarm. I estimate about thirty to forty percent of these sightings are mistaken identity. But the way these things are described, and the type of people who are describing them, I'd say most were definitely something strange, something unknown. But this is still a guess on my part. Nobody around here has had the time to really check this thing out."

"What's the scuttlebutt around the Portsmouth Air Base?"

"There's a lot. Constant reports of jet fighters being scrambled after the UFOs all the time. They don't regularly base any fighters there—the whole Pease operation is a SAC base, with just B-52s and B-47s and tankers for refueling. The fighters would have to be brought in from Westover or some other base, if there's any truth to the rumor. Then there's all kinds of stories that a couple of UFOs have landed right by the runways of the base. But there's no way of checking these out, because anybody with any real authority isn't going to say anything anyway."

Kimball offered to drive me around after midnight, and invited me to join him and Rusty, the taxi man, in their nightly ritual at the bakery. He also offered to point out several of the many spots from which reports of UFO sightings had been made both before and after the September 3rd event.

"UFO hunting has become a popular sport. All along Route 88, on the way to Hampton, and 101-C. You see cars waiting out there every other night."

"Anybody collected their stories and put them together?"

"None that I know of."

"You still haven't told me what you really make of all this."

"I'm going to wait until I see one myself," Kimball said. "And then I'll tell you."

The streets of Exeter at midnight are ghostly and quiet. The shops on Water Street, which sprawl along the bank of the Squamscott River, are dim and silent. Across from Batchelder's Bookstore, featuring cards, gifts, stationery, the faint blue fluorescent light POLICE flickers and glows uncertainly from the side of the Town Hall building. Inside, Desk Officer Scratch Toland holds a nightly rein on cruisers #21 and #22, most frequently manned by patrolmen Bertrand and Hunt on the Midnight-to-8 A.M. tour of duty.

Scratch Toland, with a round and impish face, is a veteran officer on the force, with a sharp and dour Yankee tongue and a pleasing wit. With his help, I was able to cull the names of over a dozen witnesses to UFO incidents, many more than I had anticipated, from the police blotter.

"This is interesting," I told Toland. "I didn't know you had so many leads."

"Lot of people were keeping 'em quiet," Toland said. "Afraid people might think they were nuts. Thing that brought so much attention to the September third sighting was that there were two officers on hand to testify directly."

"Do you think there are many more sightings unreported, not on the blotter?"

"I *know* so," said Toland. "Keep running into people who tell me they saw such-and-such quite a few weeks ago, a few nights ago, or whenever it was. It's getting now so that people aren't even bothering to report them."

Although I knew it was going to be repetitious, I asked Toland to go over the night of September 3 with me in detail. Somewhere, I felt, some new clues might emerge.

"When was the first you heard of this?" I asked.

"Well," Toland said, "the Muscarello kid come in. He

69

must have come in around twenty-five minutes past two, I think it was. And he was all shook up. He said he'd been watching this thing, and said it had been hovering over the field out there."

"How shook up was he?" I asked.

"He was *real* shook up," Toland said. "And he ain't the kind of kid that shakes up too easy, either."

"How did he act?"

"He was lighting one cigarette after the other, you know. And the first thing he told me—when he come in the door—he said, You're not going to believe me, but I saw a flying saucer. I kind of smiled, and I could see he was so shook up over this that I called Bertrand in. And that's when that coincidence come up. When I told Bertrand, when I told him, You want to go out with this fellow on Route 150 in Kensington and check out a flying saucer? And Bertrand, that's when he said, Gee that's funny, I just stopped by a woman out on the bypass. I saw the car stopped, I thought it was out of gas. So Bertrand says he went over and asked the woman, What's the trouble? And she told him this big thing had been following her in the air, over her car, all the way from Epping. When he told me about it, that's when I said it might be a good idea to go out with the kid."

"How did you feel about the kid when you first saw him that night? It's a pretty wild story to be hit with cold. Did you doubt him?"

"Well, I did and I didn't," Toland said. "You could tell he meant what he was saying. You don't get all upset like this over nothing. And this kid wasn't faking."

"He was so shook up you were inclined to believe him?"

"Yea," Toland said. "If he wasn't so shook up, I don't think I would've. He told me it was so low that it hovered right over the roof of this guy's house. He said it lit the whole top of the roof up, it was so low it almost hit the chimney. He said then it would sweep down like this"—Toland made a sweeping motion with his hand—"and when it did, he said he hit the road. He said it really scared him. When I figured he'd come that close to an object, sending Bertrand out didn't sound like such a bad idea."

"When was the next you heard from Bertrand?"

"When he got out there on Route 150," Toland said. The low, dim light over the police desk, the small dark room with shadows cast up from the single desk light, made it an ideal place for a ghost story, Space Age or not. "When he got out there with Muscarello, he called in on the radio. He didn't see anything, he even sounded bored. But, he says, we're going to take a walk down the field. Then the radio was silent. It was silent for quite a few minutes. And then the damnedest noise you ever heard. I couldn't even recognize Gene's voice!"

"What was the reaction?"

"Reaction? That's no word for it. He was *hollering*. I never heard him holler that way before or since. 'I see it! I see it!' he was hollering. And I started to laugh then, because I figured he was pretty scared."

"Understand he doesn't scare too easy. Is that right?"

"Bertrand? He doesn't scare at *anything*. I never heard a reaction like that in my life. He's not scared of anything—except something like this, and who wouldn't be? Bertrand will go in anywhere, he's always the first. If there's a fight or a brawl or a prowler in a dark warehouse—you name it, he'll do it. That's why I was so surprised. And I guess that's why I started laughing. I couldn't think of anything else to do."

"What about Hunt?" I asked. "Where was he at this time?"

"Well, Dave, he was hearing all the talk between Gene Bertrand and me over his cruiser radio. Dave was in the other cruiser, number 20. By the time Dave got there, the thing was just taking off over the field toward Hampton. And right after that, I got the call from the telephone operator about the man in the phone booth at Hampton."

"Tell me about that," I said. "I got part of the story from Bertrand and Hunt."

"Well, the night operator at Exeter here called in. She said she had a man in a pay phone booth in Hampton, some man who was calling in all excited. He said this huge object was coming at him from the air, with bright red lights on it. Coming right at him. And then he was cut off or hung up, she didn't know which. I called the Hampton police right away—they said they'd notify the Pease Air Force Base."

71

"What did Bertrand say when he came back to the station?"

"Well, he was all shook up. He really was. And Hunt? He didn't show it quite as much, but you know Dave. He's like that. And of course, he hadn't seen it quite as close as Gene had. Dave did call me later, though, and said that it gave him an awful weird feeling. Coming from Dave, that's quite a statement."

"Now," I said, "some of these other reports you've had since then—the ones I've taken down the names of—can you tell me about some of them?"

I was working on hearsay now, but I knew I was going to be checking most of the leads directly, and it was possible I could pick up some other helpful details. As long as I could follow it up, I was finding that hearsay could be helpful.

"Of course we've had so many since then, it's hard to remember. Let me take a look at some of the names you've got down. . . ." Toland glanced over the list I had prepared from the blotter. "Well," he said, looking over his semi-lens glasses, "this Lillian Pearce, lives right down on the Hampton-Exeter line. Just off 101-C. She'd be a good one to interview. She said she saw one in July, and was afraid to report it. Then she saw a couple more, and after Bertrand and Hunt admitted it, she reported them. The last one she saw, she said a plane from the air base was out chasing it. And as soon as the plane got near it, the lights on the object went out, and the thing seemed to disappear. Then the plane went away, and the lights came on again. And you know, it's a funny thing, we get a lot of calls like that—about a plane from the air base chasing these things. I got a call from a fellow on Hampton Falls Road, a ham radio operator. This was about a week after this Mrs. Pearce called in. There was a plane from the air base circling around Hampton Falls, and they called the ground on shortwave radio and asked for anyone on the ground that could hear them to come in. And he picked the call up, and they asked him to call in at the Exeter Police Department to see if we'd got any reports of sightings that night. They said they were out chasing a UFO, but couldn't find anything."

"What about some of the other calls you've received?" I asked Toland.

"There was a kid who goes to high school who came in here shaking a few weeks ago. Ron Smith."

"Yes, I talked to him today."

"If you wanted to see a kid shook up, you should have seen him. People don't get excited like that for nothing, you know."

"He impressed me as a pretty level-headed kid."

"He *is*," said Toland. "That's what's so confusing about this whole thing. Most of the people who've been reporting them are level-headed. And I'll tell you something. I've had three different people tell me the same story that night that Bertrand saw the woman on the bypass, and then took Muscarello out. Around eleven-thirty that night, this fellow up in Brentwood. I met him at a restaurant, oh, about a week later. And he was telling me that he woke up that night, and the whole room was lit up. And he figured somebody was coming in the driveway, or down the road with a high beam. So he got up and looked out the window. And there wasn't a car in sight, no sound or nothing. And all of a sudden, the room went dark again. And then the wife of this fellow who runs the machinery over the mill—she woke up and the room was all lit up, and she couldn't remember what day it was, but it was right in the vicinity of the time that they saw it over Kensington. The room was all lit and no cars or planes around, then all of a sudden it went dark again."

The telephone rang, a routine call. Scratch Toland hung up, lit his pipe. "A couple over in Fremont. Their kids came running in one night, said some object out in the field scared the life out of them. And Mrs. Ralph Lindsay, in South Kensington. You've got her name down there. She called in here very early in the morning, just before dawn. She said it was right out her window right at the same time she was calling. It was like a bright orange ball, almost as big as a harvest moon, she said. It just hung there in the sky, but it didn't move. And it wasn't the moon either. She talked to me for about five minutes on the phone. All the time she was talking to me, her kids were at the window watching it. Then she said it took off fast, toward Hampton. Now why would people go to all this trouble—people all over the area—if they weren't seeing something real? People don't call the police station in the middle of the night just for the fun of it."

Toland took a call on the radio from Bertrand in Cruiser #21. A door in a store was unlocked, and he was going in to check. It was now about one in the morning. Kimball and Rusty Davis hadn't come in yet, but they were expected. Outside the station, the street was dark and deserted.

Toland, smoking more matches than tobacco, went on. "The evening after Mrs. Lindsay called, a fellow phoned here after supper, around seven-thirty that night. I wasn't on duty, but Lt. Cottrell told me about it, because he had learned about my call with Mrs. Lindsay. The man said that this big, orange-red object hovered over his house just before dawn the same morning Mrs. Lindsay saw it. He told Cottrell that he never paid any attention to these things before, but that he'd been thinking it over all day long, and thought he ought to call in to the police about it."

"What about the Air Force? Did you run into them when they were investigating the Muscarello sighting?"

"They were in here one night, but they didn't say much. Close-mouthed. They were patrolling around, I understand, in a lot of different places. They got so many complaints about these objects down around Applecrest Farm in Hampton Falls, they sent the officers up to check, in addition to the Muscarello place."

"What's the Air Force's attitude? Do they seem to take it seriously?"

"They're not fooling around, I know that. Now take this sighting of Mrs. Pearce's—the first one. Several weeks before the September third sighting. We got the report that she was driving down Route 88 with her daughter. They saw this big red light in the distance, and they thought it was an accident with police cars or a wrecker, or something like that. The closer they got to it, the bigger it got. And then they began to realize something was funny. Then all of a sudden, this thing took right off up in the air. She told some friends of hers, and they laughed at her. But the Air Force didn't. They investigated, and they found that her description was identical with Gene's. Somewhere, all these pieces have got to add up."

"But what's it all going to add up to?"

"That's what I hope you're going to find out," Toland said. "Like this woman who called up here the other night. It must have been about quarter of eleven. And she asked me all about the thing. And after I got through telling her all I knew about it she said, The reason I'm calling is to find out if I see one, what I should do? And I said, Do what I'm going to do. And she said, What's that? And I said, Run like hell!"

It was nearly two in the morning when Kimball and Rusty Davis showed up at the station. There was a lot of kidding around, and then the nightly pilgrimage for the coffee and doughnuts got under way. We would have a chance to look at some of the favorite places the UFO hunters haunted on the way over to Hampton.

We piled into Kimball's car, a big Chrysler especially equipped for his newsreel and documentary camera work, with a shortwave radio, a mobile telephone, cameras, lights and film stock. It carried a license plate CBS-TV, although he worked for all three networks. "We'll check a couple of these places on the way down," Kimball said as we moved out of the empty streets of Exeter and onto the Hampton road. "But don't expect to see anything. Rusty and I have been looking every night since it happened, and we haven't had any luck. There's one spot on Route 101-C where some reports have come in—and another field on Route 88 where a lot of them have. We'll go by there first."

Rusty, in the back seat, mumbled, "As long as we don't forget the doughnuts." A shaggy, congenial man with an enormous appetite, he had heard a lot about UFOs as he taxied the citizens of Exeter and environs around the area.

Route 88, from Exeter to Hampton Falls, is dark, winding and lonely, a fit place for a tired UFO to rest, if indeed UFOs did exist. In spite of the evidence, some of it rather startling, it was hard to overcome the resistance of a skeptical outlook, born of the scientific age. And yet one of the prerequisites of science is to keep an open mind.

For the first time the idea began to grow on me that, in spite of official protestations, the Establishment (in the form of official government, Air Force and scientific agencies) was actually in as weak a position as the Protesters or Witnesses, if they could be called that. Regardless of official proclamations, the Air Force offered no definite proof of nonexistence (a paradox, of course, but everything in this case was a paradox, an ambivalence, a dichotomy). But neither did the Witnesses offer proof. They offered only conviction, sincerity, dedication, and resolute resistance to any who would call them false witnesses. What was most distressing to these people was that the Establishment—mainly in the form of the Air Force—was responsible for calling them liars and incompetents with almost unforgivable bluntness. There seemed to be shaping up here a mammoth confrontation between the Air Force and the growing number of reliable observers.

The threat of the UFO was still psychological, however. No instance of any physical harm befalling a human being had been reliably reported in the twenty-year history of the phenomenon's most yeasty occurrences. Even those observers who had had close and frightening encounters experienced no physical harm. Interstellar beings who could conquer the forces of nature to the extent of defying gravity (if thousands of observers were telling the truth), harness electromagnetic forces, and defy G-forces, which the entire NASA space program showed no indication of conquering, should easily be able to do harm at will.

The UFOs had apparently made no attempt to communicate with Earth People, unless, of course, they had communicated directly with the Scientific Elite, who, having reported it to the Government, were promptly restrained from releasing it to the general public.

And then of course the question would come up: Could scientists be squelched like this? Wouldn't some intrepid scientist say to hell with politics and everything else, he was going to bring the Truth to the public because he *believed* that truth was more important than both politics and the Establishment combined?

But if he should be so bold, wouldn't it be possible, as Gordon Evans had suggested at lunch, for the Establishment to neutralize anything he might say by subtly associating him with the lunatic fringe? Alone and disassociated from his sober colleagues, his testimony would be worthless.

On the other side of the fence, if you presupposed a benign and intelligent group of political leaders, or Air Force generals, who were faced with definite evidence and proof of the fact that UFOs of extraterrestrial origin did exist, wouldn't they, out of concern for the entire organized structure of society, feel that they must be most cautious in the manner in which this intelligence should be released to the general populace? The Orson Wells "invasion" in the late thirties, a single dramatized radio program resulted in mass hysteria. Would the same thing—or worse—happen if official government sources announced blandly that we definitely had visitors from another planet? What would a reasonable and prudent man in the position of complete authority—such as the President of the United States—do when confronted with such a decision?

There have been, I learned after I started this research, frequent and continual rumors (and they are *only* rumors) that in a morgue at Wright-Patterson Field, Dayton, Ohio, lie the bodies of a half-dozen or so small humanoid corpses, measuring not more than four-and-a-half feet in height, evidence of one of the few times an extraterrestrial spaceship has allowed itself either to fail or otherwise fall into the clutches of the semicivilized Earth People. What would any of us do if we bore the responsibility of releasing this news to the citizenry? If we were the "reasonable and prudent man" our law courts always use as the measuring stick of judgment, we would probably be very circumspect. We might even delay judgment. It could produce chaos in an overorganized society which has become so dependent on intricate interrelated mechanisms that even a pint-size back-up relay in Ontario, Canada, can plunge 30 million people into inexplicable darkness, with none of the engineering experts in the country knowing exactly why it happened. As Gordon Evans had pointed out, the Brookings report had indicated that the engineers and the scientists would suffer the greatest confusion and who else could the masses turn to, aside from the suggestion that they turn to God? For there would *have* to be an explanation—a sober, logical explanation, from "official sources." And those official sources would have to be the ordinary person, elevated into authority by the mandate of the voters. The President. Or you. Or me.

The whole question of the Space Age ghost story seems to reduce itself to an insoluble ghost story—unless physical evidence of overwhelming validity were suddenly made available; or, unless scientists who *might* have such evidence were willing to share it. The censorship of the political powers in the Air Force seems to be exercising authority far beyond the powers assigned to it by the civilian control under which it is supposed to be operating.

As I drove down the twisting, darkened curves of Route 88 in Bob Kimball's newsreel-equipped Chrysler, thoughts like these were going through my mind

CHAPTER VII

Route 88, no different from hundreds of other macadam roads in New Hampshire, took on an aura of its own because of the stories which had been reported about it. Rusty, in the back seat, pointed out a darkened field to the right of the car. "This fare I had the other night in my taxi," he said. "His wife saw it right in the field there, right behind that farmhouse, in the daytime. He said she was standing right by the house there, and she seen it go over the field, and then just flutter away. She said it was a great silver object with a dome on it."

"What about the woman in the house by the orchard?" Kimball asked from the driver's seat.

"Well," said Rusty, "she told me she was out in her yard, hanging out the laundry. This thing came right over the house, she described it like the other woman, and then she passed right out. I get all kinds of reports like this from the fares."

Kimball slowed the car down now, pulled into a dark

field on the north side of the road. "This is the place where the cars line up to watch for it," he said. "And where a lot of people have made reports from."

The three of us got out of the car. It was a small field, rimmed by the black silhouettes of trees which looked for all the world like a cardboard cutout, against the sky.

"So, this is the place," I said. "It sure is a good place for it, sure as hell out of the way."

Kimball said, "I came down here one night and counted nine cars. People standing around, looking for it. Another night, I counted fourteen cars. They were camping out here almost."

I said, "How many UFOs did you see?"

"I'll tell you when I get a picture," Kimball said.

We stood there a few moments, looking at the sky, but of course nothing showed up. We climbed back into the car, drove into the silent streets of Hampton, and pulled up behind a low squat building in the village square.

Inside the bakery, the rich smell of freshly ground coffee and hot doughnuts was welcome. Two bakers were expertly chopping circular globs out of the dough, throwing out cheerful insults to the two regular visitors and protesting that it was regrettable I had to be in such unsavory company. The doughnuts were warm and light, the coffee bracing, helping to clear the cobwebs from my head, after a day of accumulating and taping information.

Another ritual assumed by Rusty and Kimball was to deliver a parcel of doughnuts and hot coffee to the police station at Hampton Beach, the resort section of the town, swarming with visitors during the summer, now deserted and boarded up in October. We drove along the ocean, past the shells of the summer hot dog stands and curio shops, and pulled up in front of the police station, the only light visible in the entire seashore community. It was close to 3 in the morning by now, and the only sound was the echo of the breakers on the beach.

Sgt. Joe Farnsworth was on night duty, a gray-haired gentleman who tendered more friendly insults to the regulars for being so late with the coffee.

He recalled the night of the frantic phone call from

the man in the unknown phone booth, pulled out the blotter and showed me the record of it.

"There's another story, though," he said, "much more interesting than this one. It's not on the blotter because we turned the whole thing over to the Coast Guard station and they took it from there."

"Tell me about it," I said.

"Well," the sergeant said, "this was about two months ago. That would make it some time in early September or late August. I don't have the names of the two fellows involved, but the Coast Guard does, if they're allowed to give them to you. Anyway, I was cruising up on the boulevard. It was late, about four in the morning, I think. This car was parked along the side, and I eased up to it, to see what was up. There were these two boys in it, I guess they were in their late teens. As soon as they saw me, they came running to the cruiser. And they were scared to death, I mean scared to death. Both of them. And this one boy said, 'You'll never believe what I'm going to tell you!' Right away, the way they were acting, I checked to make sure they were both sober. And they were. No liquor on the breath, nothing like that. They were just plain hysterical. So they told me they were going down the boulevard, and this thing come in from the ocean right over the top of their car, and it stayed still over the car. And they stopped short, they thought it was a plane that was trying to land and they didn't want to get involved underneath it. Then this thing stopped, too, whatever it was. Right in the air. Pretty soon, they got scared and took off—and when they did, this thing did, too. But when they went up the boulevard straight, this thing suddenly came right at them. That's when they pulled over, the thing shot off out of sight, and they were too hysterical to do anything until I pulled up, I guess. So I took them up to the Coast Guard station."

"How far is that?" I asked.

"Couple of miles up the shore from here. Right on the beach. So anyway, the Coast Guard had these guys write out statements about what they saw, and everything. And they had somebody come over from the air base, I don't know who it was, and check on it. And I don't know what they found, but these kids definitely saw something."

"You don't have the names of the kids anywhere?"

"No, I'm afraid I don't. But the Coast Guard does. And the next day, the story was flying around so much I was believing it myself. Especially the way these kids were so hysterical. They couldn't have faked that in a million years."

"Any other cases come your way?" I asked.

"Oh, a couple of weeks ago," the sergeant said. "After the beach closed. About a week or two after Labor Day. We got a report, you might have heard about it, that the thing was over the marsh, back of the police station here. I went out there, but I didn't see anything. Then there's the woman who works at the high school in Exeter. And I took her to school one morning, her car had broken down. She saw it. She was going up the Expressway toward the Exeter line when she saw it, and she said the thing stopped off to one side of her car. She got petrified and stopped the car and couldn't make up her mind what to do. All of a sudden, she said, there was a big white flash from the thing, and it was gone." The sergeant paused a minute, and leaned back in his chair. "Now I still don't know what to make about all this," he said. "Do you suppose it's something the Government is working on?"

"That's one possibility. All I can say is that it's anybody's guess."

"It seems to me, and I might be wrong," said the sergeant, "that every night we got a report on this, it's been foggy, hazy."

"Most of the time," Kimball said, "in Exeter, it's been clear. So I don't think that holds up."

"That night the kids went up to the Coast Guard station, it was quite foggy. But you know—on a second thought, I don't think it could belong to the Government, because the Government can't keep its mouth shut that long. They'd be so proud of themselves if they had a vehicle that could do all this, they'd have it on TV the next day."

"Well," said Rusty, "they can't be dangerous. Because they've been around enough that they could have done plenty of damage by now, if they wanted to."

It was almost dawn when I got back to the Exeter Inn. I had an appointment with Chief Irvine the next morning at eight, followed by an interview with Lora Davis, daughter of Rusty, who had reported a UFO on Country Club Hill in Exeter not long after Bertrand and Hunt had seen theirs. Tired as I was, I found it difficult to get to sleep; everything that had happened during the long day of October 20 ran through my mind.

The possibilities seemed to boil down to one of three things: first, a revolutionary government secret weapon, unannounced and unpublicized. Second, it might be a foreign craft, Russia's perhaps, that was so fast, maneuverable and invincible that it could thumb its nose at our own Air Force, and survey the country at will and without fear of being captured or shot down. Third, it could be an interplanetary craft, coming from a civilization far advanced beyond our own.

These were it seemed to me the only speculations possible unless it could be assumed that the sightings were psychic aberrations. From the quality of the official and technical witnesses making low-level observations, such as the one Bertrand and Hunt had reported, mistaken identity could almost surely be ruled out. The Air Force explanations of some of these sightings were actually harder to believe than the sightings themselves. Psychic aberrations? Maybe—but highly unlikely. There was photographic and radar evidence, too. Bertrand had refused point-blank to believe the reports of the lone woman on the 101 bypass, of Muscarello, too, until in the company of both Muscarello and Hunt the thing suddenly loomed above him.

Of the three major speculative possibilities, there seemed to be arguments against any one of them being likely, also. If it were an experimental aircraft of our own design and making, it would be required to carry conventional running lights simply for air safety, if nothing else, regardless of its secret nature. And the Federal Aviation Agency would prohibit it, secret or not, from zooming straight at automobiles on the highway, forcing people into nervous shock. It would most certainly not be permitted to hover and maneuver in populated areas at night, skimming over housetops and cars. And if it were *that* secret the Air Force would not want it in populated areas anyway. If it were not secret, as Sergeant Farnsworth had said, it would be all over TV along with the astronauts, whose feats would be overshadowed by the power and maneuvers of the UFOs.

If the craft were of foreign origin, why had it not set off vociferous complaints about violation of air space in our country, or any other of the countries which had reported UFOs so frequently? The single U-2 which had flown over Russia at 60,000 feet had created a major international incident, blasted the hopes of a summit conference, and brought before the United Nations a case which still echoes through its halls. Logic would seem to rule out this possibility, also.

If the UFOs were extraterrestrial, why had they not attempted to communicate with us? Certainly, a civilization advanced enough to create interplanetary or even interstellar craft should be able to make it plain to us that we had visitors from space for the first time in recorded history. Unless, of course, they had already communicated with authorities who had decided to withhold this intelligence on the theory that the public might panic.

The latter possibility is at once the most logical and still most illogical (again the paradox). It is more logical than the other two only because the other two possibilities (advanced U.S. or foreign man-made craft) are so totally illogical under the circumstances. It is, at once, illogical because there seems to be no physical proof whatever.

NICAP has developed a theory about why, if the craft are interplanetary or extraterrestrial, they have not yet made direct contact with people here on the earth. It draws a comparison between what extraterrestrial astronauts might be instructed to do on investigating a populated planet and what already has been suggested for NASA by the RAND (Research and Development Corporation) for our own space exploration, now moving ahead so rapidly with unusually generous Congressional support. If the report, commissioned by NASA, represents a *quid pro quo* situation, any possible extraterrestrial visitors might be following the advice laid down by our own scientific researchers for our own astronauts. The Rand Corporation directive states flatly:

Any indication that a planet is already inhabited by intelligent creatures would signal the need for proceeding with the utmost caution. . . . Before a manned landing is made, it would be desirable to study the planet thoroughly . . . *for a protracted period of time; to send sampling probes* into its atmosphere and to send surveillance instruments down to the surface.

Contacts with alien intelligence *should be made most circumspectly*, not only as insurance against unknown factors, but *also to avoid any disruptive effects on the local population* produced by encountering a vastly different cultural system. *After prolonged study,* a decision would have to be made whether to make overt contact or to *depart without giving the inhabitants any evidence of the visitation.* [All italics are the author's.]

It is important to remember, but difficult to keep in mind, that these statements are not from science fiction. They are sober, considered proposals made by our own scientists for the benefit of our *own* astronauts in this realistic Space Age. If the recommendations apply to us, they could as easily apply to more advanced explorers. And if the UFO visitations are of extraterrestrial origin, a good part of the recommendations seems to be already in effect. As NICAP points out, though, the UFOs apparently have not followed part of the prescribed routine, in that they have certainly not (assuming for a moment the reports of sightings be true) made any attempt to conceal their operations. They have seemed, however, to painstakingly avoid leaving any physical evidence of their existence, except for the scattered photographs that have been taken, and some marks or impressions in the ground. They have not shown any evidence of aggressiveness.

The mass hypnosis and psychic illusions recorded all through history kept coming back to my mind as an explanation. What about this possibility? Frankly, I didn't believe it had any bearing on the people I had interviewed so far. It would take a pretty strong hypnotic effect to influence officers as tough as Bertrand and Hunt, with each of them predisposed to be totally skeptical before their own sighting took place. Further, it is impossible to hypnotize a radarscope and equally impossible to hypnotize a camera. There had been enough reports clearly observed on radar throughout the country, and enough pictures found to be valid to indicate that the psychic phenomenon theory was very weak at best. Constant accounts of the effect of UFOs on dogs, cattle, ignition, electromagnetic instruments, radios, and lights were also outside the realm of psychic disturbances.

I finally slept and I barely made my appointment with Chief Irvine at the Exeter police station at eight the next morning. There was not much new I could gather from him because he had been on vacation during the time of the sightings his officers had made. He could only confirm the fact that the Air Force had made several inquiries about the incident, and for some time after it had happened, Air Force officers patrolled the roads at night. He also confirmed that officers Bertrand and Hunt were highly responsible and intelligent members of the force.

I spoke at length with Patrolman Leonard Novak of the Exeter force, a husky and articulate officer whom I had met briefly the day before. As we leaned against the fender of his cruiser, he told me his experience with Mrs. Lillian Pearce, the woman who lived on the Exeter-Hampton line and who claimed several encounters with UFOs in her vicinity.

"I was driving along Route 88 one night, a couple of weeks ago," Patrolman Novak said. "And there was quite a crowd down there, down by the field where they all seem to collect to keep an eye out for these things. I stopped for awhile to listen to what was going on. This Mrs. Pearce was really kicking up a storm, talking to the colonel from the Air Force base and complaining about the fact that the Air Force didn't seem to know as much as the whole neighborhood did about UFOs. There must have been ten or twelve people from the neighborhood there, but Mrs. Pearce was doing most of the talking."

"The colonel had come all the way down from Portsmouth?"

"Not only the colonel, but a major, too. Evidently she had been to Pease Air Base that day, and was claiming to the colonel that she had seen these things four or five times, according to her. She had taken pictures of it, and they were trying to get her to give them the film. Said they'd give her a new film if she gave them the exposed roll. But she'd have none of that. She said, Oh

85

no. I'm going to get these things developed and find out what they are myself."

"Is this what all the fuss was about?"

"Not all, no. The colonel was trying to persuade Mrs. Pearce and the rest of the neighbors that what they had seen were the strobe lights from the air base runway, which is about ten miles away. And apparently the colonel had sent the major back to the air base in his car, to have them turn the runway lights on and off at a regular pattern of intervals so they could see if this was it. He was still trying to impress the people there that what they were seeing was a reflection from these landing lights. Now, the major had just come back. And he asked the colonel if he had noticed what had happened. He said that for fifteen-minute periods he had turned the runway lights *on* for two minutes, and off for three. And the colonel had to admit that, no, he hadn't seen a thing, and everybody else there said no, we didn't either. And they didn't. There was no reflection or nothing. So that kind of blew the colonel's theory."

"What did Mrs. Pearce say to that?"

"She was all upset. She said, See what I told you? See what I mean? It was quite a scene, believe me. She was backing the colonel and the major all over the place."

The incident chiefly serves to indicate that the Air Force was taking this thing very seriously, and that people were aroused enough to demand some kind of explanation. I phoned Mrs. Pearce and made an appointment to see her at home that afternoon.

After breakfast I drove to Rusty's taxi office, run by his daughter Lora while he did the driving. It was a small room in a building behind his house, dominated by an overstuffed sofa and the shortwave radio equipment used for coordinating the taxi calls. Before I began to talk to Lora Davis, a radio call came in from Rusty saying he'd just learned of a woman in Stratham, a community not far from Exeter on the way toward Portsmouth, who had made a very clear sighting of a UFO in daylight and would be willing to talk to me about it. I took down the name and address, and then turned to Miss Davis.

"I can't for the life of me remember the exact date," she said. "But it was a Saturday night, sometime after the fuss about the policemen here in Exeter and the time they saw it. A couple of us decided we'd try to get a look at it—if there was such a thing—and we stayed up very late waiting for it, up on top of Country Club Hill. I guess it must have been about two o'clock in the morning, and I first thought what I saw was a plane, with a little green light on it. And suddenly it went off, and there wasn't any green light. It had turned into a big, huge red light. Just a big red light, blinking on and off. Then it started moving in closer, I guess maybe it came within about three miles of where I was. It was much too big to be a plane, the distance it was."

"You say it had a bright red light?" I asked.

"Very bright. Much brighter than an airplane light. It was coming in from a distance, from the southeast, sort of parallel to Route 101-D, the bypass, and it was headed toward the ocean."

"Was it moving on a steady course?" I was trying to check out whether it could be a plane.

"It was for awhile, and then it stopped suddenly. Right in the air. Then it staarted off in a different direction."

"Could you make out any shape, or any pattern of lights?"

"Well," she went on, "the shape from where I saw it and from how I can determine it, was like a small cone. The top was round, and then it sort of curved under. Like a top."

"How about the surface? Could you make that out?"

"Not really," she said. "It seemed as though it had a metallic color to it. But I couldn't be sure of that. Because the lights were blurring my eyes and I didn't see it that close to be sure."

"How long were you able to keep it in view?"

"Oh, about five minutes. Maybe a little longer. Between five and eight minutes, I'd say."

"Could you describe the way it moved?"

"Well, when it moved, it moved quite fast. Not like a B-47, though, we see them all the time. Don't forget, this thing stopped right still in midair. Did you ever see a plane do that?"

"You say it had a brilliant red light. Was the object all red? Any other colored lights?"

"Just that green one at first, but that changed to red.

And then it seemed as though the red light was blinking on and off. It's kind of hard to describe."

The taxi radio came in with an inquiry and I had time to appraise Miss Davis and her testimony. She was calm in her outlook, unemotional in her reaction to the object, and appeared to be of above-average intelligence. While her observation was a little vague, she spoke with authority about what she saw, without decorating her description with unessential detail. If I had been on a jury, I would have graded her as a fully believable witness. What's more, she was aware of her compass directions, a rare attribute for a woman. She also showed some familiarity with the aircraft in the vicinity.

I checked the name and address of the new observer with her—a Mrs. Harlow Spinney, of Portsmouth Avenue, in Stratham. She and her husband were ham radio buffs, and frequently talked to Rusty on his taxi radio.

The Spinney home, with its large shortwave radio antenna, was cheery and sprinkled with good non-fiction books. Mrs. Spinney was blond, attractive, articulate. She was painstaking with details, and kept a well-organized diary.

"When I heard you were coming over," she said, "I looked in my diary to check the date of this. It was September 27, just about ten o'clock in the morning. I was driving from Exeter toward Portsmouth, and when I first saw it, it was in the distance. And it wasn't more than fifty feet from the road at that time, but I was, oh, maybe a mile from it. I thought at first it was a low-flying plane, so I hurried and got around this tractor that happened to be in the road, and got a little closer to it. It appeared to be going toward Portsmouth, not directly along the highway but in that direction. But when I got within two or three hundred feet of it, darned if that thing didn't turn around and come back so I got a *perfect* view of it in broad daylight."

By now, I was beginning to notice some similarities in the accounts these observers were giving. Without knowing each other, and without collusion, they constantly referred to the objects as "the thing" or "that thing." This had a certain convincing ring to it, because by implication it indicated that instinctively they were not confusing the sighting with a plane or ordinary aircraft. I still had no clear or vivid description of the texture of any of these objects, however, and I asked about this one.

"I'd say it was definitely metallic. Yes, it was. That's why it didn't frighten me. I thought at first, What kind of plane is that with no wings? But then I thought it wasn't frightening at all, because it looked just as if it were guided."

"Did it go fast—or did it move slowly?"

"It went slowly when I first saw it," she said. "Then I pulled up and stopped. I wanted to listen, you know, to see if I heard any noise or anything. I didn't. It was silent. It hovered, as I said, and it turned around and came back and I got a *beautiful* look at it. And then it went *furiously* off—I suppose it was toward Manchester."

Mrs. Spinney reacted with none of the eeriness the others had felt, but perhaps this might have been because she had seen it in broad daylight in a populated area. Her account was ingenuous and disarming, as natural as if she were describing a friend's new car.

"You're sure," I asked, "that this craft moved contrary to most airplanes?"

"Believe me, it didn't look or act like anything I had ever seen. Except possibly a helicopter. And a helicopter it was definitely *not*."

"Any glow or light to it?"

"No. And there wasn't a cloud in the sky, incidentally. It was a beautiful, clear day. I could see no openings in it, no numbers."

"It was smooth in texture then?"

"Yes, it was. Just about as smooth as the surface of the fuselage of a B-47 or a B-52, which go right over my house here all the time. We're right in the middle of the landing pattern, sort of. But it was so close I know I could have seen an opening if it happened to have been on the surface."

"About how long did you have it in view?"

"Oh, I don't imagine it was more than a minute or two."

"Do you have a rough idea how high it was?"

"Well, I really can't tell how high it was, but if you saw a plane that low, you'd be frightened. It probably wasn't more than a couple of hundred feet up. And you know something—"

"What's that?"

"I said to myself: Am I really seeing this thing—or is it because I want to see it? And I told myself, yes. Yes, I'm really seeing it. You really question your own eyesight in a case like this."

"What's the closest you would say it came to you?"

"Oh, I would say less than two or three hundred feet. But it went so quickly, that it was hard for me to tell how big it was."

"That's the next question I was going to ask you."

"Well, it *is* hard to tell," she said. "But if I *had* to estimate it, I'd say it was about thirty feet in diameter."

It was nearly 11:30 that morning of October 21, and I was already late for my next appointment with Mrs. Hale, the UPI stringer in the area, several miles away. I gave a mental B-plus to Mrs. Spinney as a witness, and got in my car. Driving from Stratham toward Hampton, I began to realize that I was setting a pattern for myself in this research problem. I had screened out fanatics or irresponsible observers because I simply did not have the time to waste with them. In the leads that Scratch Toland had helped me cull from the blotter, I had checked beforehand to make sure I wasn't going to get involved with anyone who could obviously be ruled out as an incompetent or fanatic. I had often heard in courtroom cases the phrase "a parade of witnesses," which seemed to signify that such a group could prove or disprove a case. In the UFO case, such a parade seemed to be the only practical way to make even a small dent in the mystery.

To be totally objective in the research, I should also interrogate "negative" witnesses. But what was a negative witness in this case? A person who had never seen a UFO? That represented most of the population including myself. Conversely, that still didn't prove that UFOs were nonexistent. How many people have seen an albatross, a white whale, a plover's egg, a pair of Siamese twins, or a cyclotron? An infinitesimal fragment of the population. Yet no one contests their existence. Why aren't they contested? Because authorities have proclaimed them to exist. But to this date, no Master Authority had proclaimed that UFOs exist, except indirectly. Oddly enough, the UFOs' greatest enemy, the U.S. Air Force, had admitted their existence because they have set up a complete, officially regulated UFO program. You cannot reasonably set up a program to investigate a nonexistent thing. The Air Force has this program, and I had already examined it in detail, in its regulation 200-2.

Nor would the Air Force have taken the trouble to spell out the subject so thoroughly in its public relations booklet *Questions and Answers About the United States Air Force.* In paragraphs numbered 148 and 149, the subject is discussed extensively, if lamely.

In answer to its own posed question *Are there really flying saucers?,* the official booklet of the Air Force says: "The term 'flying saucer' is really a science-fiction term that was coined several years ago [immediate downgrading attack on the subject]. No unidentified flying object has given any indication of threat to the national security [this, again, is tacit recognition of the fact that UFOs do exist]; there has been no evidence submitted to or discovered by the Air Force that unidentified sightings represented technological developments or principles beyond the range of our present scientific knowledge [this, of course, gives tremendous leeway. Our present knowledge includes theories by Dr. Einstein and Professor John Wheeler of Princeton and others that cope with and understand electromagnetic and gravitational forces far beyond the scope of modern engineering and its capacity to put it into practical use. UFOs, under this premise, could be thousands of years ahead of our capacity to produce such a craft, and still come within the confines of this definition]; and finally, there has been nothing in the way of evidence or other data to indicate that these unidentified sightings are extraterrestrial vehicles under intelligent control." In addition to admitting conclusively here that UFOs exist, the Air Force makes a statement which NICAP vociferously contests. We are back again, at this point, to NICAP's contention that the Air Force is, in the most simple and direct terms, lying. By the same token, of course the Air Force is calling NICAP a liar.

The Air Force booklet goes on, in Paragraph #149 to pose its own question again: *What is a UFO?*

"A UFO," the booklet, printed in 1965, states, "is an *unidentified flying object.* Since the inception of the Nation's program of investigating UFOs, for which program the Air Force is responsible, only 7.7 percent of the reported cases have remained unidentified."

Close examination of this statement indicates that there are hundreds of cases in which the Air Force was forced to throw up its hands and say, "We don't know." Under normal conditions, this would be perfectly acceptable to the general public, because it doesn't know either. But the attitude which the Air Force assumes exaggerates its own shortcomings. What the Air Force further fails to disclose is the percentage of *expert, technical, or pilot* sightings which still remain unidentified, if indeed that is any mark of particular merit. Latest *Project Blue Book* figures on this are not available.

The Public Information booklet concludes: "As the Service primarily responsible for aerospace defense, the Air Force will continue to apply the services of its highly qualified scientists and technicians to the task of continuous investigation of all reports of unusual aerial objects over the United States."

Here, of course, is the real bone of contention that NICAP has been chewing on for a good many years. The Air Force does, and there is no reason to doubt it, apply the service of its "highly qualified scientists and technicians" to the task of continuous investigation—but what does it give back to the public? The most generous and enthusiastic supporter of the Air Force would have to admit that it gives back absolutely nothing in the way of information. It has, in a very subtle manner, gone out of its way to insult hundreds, and perhaps thousands of respectable citizens.

I finally had to admit, as I drove from Stratham toward Hampton in the shadows of two B-52s which circled low in a landing pattern over my car at that moment, that I had lost my objectivity completely as far as the Air Force was concerned.

It was playing dirty pool in relation to the citizenry, regardless of what the truth concerning UFOs turns out to be.

CHAPTER VIII

Mrs. Virginia Hale—the UPI stringer and reporter for the Haverhill, Massachusetts, *Gazette*—lived in a generous ranch house on a trim residential street in Hampton, not far from the ocean. Mrs. Hale was an experienced observer. She knew every conventional flight pattern of the nearby Portsmouth Air Base, as well as the commercial air lanes reserved for airliners on their way to Boston.

She took me immediately to her kitchen window, set above her spotless stainless-steel sink, and pointed out the portion of the sky in which she first saw the unknown craft. She had kept it in clear view over a five- to ten-minute period. She pointed to a soapish smear on a pane of her window.

"I put my finger in the dishwater the minute I saw this thing in the sky," she told me, "because I wanted to clearly mark the position where it was when it first came into view. The only thing I had handy to do this was the soapy water, and you can still see it there—faintly of course. But it's there."

It was. Enough of a mark to line up a fix on a certain portion of the sky, above the rooftops of her neighbors' homes, and out over the Atlantic a short distance. It was from this general portion of the sky, I recalled, that Sergeant Farnsworth had described the craft coming in over the two hysterical young men on the Hampton boulevard that early morning when they had whisked to the Coast Guard station to make their report. I was planning to explore that event also.

"I don't know the date I saw this," Mrs. Hale told me, in the kitchen, after she had poured a cup of black coffee. "I'd say two to three weeks ago. I was standing right here by the sink, about twenty-five after six in the evening. It was dusk, it wasn't quite dark, and there was still plenty of light. The reason it caught my eye was because it was bright and because it was going slow, very slow. Not at all like the path of the planes as they come over. So I automatically figured something is wrong. Then —it stopped dead over that house—"

She pointed to the roof of her neighbor's house, just out the kitchen window. "It was about three times the height of that chimney," she continued, "and it hovered there. Now you know four minutes is a long time, and that's why I hesitate to say that. But I'm pretty sure it was that long. Then I marked the window with the smear from the dishwater, so I could remember where I lined up the spot."

We moved outside, as she reenacted what had happened. "At the moment the object stopped I came out here on the terrace. Now, I would estimate that it was out beyond the Coast Guard station which is right on the shore, just over these houses here. After it started up again, it moved much faster. The B-47s go further east and further north before they cut back. And when this thing cut back toward the southwest, coming directly back and losing altitude fast, coming in really fast, and coming, almost, I swear I thought it was coming right at me. Of course, to be frank, I was hoping it would land. And it cut over this house behind us here, and I knew I would lose sight of it. But also, it was going so fast I thought it was going to crash."

"Could you get a clear look at it this time?"

"Well, at this point I could see from underneath, too. It was dome-shaped, and underneath, it was flat. Its altitude was now about twice the height of that chimney. By the time it was over here, I could see the bottom and the front of it plainly. And here I got a full view of the bottom and the back, and tail, if you want to call it that. It didn't really have a tail, maybe you'd call it a fin. Then I went into the house and looked out the front window."

"You could definitely rule out a plane?"

"Definitely," she said. "If you're around here any time at all, you'll notice the B-47s come by here on their landing pattern, and they go just about directly over this house. Then they head out to sea, to the east, turn slightly west, and come in by Rye and North Hampton.

So I am familiar with all that. And, oh, there was one thing I forgot to tell you. Right after I saw this, there was a commercial plane moving on a steady flight pattern and I used that to contrast it with this thing, and to check the altitude and erratic movement of the object. I also checked the time, and called this girl, another correspondent, in Seabrook. I thought she might have seen what I didn't see. Now what exactly did it look like? I'd say maybe it looked like a golf ball, sliced off more than half, and with another slice taken off where this fin was. As close as I can describe, it was very bright, not like any kind of light I can think of. I know I've seen something like the texture of this light, not a regular electric light. Matter of fact, the Puritron was the first thing I thought of."

"What's a Puritron?"

"It's an ultraviolet light, an air purifier. I have one here, and I'll show you. The light was bluish-green, but more green and white than it was blue. It had very definite outlines, and that was what I wasn't quite sure of at first. It did have a little glow around it, but that could easily have been a reflection of what was coming from within."

"Can you tell me what portion the glow was coming from?"

"Well, more or less from around the rim, that's what I noticed when it was going north along the coastline. And it sort of spread up the top part of the dome."

"Was it a bright light? Anything like neon?"

"You're getting close," she said. "When I described it to my daughter—she's fourteen—she said you mean something that makes heat? But I would say more like one of these modern streetlights that glow so brightly. Except that it seemed more contained. It seemed to have more substance."

"Could you tell if the surface was metallic or not?" Mrs. Hale's description was so articulate, I wanted to get every possible detail.

"I could not say that it was," she said.

"Any portholes?"

"No, nothing like that."

"Jet trail?"

"No."

"Sound?"

"Absolutely none. None at all."

"When it stopped, you say it stopped still?"

"Absolutely."

"Did it wobble at all? Rock?"

"No."

"Absolutely stationary?"

"Yes. That's the thing that struck me It hovered only in the sense that it remained suspended. I had heard of some of the other reports, and they had said that it rocked or wobbled."

"Did it behave aerodynamically like a plane at all?"

"Well, when it came back toward me, it was going too fast for anything that I know. That's for sure. And in the pattern that it was coming, none of the planes around here would use that pattern. Not even the local ones. When it was out in the east, I thought it might have been a reflection from the chute that the B-47s use just before they touch down on the runway."

This, I noted, showed an inclination to check out her own sighting against other possibilities. It helped support the accuracy of the testimony.

"About the shape again. Could you give me any more detail?"

"Well, if you turn a real deep, very deep saucer upside down, you do come close to it, if you break out a corner on it. If I could think of the right type of light I've seen and the right type of plastic to put it inside of, that's the impression I had."

"A glow from within that left a halo effect?"

"That's about it."

"And the size of it? Could you give any estimate of that?"

"It was big."

"If you saw a B-47, which you know so well, going over in a landing pattern, how would it compare?"

"If it were strictly on its landing pattern, I would say that a B-47 would be half as big."

"What about your own personal reaction? Were you scared at all?"

"No, I was strictly too much of a reporter. But I did have the feeling, oh goodness, don't tell me that thing knows I'm here. That's really how I felt."

Mrs. Hale showed me the Puritron, an air purifier which glowed inside with a bright, greenish-blue ultra-violet light. We also experimented with putting a light bulb inside a semi-opaque plastic pitcher, which, if the light had been brighter, she felt would have approximated the appearance of the strange light of the unknown object.

I had lunch that same day with Conrad Quimby, editor and publisher of the Derry (N.H.) *News*, Ken Lord of the Amesbury (Mass.) *News*, and June Miller, of the Haverhill *Gazette*. We ate at the Cock & Kettle, a rambling early-American hostelry with an open fire, grog, and steaming New England food. They were as interested as I was in the progress of the research, but unfortunately I was not far enough into it to give them any real pattern of the scene as it unfolded.

Quimby, a penetrating and intelligent young man, had even arranged for the Sky-Lite Advertising plane to fly over Derry so that the townspeople could determine whether this was the source of many of the local UFO reports.

The results had been inconclusive, and Quimby himself believed that there had to be much more to the story. He had run into a very convincing account of a UFO incident in upper New Hampshire, and was extremely impressed by the intelligence and honesty of the person who had reported it. "The thing that gets me," Quimby said, "is that the source of so many of the UFO reports that we get, and continue to get, are *embarrassingly* intelligent. They can't be sloughed off."

He himself had talked personally to two officers at the air base, one of whom personally believed UFOs were interplanetary craft, and the other who simply said that he wasn't sure what the answer was. Neither officer, of course, could speak officially.

Ken Lord and June Miller expressed their puzzlement again. I reviewed briefly the interviews I had had, and none of the reporters at the lunch were familiar with any of the cases except the Exeter police incident. As reporters, they of course had their hands full with many kinds of stories to cover. None of them had had the time or the opportunity to probe really deeply into the mystery, and this again indicated to me that intensive research in a limited area might shed more light on the subject than had been generated before, in spite of the amassing of the worldwide and countrywide evidence. If the reports in a concentrated area turned out to show many similarities, perhaps some conclusions could be drawn about the possible behavior patterns of the objects, not readily evident from widely scattered reports.

There were already some reasonably intelligent speculations I was beginning to pick up. Ken Lord had noted some evidence from his investigations that sightings seemed to concentrate near atomic plants, although they certainly were not so limited. NICAP had previously speculated about this.

Some of the police at Exeter had said that the objects seemed to choose SAC air bases to concentrate on, but there was much evidence that UFOs were seen elsewhere. A half a dozen of the people I had talked to did bring up one point which I had not in any way checked out as yet: the tendency of the UFOs to be reported over and near electrical power lines, the high-tension wires which cut across the country to deliver power to communities. I made a note to follow this idea up further, because I had been told that several of the locations most popular for flurries of reports were at the base of these power transmission lines. And of course, if there were any truth at all to the theory that UFOs were operated on electromagnetic principles, there could be a physical affinity of the objects for the power lines, which set up an electromagnetic field around them.

Conversation at lunch was mostly speculative and theoretical. I mentioned that I was basing my research on two foundations: First, many reports of UFOs had been made in the Exeter area. This, at least, was uncontestable. Second, the problem then became one of trying to find out if they were *valid* reports.

Up to this moment, only the second day of the research, I could say that I believed the reports I had checked so far *seemed* valid. The people I had talked to, the policemen, the high school student, the taxi radio operator, the ham radio housewife, the UPI stringer—all of them had stood up under fairly intensive questioning. Their competence to distinguish between fact and fiction seemed more than adequate and they could certainly distinguish between various types of known aircraft. A reporter, like a juryman, has to make appraisals and exercise judgment as to whether he can believe and accept the testimony he hears. On sober reflection, I could find far more reason to believe these people than not to believe them.

In general, the other reporters at the lunch table felt the same way about the people they had encountered in communities within a dozen or so miles of the Exeter focal point.

Quimby, who was familiar with my column in the *Saturday Review*, asked me if I would mind coming over to Derry the next morning and saying a few words about the UFO research to the English students in his wife's class at the high school there. The subject was very popular among the students. I told him I'd be glad to, emphasizing that I was a journalist, not a UFO expert. I arranged to see him in Derry the next morning.

Meanwhile, I discovered that I was late again, this time for my appointment with Mrs. Pearce, on the Exeter-Hampton line, and I had to leave the luncheon in ungentlemanly haste.

The Pearce home is in a miniature Levittown-type development on Warner Lane, a split-level house surrounded by well-kept shrubbery with the usual quota of bicycles on the lawn. I rang the bell, and waited a moment, until Lillian Pearce, a large, handsome woman with a shock of blond hair, opened the door and let me in. I was almost stunned by what I found inside. Sitting in a semicircle was a group of a half a dozen or so of the neighbors, waiting for me, and anxious to tell me of their many experiences with UFOs. Also in the room were several teen-agers, mostly of high school age, who were ready to volunteer their personal stories. I had been expecting a single description from Mrs. Pearce and instead, I was faced with a neighborhood meeting. It was helpful, of course, because I could compare several stories with the others I had heard. For the first time in the research, I got the feeling that the UFO incidents were far more widespread, more frequent, and more recent than I had suspected.

The room was so crowded, it was difficult to keep the meeting coherent. Mrs. Pearce dropped the opening bombshell by announcing that she had encountered a low-level UFO only the evening before, as she was driving her children and those of a neighbor home from a dance. I quickly scanned the other faces—both the housewives' and the teenagers'—to see if any disbelief was registered. None was. There were only nods of assent. I was a little numbed by this, but went on with the questioning.

"This was a real odd craft last night, I kid you not," Mrs. Pearce said.

"It was definitely not a plane?" I asked.

"Definitely. It was treetop level and had an enormous span."

"Where was it in relation to your house here?"

"It was up by the next farm," Mrs. Pearce said. "Just as you turn the corner here on Route 101-C."

We were on Warner Lane, just off this road, one of the main highways from Exeter to Hampton.

"About what time?" I asked.

"About ten," Mrs. Pearce said. "These kids here were with me."

I looked around the room, at the teen-agers. If there is any proclivity that can be said to be certain, it is that of teen-agers to debate or neutralize any parent who tries to exaggerate in front of them. I was watching carefully for this reaction. "All of you saw this?" I asked the teen-agers.

They replied, almost in concert, that they had.

"It was real wide," said Mrs. Pearce. "It went right over our car. I'm not kidding you. Mrs. Deyo—Doris here —was with us."

I looked in Mrs. Deyo's direction. She nodded in assent.

"How can you be sure it wasn't a plane?" I asked.

"Do planes make no noise?"

"This was silent?"

"This was absolutely silent. This was not a plane. All of us here know planes, day or night."

Mrs. Deyo spoke. "It looked like it had a lot of little, I call them portholes, except they were square. The light coming through them was solid white."

"There were other lights on it, but they were dim,"

said Mrs. Pearce. "Several colors, red, green, orange. All over. And the surface seemed to be metal. I don't mean that metal can change shape, I mean the lights all around it, they can change the pattern, and make it seem to change shape. I say the lights can camouflage it in the air, they definitely can. I believe that one hundred percent."

"This thing just dropped down toward the car," Mrs. Deyo said. "It dropped down, and it seemed to take on red lights, and it followed us. My son was in another car near us, and he saw it over our car."

"How close over the car?"

"I mean close," Mrs. Pearce said. "Not more than eight to ten feet above it. The lights seemed to circulate, rotate around it. Airplane lights don't do this. They flash on and off."

The atmosphere in the room was tense and electric. It was still hard to control the group, to keep everybody from speaking at once.

"Let's go back," I said to Mrs. Pearce, "to your first experience. And the objects you saw closest to you."

"The first experience I had was on July 29th, this past summer. This was before anybody had seen anything around here. That I know of, anyway. And I thought I was losing my head. I was with my daughter here, my fourteen-year-old, and we first thought it was an accident down the road. With these bright, flashing red lights. It seemed to be right on the road. When we got near it, I could see this wasn't an accident. It was a huge craft, right on a field beside the road. Then it suddenly took off. My daughter won't go out at night alone anymore, since then. I'm not a brilliant brain, but I'm not stupid, either. I can tell you what I saw. I don't care if anybody believes me or not. These things I saw. And nobody's ever going to try to convince me any way different."

Like the others in the room, Mrs. Pearce was passionate in her testimony. It was a little difficult to keep her on the track, but she was a basically intelligent woman, and I encouraged her to go on.

"It's just like I told the colonel at the air base: You show me the craft, I said. He said he couldn't show me the craft, the Air Force had no such thing. I said, Then what is it? He said, It's a UFO. All right, I was told that over the phone, when I called the base after this July incident. I wasn't even going to call them. I told one of my friends that they'll think I'm nuts. According to the officers, none of them have seen these things. When the major and the colonel came down, we looked at what appeared to be a star, except that it was blinking red, green and white. It didn't appear to be a star to the major, but he didn't know what it was. The colonel did see two very puzzling red things in the sky, and he had some very, very poor excuses for it. Very poor, as far as I'm concerned."

"Was this the night when they came down to Route 88?" I asked. "When they experimented with the strobe lights?"

"Oh, the strobe lights. That *is* funny. The colonel sent the major and a lieutenant back to the air base to have the strobe lights turned on. This was after Doris and I had gone up to the air base to talk with them. We were all down on Route 88. While we were waiting to see what would happen, we were talking, and a strange object went across the sky, not low, the way the ones which have scared us, but high. I asked him, What do you call that thing there? He said, Well, that's an airplane. I said, Oh is it, well how come it doesn't make any noise? Well, it's too far away, he said. I said, No it isn't, Colonel, and there were about fifteen or twenty cars there by the field piled up. He asked me why they were there and I told him. Then I said, What kind of plane is it, are you going to tell me it's a jet? He said, No, it isn't. Well, what is it? I said. Then he sort of, you know, couldn't quite name it. Then he came up with a name, I can't even remember it. I said, I'm sorry, I don't agree with you, Colonel. I didn't. So then another object started over the road, right down on Route 88, right across the road. By the Applecrest Orchard. So the other one starts over, and I said, Okay, what's that? Oh—that's a plane. I said, Oh, you think it is. Okay. So one guy there in the crowd had binoculars. I didn't have any at this time, I went out and bought some later. I asked if he'd let me use them, and he did. The colonel looked through them and his face dropped. It did, I could tell. Now what is *that*? I said. Well, he says, you know there are passenger planes

102

that come into Boston along here. I said, Oh, you mean they stop in the orchard to have apples? That's pretty stupid. I said, I'm sorry, I don't agree with you. No, I mean it, I don't care what I say. Nobody's going to tell me I can't see something. So, anyway, one woman was standing in the background, she said, I'll tell you something, I've seen those things and they're *not* airplanes. She said, There's no noise to them. She said, I never saw a plane look like that. I believe that woman down there, she said, meaning me."

I had to admit that I was spellbound by Mrs. Pearce's vivid recollection of the scene. She continued.

"Now he's a colonel in the Air Force, he should have much more intelligence than that. So, anyway, finally he decided he had to leave. I said, Oh, Colonel, what about the strobe lights? You were trying to tell us that we were having hallucinations or seeing reflections from the air base runway. By this time, the major had returned and admitted that the lights had been turned on and off on a regular pattern, and we had seen nothing unusual at all while they were doing this."

Mrs. Pearce took a deep breath. "All I can say is that if they're from another planet, the Air Force being the way it is, I hope they're friendly people."

"All right," I said. "Let's get back to the closest sighting you made."

"This is the one that went right over my car, and I hung out the window trying to get a picture of it. And the Air Force wanted the negative. Unfortunately, it didn't come out. I would say it was as big around as a jet. The front was rounded. And it had sort of fins in the back, flat out, not upright. There was a dome shape to the top and it looked sort of like hammered metal. It had smaller lights all over it, both sides, the bottom and the top. It had larger red lights surrounding the edge of it. They were of different colors on the other parts. As I mentioned, I say it can change shape, not the metal, but the light patterns. The lights go on and off all over it. And it can glow all over. And the underneath part, like the old dirigibles, there was what I call little square windows across, square compartments on the bottom of this thing."

"How did it maneuver?"

"The thing was ahead of me. It would play tag with me, whatever you want to call it, It went ahead of me, with red, orange and white lights on at that moment. All right, the thing turned, and I stopped my car there, I had the motor running and the lights on dim, but I had stopped. Doris Deyo was on the road, I was hanging out this side of the car, out the window with a camera. That thing turned around and came directly, like this, right over the top of my car. Now there was no noise, no rush of air. I know that sounds foolish, but there wasn't. The first thing I saw then was like floodlights hitting the street, right into the middle of the street. But I felt no heat."

I encouraged her to go on.

"I think it's pretty odd," Mrs. Pearce continued, "that there's a craft flying around, that no one around the country seems to know what's going on. It's very odd. It's odd the Government seems to know nothing about it, or if they do, they won't tell you. I asked the Air Force men if it's something Russia has got, or Red China's got, or a secret of your own. The only answer I got from the colonel is that they're UFOs. They're there. They're still around, they're not gone."

I turned to another neighbor. "Tell me what you've seen."

"Well," she said, "it was the first time I've seen one. This was last night, as we were driving on the highway, Route 101-C. All of a sudden it came right across the road, it dipped right in front of the car. It had lights, we only saw two lights on this one, the width of a wingspread. They were white, or yellow. There weren't any red lights on it. It dipped, it came over the car, and went up in the sky. We lost it, it just diminished. As it goes up, it diminishes and they go so high up they seem to become stars. But not really stars, because they come down, and then up again. This one went down in the road almost, and then up over the trees. I believe they land."

Another neighbor spoke. "It's fascinating and it's weird. And none of these things have any sound to them at all."

Mrs. Pearce spoke up again. "The real close ones I've seen have been four or five feet above the ground, if not on the ground. They hover right in the fields. That's what these people up at the air base are so foolish about. I mean it's stupid. I don't know why someone can't catch one of these things or get within distance of. it."

A Mrs. Edmund Liscomb, who lived a few houses up Warner Lane from the Pearces' spoke. "The one I saw last night was a big, orange ball. Nothing but orange."

"I've seen an Air Force plane chasing one," a teen-aged girl said. "It was before dark, the sun had just barely gone down, about seven o'clock. And several people saw it, because I was over in North Hampton. It was reported by several others that day. It was light enough so that you could make out the jet plane clearly and it was tearing across the sky. Just ahead of it, and up a little bit from the plane, was this orangish-red ball, like a red ball of fire. And they were both tearing across the sky. And the plane couldn't get anywhere near it."

"They seem to send planes out after these things all the time," Mrs. Pearce added. "On the 17th of September—I made a note of it, because I've now begun to keep track of these things—we were going up to Exeter. This thing with red, green and white lights on it stopped over a house. We watched it for two or three minutes, and then a jet plane came. And when it did, every single light on the object went out. The plane went by, and the lights came on again. The plane came back, and the lights went out. Then the object went off, and the plane remained there circling and recircling the spot. And the air base tells you nothing. That's why I get sick of telling them about it."

The atmosphere in the living room had simmered down a little now, and I was anxious to turn my attention to the younger people. I spoke first with Mrs. Pearce's fourteen-year-old daughter Sharon. She was an attractive youngster, a little nervous under the questioning.

"Can you tell me what you saw, and when?" I asked.

"Well," she said. "This was in July—the one my mother mentioned to you."

"That's all right," I said. "I want to hear what it looked like to you."

"We went over to Mrs. Shaw's house, and we were coming home about eleven-thirty. And we saw these bright lights in the field. And my mother thought it was a wreck, so she started down the side of the road. We didn't know what it was, and as we got close to it, we stopped and we were sitting there for a couple of minutes. And we heard no sound at all. We just didn't know what it was. It was sitting just above the road, and it was hovering."

"How high from the ground was it hovering?"

"It wasn't over the trees."

"And about how big did it appear?"

"About as big around as a car, maybe bigger."

"As big around as a car. And could you make out the shape?"

"The lights were so bright, it was hard. But I think it was kind of oval-shaped."

"What were the lights like?"

"They were steady, they weren't blinking."

"Then what happened?"

"Well, we drove away. My mother told me to keep watching out back."

"How far were you from it when you watched it hover?"

Sharon looked out the window, pointed to a car about thirty feet away. "About from here to that car," she said.

"Could you give me a better idea as to the shape?"

"We couldn't see too well. But the top was molded, like a dome."

"It was just hovering below the treetops, over the road or over the field?"

"Over the field."

"And you and your mother drove away?"

"Yes, 'cause it looked like it was coming toward us. So we took off fast. We were really scared."

I was watching Sharon closely during the interview. There was no question at all that she was telling the truth as she saw it. What impressed me was that the people here in this modern development, with its ordinary streets, its tidy lawns, its typification of suburbia, reported so convincingly a phenomenon which, if it turned out to be true, would signal a whole new era of history. Their spontaneous reactions indicated that there was no hoax here, no collusion, no attempt to fictionalize their stories. Mrs. Pearce, the most verbal, the natural leader of the group, was vociferous and strong. She had, according to both her own and Patrolman Novak's testimony, stood toe to toe with the Air Force colonel and major, demonstrating a firm conviction.

The frequency of the reported sightings was also startling. I had come up to Exeter expecting to explore a single incident. Now it seemed to have developed into a constant, steady flow, not just from the group on Warner Lane, but in scattered places throughout the area. The press and even NICAP had not had a chance to observe and evaluate this type of single-community reaction extensively.

My talk with the Pearce neighbors and the teen-agers continued for over an hour. Reports on Route 88, on 101-C near some high-power transmission lines were the most frequent, but some of them had seen the unknown objects along Drinkwater Road, and in Kingston near the sighting by the Exeter police officers. I kept questioning their capacity to distinguish whatever objects they saw from ordinary planes, military or commercial. They insisted that regular planes continually passed over, day and night, and that the objects they were reporting had nothing to do with them.

"How would you feel," Mrs. Pearce said, "if you had a daughter who wouldn't go out the door at night because of these things?"

I figured that mass hysteria here could not be discounted, that it had to be seriously considered as part of this cluster of sightings. In the meanwhile, I was going to reserve judgment. When Mrs. Pearce and Mrs. Deyo asked me if I wanted to look over the locations they had described, later on in the evening, I said that I would. I had to admit I felt a little odd; this would be the first time I had ever gone UFO hunting, and I made a mental note to check Bob Kimball to see if he would come along. If by the remotest chance we did see anything, I would want to have a solid man like Kimball around, who, in addition to being a newsreel cameraman, was a fully licensed pilot, familiar with all types of running lights on airplanes.

I told Kimball about the interviews I had had that day, and welcomed the chance to analyze them with someone who had a technical and journalistic attitude. As a newsreel man, Kimball had covered every kind of story, and had a healthy show-me attitude. The contrast was welcome after the charged atmosphere of the Pearce meeting.

I played him some of the Pearce interview tapes on the battery tape recorder.

"This thing gets crazier every day," he said. "And just to show you I'm a complete nut, I'm going to bring my Filmo tonight and keep it on hand."

We picked up Mrs. Pearce and Mrs. Deyo at 7:30, and drove to several spots where she had said she sighted the objects. The first was along 101-C, about two or three miles west of Hampton. It was at the bottom of a moderately long hill, at the junction of the Exeter and Hampton Electric Company power lines. They crossed Route 101-C at right angles, cutting a wide swath through the woods on either side of the road.

"We've often seen them come along these lines," said Mrs. Pearce. "And right here by the poles, one of these crafts came right down over my car, dropped down four or five feet off the ground. You could see a metal surface, and the orange, red and white lights on it. Right by that tree there."

We waited for several minutes, but as we expected, nothing happened. I was interested, though, to note the location by the power lines, for it seemed to suggest that one of the theories put forward by the Exeter police might have some substance. But there were so many reports and theories that it was hard even to guess at anything. The variations in description of the UFOs could result not only from the apparent changing light patterns on the objects, but also from the tendency of all people who witness anything to report subjectively on what they see, projecting their own personalities and past experiences into the descriptions. The power-line theory was at least objective: either they were, or weren't, seen frequently in the vicinity of power lines, and this could only be examined in the light of many interviews.

We covered two or three locations on Route 88 that both Mrs. Pearce and Mrs. Deyo described as places where they had seen the objects. When we reached the field where the colonel and the major had been confronted by Mrs. Pearce's wrath, we got out of the car to see if any strobe lights were visible from the runway of the air base, over ten miles away, and to study the landing- and running-light patterns of planes which might be over the area. Both Kimball and I wanted to do this to examine with Mrs. Pearce and Mrs. Deyo the possibility of mistaken identity of planes.

Over a 15-minute period, we saw the running lights of four planes, which Kimball pointed out would be making a landing pattern for the air base. Both Mrs. Pearce and Mrs. Deyo immediately recognized them as running lights on planes, and didn't, as I had half expected, attempt to convert them into UFOs. This was a strong point in their favor, and helpful in making a better assessment of the amazing testimony given me that afternoon.

The night was dark, moonless, with a very high overcast. No stars were visible, of course, so that the winking running lights of the planes stood out clearly against the gray void above.

Just as we were getting ready to get back in the car, Kimball noticed the running lights of a smaller plane, moving at a considerably faster speed than the lumbering B-47s and B-52s coming up from the northwesterly horizon from the vicinity of the Air Force base.

"That boy is really moving," Kimball said. "If he's anywhere near the landing pattern of the field, he's breaking speed limits at that altitude."

The plane was coming toward us, moving southeast at a rapid clip. Its running lights were plainly visible, in conventional aircraft pattern. It took perhaps 20 seconds for it to get almost abeam of us, and the roar of its jet engine could now be heard. Its altitude seemed to be about 6,000 to 8,000 feet, according to Kimball. We were both watching it rather intently because its pattern was entirely different from the other planes we had observed.

Just before it drew abeam of our position, Kimball nudged me. "What the hell is that?" he said.

I looked and saw a reddish-orange disk, about one-fifth the size of a full moon. It was about three or four plane lengths in front of the jet, which appeared to be a fighter. The plane was moving as if in hot pursuit. The disk was perfectly round, dull orange more than red. It was luminous, glowing, incandescent. The plane was not closing the distance between it and the object. We followed both the plane and the object for 18 or 20 seconds until they disappeared below the southeasterly horizon.

If Mrs. Pearce or Mrs. Deyo were saying anything, I didn't hear them because Kimball and I kept up a running commentary with each other on what we were seeing as the plane moved from abeam of us until it went over the horizon.

"Check me," Kimball was saying. "What exactly do you see?"

"An orange disk," I told him. "Immediately in front of the running lights of an apparent jet fighter."

"A little to the port of it, too, wouldn't you say?" Kimball asked.

"Maybe. Not much to port."

"Do you see any running lights on the disk?" he said.

"No. Nothing but the orange glow."

"Right," said Kimball.

In almost precisely the time in which we carried on this conversation, both the plane and the object had disappeared. The whole thing happened so fast, that I'm not sure how I reacted. I said to Kimball, "Well, that sure as hell is the most interesting thing I've seen."

Mrs. Pearce, however, seemed to shrug it off. "That was nothing," she said. "Wait until you see one close up."

Driving back to Exeter with Kimball, we rehashed what we saw, so that we would neither minimize nor exaggerate it. It had happened so fast that Kimball couldn't have taken a film of it, even if he hadn't left his Filmo on the front seat of the car. Only special lenses and a tripod would have made it possible to get even some kind of a light smear. But we had seen something which was totally without logical explanation, and there was no question that we agreed on what we saw.

"What I'm trying to figure out," Kimball said as we drove back, "is not *what* we saw, because we saw it, there's no mistake about that. What I'm trying to do is to find any possible logical and familiar explanation for it. Let's set up some possible things. They were both going at about the same speed. I've been thinking, if two jet fighters were flying in formation, it could be that. And the running lights on the forward plane might have gone out, and all we could see was the afterburner of the first plane. But that's not logical, either. An afterburner would be a streak, with some blue in it. Not an orange disk. If two jet fighters were flying in formation, and the running lights on the forward plane conked out, it would immediately drop behind the other plane and let it take the lead, cut the speed, and get the hell into the nearest airport. But the jet we saw was moving under a wide-open throttle. Not full power, but it had a lot of power on. The orange disk was really too clearly defined, too round, to be the glow of an afterburner. Frankly, I don't know what the hell the answer is. I'm just trying to consider everything possible."

"You're the pilot," I said. "I'm leaving it up to you to come up with the answer."

"Well," said Kimball, "I don't have one."

Knowing that we would get no information from the Air Force, we saw no reason to report it.

Patrolman Eugene Bertrand's modest home on Pick-pocket Lane is kept cheerful and sprightly by his wife, Dorothy, and I arrived there that night of October 21 shortly after 9:30. I was still a little shaken by the experience with Kimball, still perplexed, and a little annoyed that as long as we were going to have the privilege of seeing a UFO, why couldn't we have seen one close and clear?

I told Bertrand and his wife about the incident, and then turned to Mrs. Bertrand to fill in more details about what had taken place on the morning of September 3.

"When did you first see Gene after this happened?" I asked.

"The next morning when he came home from work."

"About what time was that?"

"Oh, I guess about 8:30," she said.

"What did you think about it?"

She smiled. "I didn't believe it. Not until after the reports came in."

"Can you recall anything more?" I asked Gene. "Anything you haven't told me already?"

"Well," said Bertrand, "I keep going over this in my mind all the time. You don't get over an experience like

111

this very quickly. I'm trying to describe the lighting on the thing, because that was what made it so eerie. Like a neon sign, maybe, but a neon sign won't light up everything around it the way this did. A headlight will give off light, like a beam. But this is not the way it was. This was a glow, a brilliant glow. The trees turned red, the field turned red, everything turned red. Gave off a real spooky feeling. All the way over from the police station— it's a four-mile ride—Muscarello kept telling me and telling me what a thing this was. And of course, I was just telling myself this is fantastic, he was just imagining this. That's when I was sure he had seen a helicopter."

"How about what happened earlier that evening? Could you reconstruct it?"

"Well, I drove my car down to the station that night, it's a 1961 Chevrolet, and I went into the station and read the blotter to see what had to be done, to catch up on the news. See what cars to look for, what was stolen, general information. The lieutenant was on duty that night—Lieutenant Cottrell. I was with this fellow Dickinson from twelve-thirty A.M. until two A.M. He was a new man, and I was helping him get used to the routine. We were cruising out along the bypass, and I see this red and white station wagon parked on the side. Dickinson was driving, and I'm sitting in the passenger seat. So I told him to hold it a minute, you always check cars parked on the bypass, it's sort of like Route 95. It goes from Manchester to the beach at Hampton, or rather it hooks right up with the superhighway going to the beach. And I realize that a woman could be stranded out there quite awhile, so I had Dickinson pull over, right alongside of her, and she had her window rolled down, so I rolled my window down and said, Can I help you, madam? That's when she told me that she had been driving all the way from Epping with this flying object playing tricks over her car. So I turned to Dickinson and he turned to me, like she's a kook or something. We pulled over and waited for awhile, but we didn't see anything, and she was okay. So we left, and I didn't think any more about it until Scratch Toland called me into the station about the Muscarello kid. Then the two things sort of made sense, together."

Back at the police station, Lieutenant Cottrell was just getting ready to turn over the desk to Scratch Toland. It was nearly midnight, and it had been another exhausting day. I had not yet talked with Cottrell except over the phone at the time I was writing the column, and still wanted to hear whatever additional facts and background he could contribute. Like everyone else on the force, he was puzzled and curious about the wave of sightings, hoping that some light might be shed on the mystery.

"I was working for three weeks while the chief was on vacation," he said. "And of course this came right during this period. I frankly wish it had been some other time, myself. I won't say how many reports I had come in, but it seemed three or four times a day, I'd be getting calls from the girl in the office to come in because somebody wanted to see me. Just about every case it was reporters, newscasters, and so forth. And we had calls from people, of course, reporting what they saw. The only thing we could tell anybody was that the office did report seeing this UFO, and we had forwarded the information to the officials at the Pease Air Base."

"What happened the day of the big incident?"

"The first thing I heard about it was when I came on duty here in the morning, and read the report on it. I got in touch right away with the officials at the air base, because that's what we're expected to do. And they didn't take long to come over. They were here shortly after noon. They went with both Bertrand and Hunt to the location."

"What was their attitude? Did they take it seriously?"

"They were very serious. They went out right away on it, but they never gave us any further report. And the problem is this: If no one knows what it is, what can they do about it? I really believe something exists, now. Two police officers, together, leave written report of it. Nobody has ever been hurt by it. It hasn't attempted to do that. I wouldn't think it was coming from a nation that was out to get you. And where does it go in the daytime?"

"Well," I said, "I've got two reports of people seeing it in the daytime. One of them, at dusk."

"I've often wondered about that. But what strikes me funny in talking to Gene and Dave is the maneuverability of the thing. It defies all the aerodynamic laws. It floats, soars, goes off in any direction, turns at right angles. As I told you over the phone, if I didn't believe these guys, I'd put them in a room with some blocks to play with. And I think it would be a help if the Air Force did tell us more about this. Simply tell you enough so that people wouldn't be scared to death of it. I suppose there are people who might go along the highway, and be exposed to something of this nature, and have a heart seizure. If the Air Force would just simply *tell* somebody, it is nothing that is going to hurt them, just something we're experimenting with. That would quiet the whole thing down. I think that is all that would be necessary, we wouldn't be giving away any secrets. I really and truly wish someone would come out and say this will not hurt anybody, we *do* know what it is, but at this time, we can't say. Take the officers that night on Route 150. Both of them, we know, are in top physical shape. But how do you know for sure? I think some day the whole story will be told. I'm a firm believer there's a reasonable explanation for everything. I'm a firm believer in that. Now if there is something that the Almighty knows about that we don't know about yet, then we can all have our own ideas. But I think there will be a reasonable explanation for it."

The night shift was coming on duty, squeezing by the desk to go into the locker room for their revolvers, billy jacks, and other paraphernalia. Another night was beginning, with the quiet patrolling and routine checks going on while the town slept.

Back at the Exeter Inn, I got ready for bed and turned on a few portions of the tapes from the day. The voices were sharp, strong and convincing.

I listened until I got sleepy, then snapped off the tape recorder. I wished that I could be as confident as the lieutenant that there was a reasonable explanation for everything concerned with the case.

CHAPTER IX

Just before leaving for Derry on the morning of Friday, October 22, to see Conrad Quimby, the editor and publisher, I discovered that another friend lived in Exeter. I had not seen George Carr in years, and he had recently moved to Exeter from Massachusetts. A methodical man, with an engineering mind, I welcomed the chance to talk with him about the strange and bizarre UFO mystery, and arranged to drop by his house just outside Exeter that evening. The necessity of checkpoints like this became more apparent as the research progressed. The passion which the observers of UFOs brought into their accounts had a tendency to be overpersuasive. With Kimball and now Carr I felt I had two important controls on the situation, people in whom I had confidence, whom I had known before, and neither of whom was being buffeted by the astonishing collection of stories I was gathering.

Quimby, in his newspaper office in Derry, was another good foil against drawing conclusions too quickly from the fast-accumulating tapes I was collecting. He was a sharp and penetrating man, clinical but open-minded. He was carrying on a strong campaign for tolerance and liberalism in opposition to a competing arch-conservative paper.

News in Derry is usually gentle, as in any country area. A Kiwanis apple sale, a Harvest Ball, a PTA New England boiled dinner affair, a Cub pack meeting, or a golfer's banquet. On the editorial page, however, editor Quimby was lashing out strongly against the John Birch society and other threatening extremist groups.

Interest in UFOs was running so high in the town, he explained, that his wife's English class at the high school would probably be profoundly attentive. I again emphasized that I was anything but an expert, but that I'd probably use the talk as a device for getting the kids interested in how to dig for a story to make their themes and reports more interesting. He and Mrs. Quimby both agreed this would be a good idea.

It was the first time I had ever spoken to a high school class, and I must admit that it made me nervous. Youngsters of this age are alert these days; they refuse to take anything for granted, and they are highly sensitive to anything phony. When I started sliding off the UFO story, and into ways and means to make theme-writing fun, I think they detected my plan right away, for their interest seemed to lag. However, I stuck doggedly to it, partly because I believe the agony of theme-writing results from the failure of students to play reporter; and partly because I simply had no conclusion to state concerning the UFO story, and hated to admit it.

I was, however, struck by their interest in the subject. Why were they so intense about it? Was it something in the air, something which foreshadowed the whole trend of the Space Age? For this group had been growing up at a time when it was no longer absurd to think of astronauts, when spacemen were not ridiculous comic-strip characters in Buck Rogers suits. They were real; they were here. And if the Earth People could do it, they seemed to reason, why shouldn't some other cosmic inhabitants do the same?

Some weeks later, Mrs. Quimby sent me some of the themes which her students had written about the UFO mystery. I was interested in what the papers revealed, in view of the unproven theory that the Government was paternalistically shielding the population from the idea that UFOs were interplanetary, and likely to create panic.

"If ever a UFO pilot were to make himself known," wrote one young lady in the class, "I don't think I'd be scared of him. Of all the UFO sightings that have been made, none of them has tried to harm us. They are probably too intelligent for war.

"We have been making our way into outer space, so it is very possible that they come from another planet, and want to explore earth. . . . Fear of war is very great, and it wouldn't take much to scare the people into thinking that men from outer space were going to invade our world, but yet there has been so much talk about it and there have been so many sightings that people have been gradually getting used to the idea. I feel as if I wouldn't be scared."

Other students in the class echoed her thoughts. "I think if I saw a UFO land, I would be surprised but I don't think it would scare me at all," wrote a boy in the class.

"If I saw a UFO," wrote another boy, "I would observe it as long as possible. If it landed, I would hurry as fast as I could to the spot where it came down. I don't think I would be afraid. . . . If I had a chance to be taken away by a spaceship, I think I would go."

Others indicated that they would "like the idea," or be both "scared and curious"; only a few admitted they would be frightened. The other interesting attitude emerging was that the group, in general, seemed to take the existence of UFOs as a foregone conclusion. The younger generation, it seemed, was moving in this direction faster than the adult population.

It was nearly noon when I returned to the center of Derry, stopping at the village drugstore for a bite of lunch. I had several leads that I could follow that afternoon, but had not yet decided which to try. The thought did occur to me that it might be interesting to try random sampling, without specific police leads. If there were anything to the reports that the area was so rife with UFO sightings, a random check might substantiate this theory. If it failed to uncover many leads, then the theory might be refuted. I asked the girl behind the counter if she knew of anyone who had seen an Unidentified Flying Object, and she looked at me rather oddly, saying she would talk to me in a few moments. Meanwhile, she served me an egg-salad sandwich and a chocolate *frapp,* as they called milk shakes there in Derry, and I waited for her to come back to my part of the counter.

She returned in several minutes, apologetic. "My boss was right near me when you asked that question. And he must think I'm nuts. I've seen one myself, I have lots of friends who have seen them, and none of them look anything like this crazy advertising sign they flew over here.

My boss can laugh all he wants, but I know what I saw and so do my friends."

She went on to what was now becoming a common description: a dome-shaped saucer which glowed red, with brilliant white rounded sides. She suggested that I explore thoroughly in Fremont, about halfway between Derry and Exeter, because she had heard many reports from that neighborhood. "I get so *mad,*" she said, "when people laugh at me. Don't they think we have enough brains to know the difference between a weird thing like these objects are, and an airplane of any kind, whether it's got a sign on it or not?"

I thanked her for her information, left a generous tip, and made my way toward Fremont. On the way over, I tried to decide just how much weight should be given to the *intensity* of the testimony I was picking up. It is hard to fake sincerity and intensity, and so far, none of the people I had interviewed had shown any sign of doing this. Their marks for the "Intensity-Sincerity Quotient" would be A-plus. A certain number, on the other hand, might be said to be lacking in the capacity to document clearly what they saw. I was again vacillating about what to believe, or how much to believe.

I came into Fremont sooner than I had expected. It was a fresh and unspoiled New Hampshire town, its houses suggesting that it had changed little since the Revolution. There was a post office, a white-steepled church, a town hall, with the clean lines of pure Early-Americana. I was told that I could find Chief of Police Bolduc at the lumber mill, where he worked during the day.

I pulled up beside a long shed where logs were being rolled in and prepared for milling. A worker disappeared into the shed and returned with the Chief, a glowing, hearty New Hampshirite with a broad smile, carrying a lethal-looking pike designed to roll and handle the logs at the mill. He came at me pointing the instrument like a bayonet, then winked and asked me what I wanted.

"Well," he said, "perhaps you could find out a lot around here—and perhaps you can't. You never can tell, can you?" He winked again, and waited for me to do

118

the pumping. I was interested, I told him, in recent sightings, and low-level ones, not fleeting glimpses.

"That's a pretty tough assignment, wouldn't you agree?" he said. I agreed that it was. In spite of the fact that it was difficult to get information out of him, he was at once infectiously humorous and likable. "I'd suggest you take a run down the road a piece here and talk to the folks at Heselton's Garage. They'll keep your feet on the ground because they don't seem to go along with the idea at all. You're going to need that kind of outlook to kind of keep your sanity after you hear what some of the other folks in town might have to say. Then after you talk to the garage, you'd better go see my wife. She might have some interesting information for you."

I thanked him and drove down to the garage, where Mr. Heselton, a beefy and direct gentleman, was sitting in the small, overheated office eating a sandwich.

"You want to know what I feel?" he said. "I don't believe it. I just don't believe it. Oh, I know you're going to hear a lot of talk, and you're going to get all sorts of stories. Now take this Exeter police case. This UFO was spotted on a Thursday night or early Friday morning, September third, just prior to Labor Day. This woman claims she was followed from Epping to the Exeter line, along Route 101. This object followed her, I mean. Now I went out the following Tuesday night, on 101, just parked there, around midnight. And at no one time was there a greater span of time than three minutes that a car did not pass. Tell me, why didn't another car observe this thing if she was followed all the way to Exeter? This, mind you, is just before a holiday weekend, and I checked the highway on a Tuesday night after the holiday."

"At what time?" I asked him. I was making it a point to ask repetitive questions through all these interviews, as accuracy checks.

"The same time she did, about," he said.

"About one-thirty in the morning?"

"Whatever time she saw it. I forget, exactly. I think I checked it from something like quarter past twelve to quarter past one, something like that. And I observed absolutely nothing. There was no span of time, more than three minutes, that a car did not pass."

Mr. Heselton, I could see, was a vehement Devil's Advocate. "What have you heard around this area?" I asked.

"A lot of talk, a lot of talk," he said.

"Anybody special reported anything?"

"Well," he said with the greatest reluctance. "Bessie. Bessie's Lunch down the road here. All these stories seem to center around there. It's close to the place that everybody seems to see these things. Down by the power line, where it crosses Route 107. There're a lot of people who drop into the diner who say they have seen these things. *I* haven't, you understand. I know of several occasions, in fact I was there, when someone said 'There it is, there it is!' And it was a jet or a tower. On Route 121, there's a relay station for some outfit in Boston with a red blinker and they would see this."

The mention of the power lines again drew me up sharply. Fremont was a good 15 miles away from Exeter, and I felt there was probably little communication between the communities in the way of comparing notes about the electric power-line theory. Perhaps I was reaching one common denominator in connection with the erratic behavior of this puzzling phenomenon. It was still too early to tell, however.

"Any reliable people reporting them?"

"What these people say, who's to say what's reliable? There's a fellow, a friend of mine, called me the other night, his car was over here being repaired. He told me about this sighting that he had made, and he became fairly indignant when I sort of doubted him. He firmly believed that he saw something. Claimed he very definitely saw something."

"What did he describe?"

"I'm not going to describe what he saw, because I didn't see it myself. And I don't think it's rightly good to give you his name without his permission. I will say that he said he never would have seen anything if his electric power saw hadn't stalled. But the damn power saw stalled, and he looked up and there it was. So he watched it for quite awhile. Apparently, right about that time, a neighbor called to tell him to look. He was seeing the same thing."

"What about some of the other stories you've heard around Bessie's Lunch?"

"Well, as I said, there's a power line down there, see.

Few hundred yards below it, and maybe some nights, there might be fifty cars there. And out of the fifty, there might have been fifteen to twenty people who see it. This is because some of 'em get sick of waiting, and might not stay long enough to see it. But there was a man and woman down there, in their forties, I'd say, and they come in here and told me. They can't describe it. He said it was an object flying along in this fashion with a bright light on it, you couldn't hear a sound from it. And still it was there quite close to him." Like many others, Mr. Heselton was not quite so skeptical as he appeared to be at first.

"Just the other night, some other people saw it along another section of the power lines. And it sounded like the same thing, with a bright light, and then an orange and a red one. And it was seen again, near the same place, only a couple of nights ago. It moved over near the trees, they said, and it goes down low behind the trees and goes up again. And when they see it, they say that you see it for a few seconds, and it's gone. Someone I know stayed there for weeks, down by the power lines, just to catch a glimpse of it. But how can you describe it if you don't see it yourself?"

Although Mr. Heselton had warmed up considerably, I was anxious to see what I could find out directly from Bessie's Lunch. Mr. Heselton warned me that if I "passed the power lines, I had gone too far."

The power lines again. I drove through the village, which looked as if it were out of a Currier & Ives print, and discovered Bessie's Lunch in a lonely wooded clearing not far out of the village. It was a rustic diner, catering apparently to passing truck drivers, tourists, and local residents as well. It was homespun and friendly in atmosphere, with barely enough room behind the long row of stools to stand. A tall, angular Yankee behind the counter turned out to be Mr. Healey, husband of Bessie, in whose honor the diner was named.

Mr. Healey was friendly, but reserved. I ordered a cup of black coffee, and finally confessed that I was on the track of UFO reports, and perhaps he could help me.

"Understand you got several reports down here about them. Is that right?" I asked.

"Where'd you learn that nonsense?" he said.

121

"Couple of people up in the village," I said.

"You hear all kinds of stories these days, you know," he said, and continued cutting some pie and cleaning up the counter. A couple of truck drivers came in, ordering apple pie and coffee.

Finally, I tried again. "Had any recent reports near here?"

"All depends," he said, "what you mean by reports."

"Well," I said, "people who seem to be sane enough, who might have seen some of these unidentified flying objects and might have talked to you about them."

I noticed that he was eyeing my tape recorder, slung over my shoulder in a tan leather case. "Watch'ya got there, a camera?" he said.

"No, it's a tape recorder. I'm trying to get all the information I can on these things. Good and bad."

"You from Boston?" he asked.

"Nope. New York."

"How do you get people to talk for one of those things? Don't they freeze up?"

"Not really," I said. "I'm taping our conversation right now." I figured the only thing for me to do was to put my cards on the table. Another man came in, sat two stools down from me, ordered coffee.

I seemed to be getting nowhere with Mr. Healey, so I turned to the customer, apparently a resident judging by his friendly greeting to Mr. Healey.

"I was just asking Mr. Healey about any reports of Unidentified Flying Objects," I said to him.

"What'd he tell you?" asked the newcomer.

"Nothing, yet," I said.

The newcomer smiled at Healey. "For gosh sakes, why don't you tell him about what Bessie saw?" he said.

Mr. Healey shrugged. "I don't want to put words into Bessie's mouth."

"Is she here?" I asked.

"Nope. But she will be soon."

"I better have another cup of coffee, then," I said.

Mr. Healey drew another. "We get so many of these reports," he said, "that I don't know what to make of them. That's why I'd rather have Bessie tell you herself."

Mr. Healey liked to warm up to a subject slowly. The

newcomer, a Jim Burleigh, had also heard a good many reports.

"Ran into one couple here," said Mr. Healey, "who saw it pretty close. Right along the power lines down here. They all seem to describe it pretty much the same, that's what gets me. No matter what place they see them in. If the people were making it up, I don't think they'd come in with the same descriptions. This couple who come in from South Hampton or Hampton, I don't know which one it was. I've known the father ever since I was a kid, and I know he wouldn't lie about it. And his was the same description as all the others has given—dozens of 'em. And we have so many that come from different parts dropping by here. We had a woman in here who come all the way from Epping. She claims she saw it, and she described it the same way: a round flying object with bright lights, and then it's got this orange and red light. And she said it flies along that way—no noise, not one of them. They all say close to the same thing, that's what gets me."

"About how many people have talked to you about them? Besides your wife?"

"One time a woman come in here," he continued, "a woman pretty high-strung, you know. Nervous. And she was, oooooohhh, all excited. You wonder. And then somebody comes in afterwards and tells you the same thing. I saw it! I know I saw it! It was so quick I couldn't tell! I can't describe it! There was another fellow. And his wife. I don't know their names. He was driving along and all at once he sees this thing come out from behind the treetops. And his wife yells, 'My God!' and she sees it too. You know it's a funny thing, it's hard to be called malarky. It really is. And this man's at least four times come down here to try to see it again. To see if he could make out more, to see again what it was like. Out around the power line. Whether it's due to some atomic energy stuff that would be liable to be attracted that way, or what, I don't know."

We were interrupted when Bessie, a plain and honest-looking woman, came in with her daughter, a smiling girl in her twenties. I lost no time in questioning her daughter, who mentioned her own sighting first. It had happened as she was standing in her backyard in Fremont.

"It was just a round thing, you know," she said. "And it was all red. But underneath you could see silver things hanging down from it."

"What did it do? How did it act?"

"Well," she said, "first it was staying stationary, and then it would go up and then it would go back down amongst the trees."

"It was that low?"

"Oh, yes," she said.

"About how far from you was it?"

"Oh, dear," she said. "I'm not good at miles. But it was so that you could see it real plain."

Bessie herself first saw the object with her other daughter.

"The first one I saw," Bessie said, "went right down in back of the trees. It was white, and then it turned red. Dark red. But first it looked greenish-like. And then there was a plane that seemed to be trying to circle it. And I was with my other daughter, we both saw that. She has seen it more times than that, too. We saw it two nights in a row, the same time of night. Early evening. I went out Tuesday night—just last Tuesday, out at the clothesline, and I said, Gee, am I seeing things? It was really close. That night it was round, just as big, and you could see these silver things coming down from it. So I went in and called my neighbor, and I said, Come out on the field, quick. But her husband yells, We can see it better from the attic, and he called down he could see it real good. Then it went down behind the trees, and came up again. It's just like the one we saw the other night. It went right down the power line. That's what it always seems to do—hover over the power lines."

Bessie could not be called an expert witness, but there was no question that she recalled the incident vividly and genuinely. And here again the power lines were indicated, miles away from Exeter.

"It changes lights, you know," Bessie said, echoing Mrs. Pearce's contention. "When my husband came out in the yard with me, it was bright red, with orange around it. And gee, then it moved away as fast as it could go. But it hovered before that, like they say. And this plane was flying around, looking like it was trying to get it."

"Could you make out any more detail?" I asked.

124

"No," said Bessie. "When I first saw it, it was white, sort of round-like, and then it kind of glittered like a gleam, and then all of a sudden, it was red. Not a real red, but more like an orange."

I thought back to the sighting Kimball and I had made. I didn't mention this to her, but her description jibed closely with what we had seen.

"Three years ago," Bessie said, "before there was such a fuss about these things. This friend of mine, her kiddos were playing in this field with the neighbor kids. And one little boy, he stutters, and he came in, you know, and all the kids yelled at once—Oh, Mommy, a spaceship landed up in the field. And the mother says, What are you talking about? And the little boy said, Yes, he said, yes! And she said, Oh, you kiddos go out and play. And then when all of this started up, she said, I wonder if those kids did see something?"

I asked Bessie about the date of her most recent sighting. It was the previous Tuesday, October the 19th, about 6:15 in the evening. At first the thing was high, and then it came down directly over the power lines.

Jim Burleigh spoke now, recalling a recent evening when his sister phoned him to come down to her house quickly. She lived, he said, right at the base of the power lines. There was a beacon there, which flashed, but everybody knew about that. "When I got down there," he said, "this object was up higher than the beacon, and traveling along at a good clip. Right straight along the power line. It was far away when I got there, so it only looked about the size of a baseball, and then it started going along the tops of the trees. I watched it closely to see what it was, and at that time, it looked like a big orange flare. Like a globe. And at times the light seemed to change. Pulsate."

"Sure it wasn't a plane?"

"Nossir," he said emphatically, "it wasn't a plane. There was no sound from it, and a plane couldn't travel that slow, then all of a sudden speed up. A helicopter could, but a helicopter would make a lot of noise. This here thing would go along, and then stop."

"What about the other people around here who have seen it? How do they react?"

"Well, I'll tell you this much. Some of them get excited, some of them say they get a little scared. Me, I'd like to see one close up."

Jim Burleigh finished his coffee and agreed to take me to the Jalbert family, a few hundred yards down the road. It was a small house by the side of the road, not more than forty or fifty feet from the poles of the high-tension power lines which crossed the road at that point. The lines, part of the now-famous Northeast Grid, inter-lock communities with electrical power, and permit differ-ent utility companies to exchange power when a peak demand requires "borrowing" electricity from another community. Some transmission lines are mounted on huge, gaunt steel towers; others use oversize lighting poles, as was the case here. When they are constructed, a wide rib-bon of clearing is made extending dozens of feet on each side of the lines, in order to keep the wires free of any entanglements with foliage or tree branches. This creates, in effect, wide highways or swaths of clearing which sweep across the country.

Before we went into the Jalbert house, I examined the power lines carefully. The swath must have been over a hundred feet wide, and you could look down it in either direction for several miles. Overhead, some ten or twelve heavy wires were suspended, sweeping along the open swath until they disappeared in the distance.

Mrs. Jerline Jalbert, a pleasant and unassuming widow, had made a modest home for her boys, Joseph, Jr., six-teen; Jerle, fourteen; Kent, twelve; and a smiling four-year-old. They were bright kids, standing high in their classes at school, innately friendly and curious. The en-tire family often stood watching by the power lines at dusk. Mrs. Jalbert told me what she had seen the pre-vious week.

"It was a funny-looking shape," she said. "Very hard to describe. This was Tuesday night. About quarter of seven when I saw it. We had just been outdoors and we happened to look and we saw this bright red thing in the sky there. It was really close, because you could see something hanging down from it that night. I don't know what it was. When I had gone in the house to call a neighbor, it had moved across the field by then. Then it slowly disappeared out of sight."

"Can you recall the shape a little more clearly?"

"Well, it was big and it was round. Like a glowing light. You'd think it was just like the moon rising out of the sky, but of course it wasn't that. It was the size of the moon, or bigger, though, when I first saw it."

"What was your reaction?"

"It doesn't scare me any. I'd just like to know what it is."

"How about the way it moves?"

"Well, it does both. First it goes fast, and then it goes slow. Slows right down. Then it seems to go up and down. It's the darndest thing."

"Now this thing that was hanging down. What was it like?"

"It was silverish. Several things. And you could see them, because it was glowing in that part of it."

"How long were you able to watch it?"

"A good half hour," Mrs. Jalbert said. "And you see, this is only one time. We see it regularly along here. Always seems to be somewhere near the power lines. It often comes around seven o'clock, and by quarter of eight it's gone. Monday night we saw it—" She turned to Jim Burleigh. "Was it Sunday I called you up about it? Anyway, it goes way up in the sky finally, and it gets smaller and smaller as it goes up, and gets more orange. And a lot of times, this airplane comes out and chases it."

I turned my attention to Joseph Jalbert, the sixteen-year-old.

"When we saw it the first time," he said, "it was even with the power line. Right beside it."

"That low?" I asked. I was fascinated because for the second time in as many days I had run into a cluster of people who reported seeing the objects regularly, people who had no connection with Mrs. Pearce's group, who were not even aware of the others' existence.

"All of a sudden," Mrs. Jalbert added, "it'll disappear. Then, just as sudden, it'll come back. Then little red lights will sometimes come on top of it, and one on the bottom. Off and on."

"Now you say it seems to stay pretty close to these power lines?"

"Yup," said Mrs. Jalbert. "It seems to stay over these

127

lines most of the time it's been down through here. It's always over those wires."

"We were looking at one with field glasses one night, a guy in a car down here had some," said Joseph. "We were watching it go up and down. You'd see a red light and when you'd be looking, it would turn white."

"Now you're sure this wasn't a plane? Running lights?"

"No," said Mrs. Jalbert, "we all know planes around here. The boys can name every part of a plane. And a plane wouldn't be orange. This is orange, just like Halloween orange. And no noise. We never hear any noise."

Young Joseph spoke up, the sixteen-year-old: "Remember the time Mr. and Mrs. Bunker were down here?" he asked the others. "It was what? Three or four weeks ago? Me and Kent were down at the power line. There was seven or eight people down there with us watching for this thing. And it come around about quarter of eleven that night. It come from way down over that end of the power line, it was going right along the trees. And there's a big oak tree out there that's dead. When it got to that tree, it went right up and over—no noise at all, just a red light and two white lights, like a house window when it's lit. We didn't see it anymore, but Jerle, my brother, he was in the house, he saw it out the back window, and he saw a blue thing come out of it, and that was it. That right, Jerle?"

Jerle nodded.

"When you see it, it's sort of a round shape, and when you had a chance to see the bottom part, where these windows were, there was a big red light sitting there. And you'd see it and one time you'd see a red light, the next time you'd see a white light, then a red light, then a white light."

"And oh, so white," Mrs. Jalbert added. "There's no airplane with a light that color."

"You know that one time we saw it so close," Kent said, "it was so quiet you could have heard a pin drop. It showed up light enough so that you could have read a book."

I turned to Joseph. "What kind of feeling do you get when you see it?"

"A shivery feeling," he said.

128

"How about you, Kent?"

"I don't know. When it's going over you like that. and you don't know what it is, you just don't know what to think."

"It does give you a funny feeling," Mrs. Jalbert said. "I have the feeling if it should land, I don't know what I'd do, whether I'd run, or what."

"How about the size of this thing? Any estimates?" Joseph said, "I'd say it was as big around as a car."

"You're sure there's no sound?"

"No sound at all."

"You know the running lights on a plane, Joseph?"

"I sure do," he said. "Nothing like that at all. Nothing."

"How about the surface of this thing, Kent?" I asked.

"You really can't tell. The lights are too bright. And when it's orange, it just glows. Like a light bulb."

Jim Burleigh, who had been listening in the background quietly, spoke again. "You asked how fast it travels," he said. "I was up to my mother-in-law's, about three miles from here, and they called up and said they had spotted this thing over the power line. I didn't have the time to go down, but it was moving so slowly then that it was in sight for about half an hour."

Joseph raised his hand politely, as if he were in school. "I have a theory about it," he said.

"All right," I said. "Let's have it."

"I think it's going over those power lines to recharge its batteries, or something like that. Taking all the electricity from the wires."

"That's a very interesting theory," I said.

"I also think they have a kind of radar, like bats, because they never bump into anything. They give you a real spooky feeling. And one time, when one came by close, my radio went out for a few seconds on me."

I turned off my tape recorder and chatted informally for awhile, trying to appraise all this testimony. The descriptions of the objects at a distance fitted Kimball's and mine. The plane chasing or looking for the object also fitted in with what we had seen. The youngsters were bright, exceptionally intelligent, as was Mrs. Jalbert in her quiet and unassuming way. I was forced to conclude that there was a great deal of truth in what they were saying, allowing for the exaggerations of enthusiasm. Their response to questions was totally spontaneous. But were they mistaken?

Still, what they said jibed with information from many other people I had interviewed, without any possible collusion. And the boys were keen and up on airplanes. Youngsters of this age are often far more familiar with aircraft than their parents. Their eyesight is better. And they checked each other out regularly in what they were saying, not in any conspiratorial way, but to verify their own recollections.

I jotted down the names of a Mr. and Mrs. Bunker, whom the Jalberts thought lived fairly near, and they also felt that it was worth while for Kimball and me to come back that evening at 7 o'clock to see if by any chance we could see another UFO. I doubted it, of course, but we had doubted we were going to see anything when we went to Route 88 with Mrs. Pearce and Mrs. Deyo.

I called Kimball from the Jalberts' house, and we arranged to have a quick early dinner in Exeter, in time to return at 7 that evening.

When we reached the Jalbert house after a hurried snack in Exeter, the weather was miserable. There was a low overcast and it was extremely hazy. The power lines stretching across the road were swallowed up in mist within a few hundred feet. The tall, oversize poles, four abreast, stood at quiet attention like a halted company of infantrymen.

Joseph, the oldest Jalbert boy, was gloomy and pessimistic. "We almost never see them on nights like this," he said. "I know just how you feel. You can't believe it until you see it. And this is a bad night for it." He was apologetic.

"You didn't believe them until you saw them?" I asked.

"Nossir," said Joseph. "Not at all. When people came down here in their cars and told me about them, I thought they were off their rocker or something."

"When did you change your mind?"

"Well, I said to myself, gee, they're making all of this up. They had to be. Because here we were, living right here, and why hadn't *we* seen any?"

"You say a lot of cars suddenly started coming down here?" There were no cars except ours tonight. In addition to the mist, it was raw and cold, and I was glad I had brought my parka.

"Yeah," said Kent. "They all started coming down here, a whole mess of cars. And just sat here, waiting and watching. They kept telling us about it."

"How long did this go on?" Kimball asked. He had put his Filmo back in the car now, the mist was so thick.

"Well, they must have been collecting down here a week," said Joseph. "Until I decided to come down here and see for myself."

"How long ago did the cars first start coming down?" I asked. Joseph was an intelligent kid, and I was interested in the fact that he had been a full-fledged skeptic before all this started.

"Four or five weeks ago, I guess," he said. That would have made it in the latter part of September. "The cars would come down here, and then the next day at school, everybody was telling me, Hey, we were down there with my father, and we saw this and we saw that. And you know what I said? I told them they were crazy. So finally after about a week of everybody telling me in school about all this, me and Kent decided to come out of the house and see what was going on. So we came out here, and we said we're not going to leave till we see such a thing. And finally I was getting so I knew it wasn't true. And then when I saw it—right then I changed my mind. Right then and there 'cause I knew it wasn't a plane when I looked at it, because of the light structure. And how it looked when it spun around. Ever since then, I've believed them."

"What do people tell you when you tell them about it?"

Joseph thought a moment, standing there in the cold, dim glow of the parking lights of Kimball's car. Then he said, "They tell me I'm nuts. That is, until one of them comes down and sees it. Then other people call *him* nuts. You got to see it to believe it. That's all there is to it."

After nearly twenty minutes of fruitless waiting, Mrs. Jalbert came out of the house to join us. "I don't think you'll have much luck on a night like this," she said. "I'm sorry."

Kimball and I couldn't help smiling. Everybody who had reported "The Thing" seemed to feel such a personal responsibility for it.

I had not yet talked to Chief Bolduc's wife, as he had suggested, because of the unexpected activity resulting from dropping by Bessie's Lunch. Kimball agreed it would be a good idea to stop by at the Bolduc house to see what we might uncover. We were not really disappointed that we saw nothing at the power lines, and we were already batting .500 in the two times we had somewhat sheepishly looked for the objects.

Chief Bolduc and his numerous family lived in a rambling old farmhouse not more than a few hundred feet from Heselton's Garage. Kimball and I were admitted by the Chief, congenial as ever, into the sprawling country kitchen, where an assortment of children and adults were in varied stages of finishing up dinner. Mrs. Phyllis Bolduc, plump and cheerful in spite of the confusion, was as cordial as her husband.

At the head of the large kitchen table was Meredith Bolduc, the twenty-two-year-old daughter-in-law of the Chief, who was sitting in the corner in an easy chair. Jesse Bolduc, married to Meredith, leaned back against the wall in a wooden chair underneath a rack packed with hunting guns, while children and grandchildren of assorted ages made occasional excursions in and out of the room off the kitchen which housed the television set. The scene created the impression of a Yankee version of a Bruegel painting of friendly family confusion.

I told the group that the Chief had suggested earlier in the day that they might be able to give me some information on Unidentified Flying Objects.

Meredith, an attractive young housewife with short black hair, spoke first. "Go no further," she said. "I tell you that the experience I had is enough to make your hair curl."

"Tell me about it," I said, slinging the battery recorder off my shoulder and turning it on.

"Oh, dear," she said. "Am I going down in history?"

"Doesn't make you nervous, does it?"

"Not really. Maybe a little."

"Just relax and forget about it."

"It's these men of mine here who really make me nervous," she said, referring to her father-in-law and husband. "But anyway, I know exactly what I saw and I'm going to tell you about it, no matter how much they kid me. Actually, they know better."

"You're darn right they do," said Mrs. Bolduc. "They know this is no joke."

"Anyway," Meredith Bolduc continued, "this thing was coming up the power lines toward the road, this was going from Fremont toward Kingston, at the power lines right down near the town line. It was coming, and it didn't stop. I just kept on going on to Kingston, to my folks. And when you see one of these things, you don't forget them. This was last week, just a few days ago. But I saw it much closer two weeks ago Wednesday, that would make it—that would make it October sixth. This is the closest it ever came to me."

"Where were you at the time?" I asked.

"On the Raymond road. Driving."

"Did you stop?"

"No. I didn't know whether to goose the car, or turn around and go home."

"It was close?"

"Yes. Came right down toward the car."

"What was your reaction?"

"Scared! Scared to *death*. In fact, a couple of minutes after that, I saw a light shining over my shoulder and I turned around and jumped a foot—but it was only the moon!

"This was the only night I was really afraid of it," she continued. "The other nights it was fascinating, it was way off in the distance. What good is it going to do to reach for a gun or to goose your car and make it go faster?"

"About how high up was it when you saw it that close?"

"I'd say a couple of treetops high. You just had to look up a little, right in front of the windshield, and there it was."

"Could you make out any detail?"

"Well, it was bright, and white, with sort of fluorescent

red around the rim. Like a big light bulb, the way the white part of it shone. It might have been more whitish-yellow, the main part of the thing was."

"What about the shape?"

"It wasn't flat, but it wasn't round either. Not oval like an egg, but it was oval—not quite as oval as an egg. You could tell it wasn't round, but it wasn't square and it wasn't flat. It was a funny shape."

"Where was the red?" I asked. I was continuing to ask the same question more than once, as a double check on accuracy.

"On the outside of it. Around the rim. And I'll tell you this much—I don't particularly care about seeing it that close anymore."

The men chuckled. Meredith reacted quickly.

"By God, you guys laugh!" she said. "But wait until you see it up close! And I'll also say this: I absolutely refuse to drive alone at night anymore."

"Now both our older boys saw it," said Mrs. Bolduc. "One of them told me it hovered right over our house here."

"That's right," said Meredith, "the night it put the lights out."

Kimball sat forward on that statement. "It put the lights out here?" he asked.

"Well," said the Chief, and now he was serious, "we have one of those automatic lights out by the barn—outside light, lights up the whole area. It's got one of those photoelectric cells on it, so's it goes off when the sun comes up. This one night, Mrs. Bolduc saw the whole bedroom light up with this bright red light. And the next thing you know, the barn light went out, and then went on again when the thing went away."

"Damn interesting," said Kimball.

"Yeah," said Mrs. Bolduc. "I saw it right by the house. Looking out my bedroom window. I said, there's that saucer again. Seems so that it's getting that every time I look out my window, I seem to see it. And I've seen planes circling around after it twice. That was the time we watched it with binoculars, Joe, remember?"

"What did it look like through the binoculars?"

"I put the binoculars on it, and it looked like the shape of a football, with lights around the middle."

My mind went back to the report from Cherry Creek, New York, hundreds of miles away from Fremont, New Hampshire. The description was almost identical with the one given by young Harold Butcher, as the bull twisted the metal pipe out of shape with his nose ring, and the radio interference blocked out the program. Here in Fremont, the light in the barnyard had gone out. I had to conclude that these similarities couldn't possibly be collusion or coincidence.

"And you know Carol McFarland—that's Mrs. Herbert McFarland—she lives just up the line there, she says that it followed her home on the Red Brook road, and that road is just down below the power line. She said this thing followed her all the way home. And you know something—there were so many people down there by that power line one night, it looked like a beach party down there, it really did. A beach party. One woman was there with a nightgown on, with a baby in her arms."

"I'll tell you this much," said the Chief from his easy chair. "It's gotta be something. It's just gotta be something!"

Kimball and I were silent on the first part of the drive back to Exeter. Finally I spoke.

"*Now* what do you think?" I asked.

Kimball just shook his head.

"I certainly never expected to run into so many reports, two days in a row," I said.

"I never expected to run into so many reports two years in a row," said Kimball.

"All these things that keep repeating themselves," I said. "Like where do the cars always seem to congregate?"

"By the power lines," said Kimball. "Both Fremont and Exeter."

"How many people have had the damn things come right at their cars?"

"Let's see," said Kimball. He was driving slowly because the fog was still rather thick. "There's the woman that Bertrand reported on the 101 bypass. There's Mrs. Pearce, down on the Exeter-Hampton line. There's the two young fellows the Hampton police took to the Coast Guard station. Muscarello, he wasn't in a car, but he had to dive down on the road to get away from it. Actually, it came right at Bertrand, too, wouldn't you say? When he was out on the field with the kid."

"Well," I said, "he started to pull his gun on it."

"That's close enough," said Kimball. "And then there's that electric light bit. In the barnyard."

"Could you call that physical evidence?"

"In a way, I guess you could," said Kimball.

"I think I have to say that I'm convinced that these people believe what they saw. Now I guess the question is: Did they see what they believe?"

"I think we have to admit that they did. I wouldn't have said this two days ago, except for Bertrand and Hunt. I know them well enough to know that they wouldn't report it if they didn't mean it."

"Then if all this is true, and if it could be deduced that these objects are interplanetary, why aren't we able to break the story? I know the answer to that, it's just a rhetorical question. There is overwhelming evidence, but still no proof. It's still a ghost story."

Kimball was silent a moment, then: "I'm trying to be impartial and completely objective about it. I'm trying to give it, on purpose, as much of a negative viewpoint as I can give it. In other words, I say to myself: It must be something else. But I *can't* prove it's something else, any more than I can prove it *is* what they say it is. I've got to look at it from the wrong side of the street, from the wrong side of the tracks, to make it seem as if they were seeing a star, or a plane, or something normal. But let's face it, it's *not* something normal, and there's no use in kidding ourselves. People just don't get wrought up like this over an illusion."

"It sure as hell seems unearthly," I said.

"I try to do that—I get myself in the complete negative—like let's go against it. You've got to avoid conning yourself into believing things you shouldn't believe. But it turns out you sit and talk to all these people and you're the one who's crazy, not them. Because all the damn stories fit together."

"One thing that makes it difficult," I said, "is that not one element, or one interview, is enough to make a story. But a consensus, an *accumulation* of the stories is. It's the collection of these damn tapes that's making it hard *not* to believe this thing. Not just one tape, but dozens."

"And then you've got to add to that, the thing we saw."

"I know. I think we can both agree that we weren't seeing things."

"Definitely no," said Kimball. "We were not seeing things."

"We could see the running lights on the plane very clearly, right?"

"Very clearly."

"So there was absolutely no danger of misinterpreting what we saw as a plane. And yet the object was moving the same or faster speed than the plane right behind it. And it was overcast. We couldn't have confused it with a star or planet or anything else. To me it looked like a miniature sun on a foggy evening, very dull red orange, and moving like hell. I guess we have to agree we saw it, that we can't rule it out."

"The thing that makes me mad is that it would have been impossible to get a picture of that. It was too high, too dim. If we could just find one down closer, I'd be happier."

A close, low picture would help. But it would be a matter of extreme luck and infinite patience. After Kimball dropped me off at the Inn, I decided to stop by the home of George Carr, play him some of the tapes, and get an entirely fresh viewpoint. Carr, who had worked with and developed many new techniques in high-vacuum processes, possessed a very shrewd analytical mind.

In his living room with a glowing fire to take the chill off the evening, I went over the story with him, played him portions of several different tapes.

He was impressed. "But you still have to get that physical evidence," he said.

I agreed. I told him of the many NICAP reports of impressions on the ground, singed grass, melted ice impressions, and the photographs. He felt that the impressions could be too easily faked or mistakenly identified, and I was inclined to go along with him on this. The pictures, though, were most interesting if the background of the photographer, the circumstances under which they were taken, and the examination of the negatives were fully explored. I told him about the picture NICAP had sent me from the amateur astronomer near Pittsburgh, in which the shape of the object was clearly defined, with the moon in the background as a checkpoint, and the tree line also easily discernible as a further checkpoint. Carr felt that a study of that photography would be a major step in establishing some kind of physical evidence to go along with the hours of testimony recorded on the tapes.

I decided that I would clean up whatever loose ends I could the next morning, see my agent and editors in New York, and then leave for Beaver Falls, Pennsylvania, where the rather startling picture had been taken. I knew that NICAP had already investigated the circumstances very thoroughly, along with the negatives involved. On the other hand, I could not include a major point in the book unless I explored it first hand. At the same time, I made plans to go to Washington to talk again with NICAP, and perhaps get some basic information from the Federal Aviation Agency regarding the regulations for experimental aircraft. It was hard to understand why, if the theory that these objects were experimental aircraft of the Air Force were valid, they were permitted to so upset citizens in populated areas. And why was the Air Force apparently sending fighters after them? And again, why were they permitted to fly in conventional flight lanes without rigidly prescribed running lights? Regardless of military secrecy, there are some safety precautions which cannot be violated, and the consideration of these questions made the secret-aircraft theory seem extremely flimsy.

CHAPTER X

Saturday, October 23, was my fourth day in and around Exeter. There were many details I had not had the chance to follow up, but some of them would have to wait until after I had returned from Pennsylvania and Washington. What about the two men who had been taken to the Coast Guard station at Hampton, almost in shock? What about the dozens of other names from the Exeter police blotter, which I had been unable to follow up individually? What about a thorough random-sample questioning, a cold-turkey probe to get a clearer idea of the probable incidence of these sightings? What about the power-line theory? What information could I get from the local power companies? What about a personal call at the Pease Air Force Base in Portsmouth, even if the results were to be negative? What about Muscarello, the eighteen-year-old boy who had started all this? He was a boot trainee at the Great Lakes Naval Training Station in Illinois, and impossible to reach by phone.

I followed several leads that morning by phone, with the stories jibing closely with the accounts I had already recorded from the others. Again, there were several independent mentions of the power lines. In spite of different wording, the description followed the same pattern and the sincerity and conviction were there on the phone, as in person.

Stopping for a second cup of coffee on my way up to the Muscarello home to talk to his mother before I left, I glanced through the pages of the Manchester *Union-Leader*, and came across a headline which by now had become almost commonplace: INDEPENDENT OBSERVATIONS: TWO MEN IN SUNCOOK WATCH FLYING SAUCER. The article stated:

> A vivid report of actually observing a "flying saucer" through binoculars was made yesterday by Oscar J. Augur of Cemetery Road yesterday, as he recounted the details of the rare experience.
>
> What gave added credence to Augur's story was the uncovering of another person who had sighted a "flying object" at about the same time and about 15 minutes later.
>
> Augur said he was driving south on Pleasant Street, Hooksett, at about 6:50 P.M., and when he neared the intersection with Merrimac Street he noticed a bright object over the Merrimac River on his right.
>
> "I hurriedly got out of my car and with a pair of binocu-

lars, I unmistakably saw the saucer as clear as day," Augur excitedly recalled. "There was no mistaking the vehicle as I observed it for several minutes as it maneuvered erratically in the valley. The top of the saucer was domed shaped and glowed red while the rounded sides were bright white.

"It was still light enough at the time for me to see it plainly as it maneuvered about," Augur related.

The article went on to relate the story of another resident who observed it at an altitude of 300 to 400 feet, and about 300 yards away. "The object remained stationary for about a minute," he told the reporter, "and then it began to sway slightly from one side to the other and suddenly moved quite rapidly in a southerly direction. The only sound I heard was a hissing sound like we hear coming out of a steam radiator valve."

I was tempted for a moment to drive to Suncook, some 30 miles west of Exeter, but then thought better of it. The stories matched so closely to the dozens I had already recorded that nothing new would be added. Descriptions from any reliable source could almost be predicted, it seemed.

Mrs. Dolores Gazda, Muscarelio's mother from a previous marriage, lived in a modest but spotless apartment on Front Street in Exeter, about a mile out from the center of town. An outdoor wooden stairway with a small landing on the top led to the door, and she sat me at the kitchen table for a cup of coffee. She was young-looking and trim, barely old enough, I thought, to have an eighteen-year-old son.

"Do you want me to tell you something interesting?" she said as she poured the coffee. "When this whole thing started, I told my son I really couldn't believe him. He had been out all night, and he came walking into the house at about four in the morning. I was really concerned, and very upset. You see, he'd sold his car because he was going into the Navy in a few weeks, so he hitchhiked all the way to Amesbury to see this friend, and that's how the whole thing started. Well, of course, I could hardly believe this fantastic story, but when the two police officers told me what they went through, I knew that all *three* of them couldn't be pulling my leg. Well, he told me that this photographer from the Manchester paper had been over in the police station and took his picture, and the story was going to go into the paper. And I went all to pieces. Because I knew that dozens of people would be coming up here, trooping into the house, and I hate any kind of publicity and that sort of thing.

"I had no sooner said that, later that morning, when all these people started coming to the door. And then the people from the air base started coming, and then the Navy, and it just doesn't look right, plus half the time my son wasn't here and I was stuck talking to them. So finally he saw all the people—there were ten in the living room alone one afternoon, they all came at once. He began to see what I was talking about, and he understood it. He said, If you want, I'll talk to them somewhere else. I told him, I don't mind if you're here, but I don't want this a continuous thing.

"Well, things started calming down a bit, and then his curiosity began to get under his skin. He was just as determined as he could be to see that thing again. He knew that some people doubted the story—although why they should I don't know, with two policemen seeing it at the same time with him—but he got some of his friends together, and they'd go up to Route 150, near where he first saw it, practically every night. And one time he said he sat there until the sun came up, and they saw one in the daylight. He said it was definitely a saucer shape, and it had a bluish hue to it. He said it must have been some kind of metal to give off that color. And while he wanted to see that thing again, he did get a little sick of telling the same thing over and over again to people. The newspaper reporters would keep him talking for hours. He said, You know, Mom, I want to cooperate, but I am so tired of telling the same story over and over.

"And of course, I got interested in all this myself, and I used to go up there with him with some friends. We didn't have much luck at first, but two of my friends told me they were coming out of the Exeter Hospital one evening, and there it was right over the hospital. Right over the hospital! Somebody in the hospital called the police that night, and they said it was bothering all the electricity in the hospital—lights and equipment.

141

"Now my son says it was as big as a house, and that's about the description of it when it was over the hospital. And then one night I went down with these friends on Route 88. I still hadn't had any luck, all those nights I went with Norman. But this night, we weren't there more than ten minutes, when all of a sudden, this thing, you couldn't see what it was shaped like, came out from behind some trees, like if it was just parked and rose. Now I describe it as being beautiful. It went right along the top of the trees, oh, several hundred yards away. It was hard to tell the distance. It was huge, it looked awful big even from that far away. What it looked like to me, there were lights on the bottom going around it like pinwheels. Red ones. And it was very bright and it was beautiful. Since then, I've seen it right over the house here. And the other night, the whole neighborhood was shook up. I could see it right here from the landing. And I went and told all the neighbors, and they all saw it with me. It was very low, and spinning like always, with these red lights. So a few minutes later, an airplane came over, and made a circle around it. And darned if that thing didn't just turn around and take off like a bullet."

I arranged to meet two of Mrs. Gazda's neighbors, and they confirmed her story. Meanwhile, I asked Mrs. Gazda about the Air Force investigation.

"Well," she said, "at that time, I could only tell them what my son had told me. When he came in, they took him to a restaurant to talk. But they were very interested. Very. When I started asking questions, though, they just started asking back. Now why do you suppose they're so interested? If the things were their own, I don't think they'd be wasting their time talking to Norman and me, do you? I frankly think they don't know any more than I do. I think they feel that everybody would be scared to death if they turned out to be interplanetary, that's what I think. But I've seen them and I'm not afraid. The only time I might be afraid, if one of them should ever land near me, would be radiation. That I might worry about."

Mrs. Gazda got up from the kitchen table, poured another cup of coffee.

"One thing that interests me is the way they seem to

142

change color. From white to this special kind of orange, and the red, too. And maybe you can tell me about this: Has anybody ever mentioned to you about these things following power lines?"

I told her I was investigating that.

"And also water. I've heard some people say they look for water, but of course that's all just guessing."

It was nearly two in the afternoon when I checked out of the Inn and began driving toward my home in Connecticut. I had to admit my head was spinning.

I had talked with and interviewed, either singly or in groups, nearly 60 people. I had nearly 20 hours of tape recordings.

Driving along the broad, straight superhighway toward Boston, I tried to summarize in my own mind just what specific conclusions could be drawn from these long and involved days in and around Exeter. What had I been able to gather that was irrefutable evidence?

First, it was uncontestably true that the Unidentified Flying Objects had been reported and verified in many cases by more than one reputable person at regular intervals over a wide area of southern New Hampshire.

Second, it was uncontestably true that the reports were coming in very frequently.

Third, it was uncontestably true that many reports indicated the objects sighted over, near and along highpower electrical transmission lines, although sightings were not confined to such locations.

Fourth, it was uncontestably true—to Kimball and me, at least—that we had seen an object that could not be identified as any known aircraft in existence.

Fifth, it was uncontestably true that some people were in actual shock or hysteria as a result of extremely lowlevel encounters with these objects.

The tape recorder was beside me in the front seat of the car, as I circumvented Boston on Route 128, and continued along the Massachusetts Turnpike. I picked up the microphone and began dictating a memo to my agent and editors in an attempt to give them a brief picture of the progress of the research to date. I indicated that I could not understand why some kind of major newsbreak should not be forthcoming on this subject in the light of the material I had gathered.

"I say this after several days of intensive research in Exeter, in which I interviewed nearly sixty people and tape-recorded hours of testimony," the memo began. Then it continued:

The people who have given this testimony have been checked out as far as character and reliability are concerned. For the most part I would say that their judgment and capabilities range from average to better than average.

The testimony adds up to this:

There is overwhelming evidence that UFOs or "Flying Saucers" do exist.

They seem to exist in uncountable numbers.

They move at incredible speeds and in aerodynamically impossible patterns.

They are reported, checked and verified almost continuously.

They hover for considerable time, often at less than treetop level.

They have been reported to have landed.

At low altitude, they sometimes assume a domelike shape with an inner red or white glow. A pattern of red pulsating lights is frequently observed in some cases; in others a red whirling pattern is reported around the edge.

They are usually absolutely silent, although in some cases, a high-frequency hum is heard.

They move almost directly overhead of cars and people, at times causing fright and panic.

At least four women, living in widely separate areas, are afraid to go out alone at night, and they refuse to do so.

At least four people report extremely large objects—60 to 80 feet in diameter, rising up silently from behind trees.

The low altitude movement has been reported to consist of a yawing, kitelike motion, wobbling in the air and moving slowly back and forth, sometimes with a fluttering pattern, like a leaf.

At times, it is reported to throw a brilliant red light glow, which paints the side of white houses a brilliant red. It can light up a wide area on the ground around it.

At high altitudes, in some cases, it seems to assume a shape of a small disk, in the relationship of a pinhead (star) to a tennis ball (UFO).

Reliable, but off-the-record information from the Pease Air Force Base in Portsmouth indicates frequent radar blips and fighters are *constantly* scrambled to pursue these objects. This information is not official, but it comes from a reliable source.

The objects are often reported in the vicinity of high-power transmission lines: Some of these locations have been crowded with cars many nights, with group sightings sometimes reported.

No one has ever been harmed physically by any of these objects, although psychological trauma has been evident.

The area covered by the research extends from Hampton, N.H., on the coast some 20 miles west to Derry, N.H., near Manchester.

In most interviews, I was able to determine the reasonable capacity of the respondent to differentiate between a helicopter, balloon, jet, prop plane, planets or stars. Some sightings have been described in daylight.

I tried to take it easy over the weekend, but wasn't very successful. It was frustrating and annoying to have so much evidence, without a shred of proof. I reviewed the tapes again, trying to discover false notes in the voices of the people I had interviewed. This quality was simply not present. The observers were not fictionalizing, they were not lying. In dealing with many people over so wide an area, it seemed impossible to create a hoax. For the most part they were sober and reliable people, and their voices and convictions were loud and clear. Then there was the sighting that Kimball and I had made. Not so close and near and traumatic as some of the others but it *had* happened, we had checked each other out, and it was clearly a craft or object which neither of us had ever seen before. Kimball, as a pilot, was more technically qualified than I but we both were rational (we hoped) and accurate observers who had made every effort to rule out mistaken identity and illusion.

On Monday, October 25, I went to New York with the tapes to play them for my agent and editor. This was helpful, because I had become so involved with the project that I was beginning to lose some of my objectivity. They were impressed with the tapes, as I had been. They agreed that it would have been impossible for the people I interviewed to have faked such similar descriptions even if they had tried. They were puzzled, as I was, by the unanswered questions, the loose ends, the seeming paradoxes. If the trip to Pennsylvania and the

145

full investigation of the photograph added even the slightest clue, we all agreed it would be worthwhile. Most important were a) the character and reliability of the photographer, and b) expert analysis of the negatives.

Two days later, October 27, I drove from Pittsburgh north some 30 miles to Beaver, Pennsylvania, in a rented car. The *Beaver County Times,* an extremely able newspaper covering a large population in the Pittsburgh area, had covered the picture and story in depth, I had learned, and I planned to talk to their reporter first before interviewing the youthful photographer directly. NICAP had informed me that the newspaper story and the investigation by their own representative had tallied completely.

Autumn was in full swing. I drove through the narrow twisting roads, typical of the western part of Pennsylvania, laid out in curves by the Alleghenies, which rimmed both sides of the road. I was so conscious now of high-tension power lines that I scanned the tops of the hills on each side, noticing a string of the power-line towers parading across the tops of the hills. Later I learned they carried power from the Shippingport Atomic Electric plant near Pittsburgh, the first atomic power plant in the country. Naturally, I speculated on whether this might have anything to do with the appearance of the UFO which had been so clearly photographed.

One especially interesting thing had shown up in the picture: under the upside-down luminous dinner plate shape was a whirling halo, a misty cloud extending beneath it like a ghostly tail of a kite, which had not been visible to the naked eye but which had shown up on the photographic negative clearly. Since film will pick up some invisible infrared and ultraviolet light, this might provide a clue to the power source of the objects.

I found Tom Schley, reporter for the *Beaver County Times* who had covered the story, at his desk in the large, modern building of the paper.

He had plunged into the subject cold, and was as mystified as I. He was convinced that the seventeen-year-old James Lucci, who had taken the picture, was sound and able, an amateur photographer who often took pictures of the stars and moon as part of his hobby. His father was a professional photographer for the Air National Guard, and both the family and the boy were highly regarded in the community. At the time of the observation and the taking of the picture, James Lucci was with his brother, and a third witness, Michael Grove, saw the UFO from his home across the road.

NICAP had discovered in its investigation that James was making time exposures of the moon in the driveway of his home in Brighton Township, Beaver County, at about 11:30 P.M. A round, thick object, glowing brighter than the moon, came into the field of the camera from over a high, steep hill behind his house. Realizing the camera must have caught it, James closed the shutter quickly, wound the film down for another shot. Before he could get a third shot, the object climbed rapidly out of sight.

The entire Lucci family was afraid, as many other people were, of ridicule and publicity, but friends persuaded James to bring the picture to the *Beaver County Times,* where three photographers superimposed negatives and made other tests which showed the UFO had slowly moved closer, left to right, as described by the witnesses. After a full evaluation, they labeled the photograph genuine. The boy's character was vouched for by the Chief of Police, Brighton Township, the high school principal, and Beaver County police.

Lucci took the picture with a Yashika 635 camera, with Altipan 120 film (ASA 100). The lens opening was f 3.5, set at infinity, exposed 6 seconds. The film was developed 12 minutes, with fresh D 76, 70 degrees, with agitation.

At lunch, the reporter filled me in on the background of the story as he covered it.

"The pictures were taken," Schley told me, "on a Sunday night—August the eighth. And young Lucci was finally persuaded to come in to the paper a day or two later. He showed them to some photographers here, and they studied them carefully. They became very interested, and they took one negative and laid it over the other one and matched them up. And when they did this, the edges, the tree line of the hill, all matched. The moon matched, too. And in one picture, the object was farther away on the left. In the other, it was closer and to the right of the moon, which indicated some movement between the two pictures.

"We all got interested in it here on the editorial staff, and they had the boy come back and talk to me. And I sat and talked to this boy and a friend of his, I can't remember his name. And after I talked to them, and since I was a little skeptical myself, I contacted the Air Force because I never had had any experience with these things."

"How far's the Air Force base?" I asked him.

"Pittsburgh."

"Any Strategic Air Command base around?" I was probing for any correlation between this incident and the one at Exeter, which of course had been so near the Pease Air Force S.A.C. base.

"No," said Schley. "It's not an S.A.C. base."

"How about high-tension lines?"

"Lots of high-tension wires around here. They go all across the mountains. I'm not sure about the place where the picture was taken, I really didn't check for that. Anyway, in spite of the fact that the boy was obviously sincere and intelligent, I was naturally a little skeptical. I had never, as I said, handled any of these reports."

"That's when you contacted the Air Force?"

"Right," Schley continued. "So I contacted the Air Force and I got a little bit of what I now call a runaround. My city editor was pushing for the story, he didn't want to wait till the next morning, so I called the Air Force back and put a little pressure on them. I wanted to talk to someone right away, not wait all night. So I finally got hold of a lieutenant at the Pittsburgh air base. And I asked him my questions. And he said he would have to call back. And he did. My questions were: Were there any UFOs reported recently, a matter of a couple of weeks? He said, Yes, there had been several. Then I got more specific. How about that particular night? Especially around 11:30? His answer was yes. There was one reported at that time. And I asked where was it. His answer was: Nearer to Pittsburgh."

"You're lucky you got that much from him," I said.

Schley smiled. "That's what I found out later. Then I said to the lieutenant: Could you tell me if this was a naked-eye sighting? Or a radar sighting? What type was

148

it? Well, he said, I can't say any more on that. Of course, here again, I didn't know the Air Force position on this. So my immediate suspicion was that they got something on radar because why would they hesitate to tell me if somebody said they saw it? So then, a few days later, I went ahead and wrote my initial story about what the boy said he saw, and we ran both pictures. Apparently someone sent a copy to NICAP in Washington, and someone sent one to Bill Weitzel, the subcommittee chairman down in Pittsburgh. He came down and began investigating, and he struck me as a pretty thorough and accurate man. I had never heard of this outfit before."

"They impress me as being very careful," I said. "From what I've seen, they try to knock a story down before they'll accept it."

"This is my impression," said Schley. "As far as my experience goes, I've met two of their people, and both of them impressed me very much in their serious attitude. They were very thorough in their examination of the material. They almost seemed to try to *disprove*, as you said. And I was very impressed with this. They spent five or six days here. And I got more interested in the story myself. We had a few other reports that came in, too."

"Any below treetop level?" I asked.

"No, nothing below that level," Schley said. "But I picked up a very interesting story from a couple who had sighted one of these things. This is really weird. At the time they saw this thing, their dog started acting very strangely. The wife said it was always a very friendly dog, and it began to try to hide, and it was cowering in the cellar. Its hearing seemed to be affected. As though it was hearing some sort of high-pitched noise they couldn't hear."

My mind immediately went back to Exeter, to Gene Bertrand's vivid description of the animals on the Dining farm. More bits and pieces of the puzzle seemed to be coming together—but we were still far from any kind of convincing proof.

"You see," said Schley, "the thing is this: As a newspaperman, I don't like to be taken in, and this is immediately the suspicion that you get with a story like this. So that's why I was particularly concerned about the whole thing. I did everything I could to discredit the story before I wrote it, but I couldn't. If I had, I would have backed off from the story fast."

"That's just about the way I feel," I said. "If I could explain this thing either way, I'd be happy."

* * *

With reporter Schley's help, I was able to catch two of the photographers on the newspaper who had made the examination of the Lucci negatives, Harry Frye and Birdie Shunk. We joined them in the cafeteria.

"How do you go about checking out the negatives?" I asked.

"The only way," said Frye, "is to make completely sure that there's no double exposure involved, or anything like that. If the negative is faked by a double exposure you have overlapping images. Now I studied the negatives for considerable time and I don't think they could possibly have been double-exposed. Everybody else in the department agreed on this."

"It wasn't a lens-reflection freak in the development, either," Shunk added. "We examined the negatives thoroughly for that possibility."

"After we all had studied them, we couldn't help but come to the conclusion that the image was a definite picture. There was no other way it could have been done."

"How did you go about matching up the two negatives?" I asked.

"Well," said Frye, "we put the two negatives, two separate exposures, we put them together and lined up the trees, the horizon line, the moon, and other things that were in both negatives. And you could see where the object had moved across the film. From my judgment, the object had moved from a position closer to the camera to a position a little farther away and across."

"And that would have been difficult to fake?"

"It would be, yes," said Shunk. "It would be difficult to fake it in another way—to put something up there and photograph it, and still get the things that are seen in the background. Just about impossible, I'd say. You also noticed that tail of mist coming down from the object."

"That wasn't seen by the naked eye," I said. "What

150

sort of thing does a film pick up that the eye doesn't? Infrared? Ultraviolet?"

"Ultraviolet will appear on a film and not to the eye," said Frye. "It would tend to produce a white image."

"Then is there a possibility that these rays coming down from the object could be ultraviolet?"

"Well," said Frye, "this is something I couldn't answer. It could be, and it could be also something else. There is a lot of light outside of the visible spectrum that you can photograph."

"How about infrared?" I asked.

"That will also photograph on a plate to a certain extent, especially with certain film."

"We discussed ways that the picture could have been faked," said Shunk, "and we couldn't come up with a logical way you could do it."

"In other words," said Frye, "if somebody asked us to go out and duplicate this picture, we would find it impossible."

I thanked Schley and the photographers for their information, and then left to see James Lucci and his brother, John, to reenact the way the photograph was taken, and to see what other information I could pick up in their neighborhood.

James Lucci was quiet, soft-spoken, shy. His brother John was twenty, three years older. He was a student at Geneva College nearby. Both were articulate and friendly. The Lucci house nestled at the bottom of a steep hill, so typical of western Pennsylvania. I got both boys to take me to the exact spot where their camera had been set. It was in the gravel driveway, directly beside the house, and we stood there, looking up at an angle toward the hill. The trees stood out sharply in silhouette against the sky, the same tree line which had showed up in the pictures.

I asked James Lucci to point out the exact spot where the object was when the picture was taken.

He pointed to the high ridge, at about a 45-degree angle from where we were standing.

I looked up, following the direction of his finger, and caught my breath.

For immediately below the part of the sky he indicated

151

were the sweeping wires of a high-power transmission line, extending from a tower on top of the ridge and stringing across the valley to the next hill. It was Exeter all over again, this time with a striking photograph to go with it.

I found it a little difficult to remain calm, but I asked the Lucci boys to give me the details of their story.

"I had set the camera up that night," John said. "My brother and I both work together on this. Last winter, I had taken a picture of the moon through an icicle, that turned out to be beautiful. This time, we thought we might get an interesting effect by shooting the moon through the very faint haze, or thin overcast, that was around that night. It was just sort of nice and misty, but you could still see the moon through it. I let my brother handle the camera that night, because we take turns doing it. It was about eleven-thirty. And all of a sudden, the bright, round object came up over the trees. And it shocked us, it really did. We didn't have a shutter cable, but he took the time exposure, and then wound it down to the next picture. And he got a second picture, as it hovered in different positions. But before he got a chance to get a third picture, it shot straight up in the air and it was gone."

"Fast?" I said.

"Just like that," said John. "Boom. Gone."

"Which of you saw it first—you or James?"

"I don't know who exactly saw it first. We saw it at the same time, I guess."

I turned to James, who had been at the camera at the time, and who had actually taken the picture. "You were the one who took the picture. Did you see it through the viewfinder?"

"I was looking through the camera when I saw it."

"What did you do?" I asked. "How did it work technically?"

"I had my hand over the shutter to make a time exposure of the moon, and the object came right into the frame," James answered. "I waited for a couple of seconds and it stopped. I wound the camera down, and took the next picture. I was going to take another one, but it went up. It took right off."

Now I turned back to John. "You saw it with your naked eye, rather than through the camera. It was coming over those trees, you say?" I pointed up to the top of the hill.

"It was a big white light," he said. "I couldn't make out a very clear outline. But it was brighter than the moon. We were just standing here and it just crept up over the trees. It didn't just pop up, but it didn't just creep up. It came over the trees like an airplane would go. Then it stopped dead in the air."

"Any sound?" I asked.

"No," said John. "Absolutely no sound at all. It's dead quiet out here in the middle of the night, and I was standing right here, and I didn't hear a thing."

"Any other lights, other than the white light?"

"No."

"Any pulsating lights?"

"No."

"What shape?"

"Disk shape. Just like the picture."

"In its motion, did it seem to—what? How did it move?"

"It would stop," said John, "and it would just move around in different areas. Hover here, hover there. It would hover for a brief moment, then move to a different spot. It didn't seem to wobble too much."

"The light was all uniformly white?"

"Yes," said John.

"Did it look as if it were luminous—lit from the inside?"

"I couldn't tell," John said. "It wasn't a reflection, it was its own light. But I couldn't tell whether it was outside or inside."

"Did it have a clear surface?"

"We still couldn't tell. It was misty that night. You couldn't tell the surface actually. It was just like a big, disk-shaped light."

I spoke to James. "What did it look like to you? You saw it just through the viewfinder? Or with the naked eye, too?"

"I just saw it through the camera."

"What did it look like to you through the camera? Beyond the details you see in the picture?"

"It was hard to tell," said James. "I was trying to focus at the same time I was taking the pictures."

"What about that haze underneath the object in the picture?" I asked. "I understand you couldn't see that with the naked eye?"

"That's right," John said. "You couldn't see that."

"Tell me about your own reaction to the thing," I said to John.

"I didn't know what to do. I was scared to death. I was standing right here when the thing first came up. I didn't realize what was happening at first. And then it started to hit me. And I didn't stand around here long, I'll tell you that much."

"Can you remember what you said to James when you saw it?"

"I can't actually remember my exact words, but I didn't want to stick around. I wanted to get back in the house."

"How did you feel, James?" I asked.

"I just picked up my camera and ran into the house and developed my film."

"How did the experience affect you?"

"I guess I felt more happy than scared."

"I was more shocked than that," his older brother confessed.

"Now," I asked. "Can you tell me again as to where the object was in relation to those high-tension power lines?"

John studied the area a moment. "I'd say it was right up there, directly over the wires. Not more than fifty or sixty feet."

We went into the house, and I again studied some prints of the pictures. The object was bigger than the moon in the background. The disk shape was clear and unmistakable. They were the clearest photographs I had seen of the objects, and the shape was very close to many of the descriptions given in Exeter. The light in this case was uniformly white, as reported by the brothers, but there had been so much testimony to the effect that the lighting patterns changed frequently that this didn't seem significant.

I asked the boys about other sightings and they told me there had been several that they had heard about.

"There's a fellow and his wife who live right up over the hill from here," said John. "He said he and his wife were watching television one night, and the dog started acting up. Then the TV picture got all scrambled. He went outside, and he told us he watched one of these things—he described it very much like the picture—for a long time."

"Where does this fellow live?" I asked. Again, the disturbed animal behavior, I noted.

"Right up over the hill behind the house here," John said. "I know that during August and September, there were a lot of reports around this neighborhood. People were calling in to the police and the newspaper every other week, practically."

"Do you know these people—the ones whose dog was scared?"

"We know them slightly," said John.

I asked the boys to take me up there, and they agreed.

Mr. and Mrs. Donald de Turca lived in a spanking new development on the top of a hill about five miles away from the Lucci home. Mrs. de Turca was at home, preparing dinner for her husband who was due back any minute from his job as an officer for the Pennsylvania Turnpike Commission. Mrs. de Turca, an attractive young woman, was a case investigator for the Department of Welfare.

"It's been so long since we talked about it," she said. "The date was August 11, on a Wednesday. Both my husband and I made a big note about the date, because it was such an amazing thing, so hard to believe. Of course, I had gone to work that day, and we had gone to my aunt's house to visit. When we came back, it was around midnight. And it was beautifully clear that night. As we were driving along, my husband said, Look how clear it is. And he turned off the headlights for a moment. The moon was so brilliant you could see everything. We stopped at the house, and we have a dog, and my husband said, I think I'll take the dog for a walk. And he did."

Donald de Turca arrived at this moment and told a graphic story of how he had stepped outside the door with the dog just as a huge, disklike object hove into view not more than 200 or 300 feet above his neighbor's house. It appeared to be 60 to 70 feet in diameter, and he showed me a sketch which he had done before the NICAP investigator had shown him the photograph taken by the Luccis. It was almost identical. The object he reported differed in description from the photograph in only one way. At the time he saw it—it hovered for nearly half an hour—there appeared to be brilliant red lights whirring around the rim. In addition, the object gave off a clearly discernible high-frequency hum. And down the street from the de Turcas' was a section of the high-voltage transmission lines. Mr. de Turca, a former paratrooper, knew the configuration of nearly every aircraft.

"I had such a long time to study this thing," he said, "and it was so low, that there couldn't be any remote possibility of mistaking this for a plane or helicopter or balloon. Then there was the dog. He ran around in circles. You can't fool a dog, can you? He almost went crazy."

Standing on his lawn, he pointed to a neighbor's house. "It came in from the west, directly overhead, right overhead here," he said. "Then it zigzagged a few yards, hovered a little, and came back. But it remained nearly all the time in the same area, right over that house there, three or four rooftops high. When it took off, it didn't make any sound. Took off real quick. Faster than a jet. And this was the first time I observed it moving in a straight line."

With this and other accounts covered by reporter Schley, it was apparent that events in Exeter were being repeated in western Pennsylvania. The parallels were startling not only in description, but in other ways: the behavior of animals, the changing of light patterns, the hovering, the fast and slow movements, the quick change of course, the blinding speeds, and the attitude of the local Air Force.

But most startling to me was the appearance of the objects over or near the power lines. Whatever clue this might be, the observation had been repeated too many times to be treated as incidental.

CHAPTER XI

On Thursday, October 28, I had been invited by Dean Rusk, along with other journalists, to a National Foreign Policy Conference for Editors and Broadcasters at the State Department in Washington. It was a conference I wanted to attend, and I planned to cover it, as well as visiting with NICAP to try to get any up-to-the-minute material they might have. Because of a late arrival from Pittsburgh, I had to choose between the two. Somewhat reluctantly, I decided that the UFO story was developing so fast that it transcended even the precarious international situation in impact. I could not help feeling that something was bound to break soon in the story, and any interruption of the research would be unwise.

I met Richard Hall, the assistant director of NICAP, for lunch. A young, soft-spoken and intelligent man in his thirties, he filled me in on the overall activity of the organization, that Major Donald Keyhoe had founded in the face of an antagonistic national press.

"Is there any pattern of sighting throughout the country you've been able to discover? Any special areas where they concentrate?" I asked him.

"About the only thing we've been able to discern," he said, "is that the sightings seem to concentrate in small geographic areas during any wave. But that concentration area will shift around. In 1960 there was a concentration in northern California. Other times, it's been over the Midwest. In 1952, there was the famous cluster of sightings over Washington, involving radar at the control towers of the airports in the area. But there are always outlying reports, too. We don't have any idea what they're up to."

We were talking about a map of the United States in his office, with markings—by pins of different colors—of récent reports on it. "What do the yellow pins represent?" I asked.

"The yellow ones are reported landings or near landings. We've found a lot of people are reluctant to report these because of ridicule. When you've talked to as many witnesses as we have here, from all walks of life, you begin to notice people like the small-town school principal who came in here. He had sighted an object, very close to landing, several years ago. He didn't want to be ridiculed, didn't want his position to be jeopardized. He came in and unburdened himself to us because he knew he would have a sympathetic hearing, and he described, unknown to him, things that had been seen by many other people across the country."

"I've been wondering about that myself," I said. "I've been tape-recording a lot of testimony. These people are sensible, reliable. In a courtroom, their testimony would have to stand up against any judge or jury. This is what puzzles me."

Hall smiled. "On the basis of legal-type evidence, this case would have been proven a long time ago. Of course, what most people are waiting for, and what most scientists are looking for, is hardware. They want a piece of one or something they can analyze before they will commit themselves. But I don't think this is very becoming to the scientific fraternity, to want something in hand before they at least study it."

"NICAP, I understand, has reached the hypothesis that UFOs are probably extraterrestrial. Have you any further speculation?"

"Except for our published statements, which we think are a reasonable hypothesis that these could be spaceships, that's about all we could say."

"Is there any scientific agency that is willing to investigate on this?" I asked.

"Not as an agency, no," Hall said. "We have a great many individuals all over the country in government, agencies, Cape Kennedy, Huntsville, and so forth, on an individual basis."

"What seems to be the main resistance to studying the subject?"

"The lack of governmental recognition to the phenomenon, and the fact that it is debunked officially."

"The Air Force remains absolutely inflexible?"

"Since 1952, yes. At that time they were much more open about it."

"What's the most interesting confirmation they ever gave the subject?"

"The famous *Life* article in 1952 was reported to be encouraged and sponsored by some high-placed generals in the Pentagon. They presented some of the better cases in their files to back it up. And they're similar in character to the reports we're getting today. But again they suffered from lack of concrete evidence. It was a very strong suggestion that we had interplanetary visitors."

"What about the Federal Aviation Agency?" I asked. "Certainly these things are violating safety regulations for any craft—experimental or not. Have you learned anything from the FAA?"

"We tried to get a Congressional investigation to look into this, particularly in one case. An American Airlines captain in 1956 took his plane off course to pursue a UFO, which is against all C.A.B. regulations. The Senatorial committee found the case very interesting, and listened attentively to our tape-recorded interview with the pilot, stating that he had done this. He denied this later publicly. But the committee said that they would be accused of digging skeletons out of the closet if they used it. So nothing came of it. The FAA, again on an *individual* basis, is very interested. We get very good cooperation out of the FAA when we make inquiries about radar trackings. As far as we know, there is no organized attempt to gather the information. We've had people who call the airport when they've sighted something. And often they would be put on to an FAA man who is interested in gathering the information. We suspect it is just a matter of individual curiosity."

"Are you able to speculate on government lack of interest, or apparent inactivity?"

"Frankly," Hall said, "I think they have a tiger by the tail at this moment. They started out with immediate secrecy when they started getting these reports, and they've gone on for so many years denying that there is anything to it, that it would be very awkward and embarrassing to admit that there was something to it, all of a sudden. And if they did, they would appear awfully stupid in the past. Now the way we feel today—we have the choice of two views. One, they are *not* aware of what's going on. This seems highly unlikely. Number two, they are *well* aware of what's going on. And for various reasons, they are suppressing it. A third alternative is that there is nothing at all to it. That would be the hardest of all to accept."

I recalled the sighting Kimball and I had made. "What about the reports of Air Force fighters scrambling after the objects?"

"The business of people observing aircraft, usually military aircraft, chasing after UFOs is a quite common report. And very often, all authorities will deny that they have any planes up chasing anything. They profess complete ignorance."

I sketched for him the sighting Kimball and I had made, mentioning the fighter plane and a description of the object.

"This happened over Washington last January, when we were having a flurry of sightings in nearby Maryland and Virginia. A group of Signal Corps engineers downtown on Constitution Avenue saw a group of shiny oval objects in the direction of the Capitol building in the late afternoon. Not directly above it; you couldn't tell the exact distance. And chasing these objects was a sweptwing jet. It was apparently in hot pursuit. All the Washington papers inquired about it, and it was completely denied that any military craft were up chasing anything. We got indirect confirmation, verbal confirmation, that something was tracked on radar at the National Airport, but we were not able to document the military part of the story. I think what has misled most of the general American public are the crackpot reports, which are extremely wild. We keep away from these completely."

"From some of the material you sent me," I said, "I understand you have some landing reports that aren't completely wild. Like the one in Buffalo, where they found a blue dye."

"Yes," said Hall, "we got there before the Air Force and interviewed the witnesses. But the sample wasn't found until the Air Force was there, and they got to the sample first. There was some left which we got, and we had it analyzed. The report is all in obscure chemistry jargon, but they state there is nothing particularly unusual about it. Titanium was one of the major constituents, which was a little surprising to us. But it didn't prove anything."

"What other landing reports has NICAP investigated in full?" I asked.

"The landing in New Mexico, where a police officer by the name of Soccoro saw it, was interesting. He had a particularly high standing in the community, which made his story quite believable. He was the one who saw the egg-shaped object on the ground. We got soil samples, we got a shiny material that was on a rock right adjacent to one of the imprints that was left."

"What kind of imprints were they?"

"They were rectangular, four of them. And it looked as if, assuming this was some kind of craft with a landing gear, it looked as if the landing gear had scraped down along this rock and left some metal on it. We had that analyzed at a Washington government laboratory, very well equipped, on an off-the-record basis. And they identified this substance as silica, which is very surprising because we were not aware that silica could give this shiny metallic appearance. But they say it can under certain weather conditions. So again it was inconclusive. If it proved to be a metal, even if it wasn't a particularly unusual metal, it could have been interesting."

"Tell me a little about some of the scientists who have been working with NICAP," I said.

"Well," said Hall, "the most prominent scientists who are associated with the UFO subject, or stick their necks out to some extent, are in general the type who have a little more daring and imagination. Dr. Carl Jung, the famous psychoanalyst, before he died, was a member of NICAP. In his final letter, he said that he had read Major Donald Keyhoe's last book, and he had pretty much concluded that we were dealing with real objective phenomena in the sky, in contrast to some erroneous quotes about his own book that he believed that they were only psychological manifestations. But this impression about Jung's book was incorrect. Because if anyone had read it carefully they would have noted that all he said was that he had to deal with the psychological aspects of it, because that was his field. But he left open the possibility of the reality of the thing. A very prominent scientist on our Board of Governors is Dr. Charles P. Olivier, President of the American Meteor Society, and Professor Emeritus of Astronomy at the University of Pennsylvania. He doesn't take any position as to the nature and reality of UFOs. He stated that he believes there should be a much more thorough and careful investigation of the subject. And as such, he's one of the few astronomers willing to endorse the basic scientific principle to investigate and study before passing judgment. We have numerous members who are also members of the American Association for the Advancement of Science, including my brother, Dr. Robert A. Hall, who is program director for the National Science Foundation for sociology and social psychology. He's one of NICAP's special advisers. Then there's Dr. Leslie Kaeburn, a biophysicist on the faculty of the University of California, and a member of our panel of special advisers. There are many others—competent professional scientists who are willing to take a position and at least willing to encourage further investigation of the subject, and not entirely satisfied with government findings."

"Have you found your job frustrating?" I asked.

"It has been frustrating in past years, but recently there has been a swing in the other direction. If this keeps up, I don't see how Congressional hearings can be avoided."

"Where does the resistance to the subject come from about a Congressional hearing?"

"Well," Hall said, "Congressmen in general are likely to take the Air Force as the best authority on the subject. They may be, of course, but they're not letting anyone else know what they know. Also in 1961, there was a three-man group set up in the House science committee to explore the possibility of hearings. And the information we had at that time was that they feared they would be laughed at and ridiculed if they brought the subject out into the open. But I don't follow the reasoning on that. They investigated V-girls in Baltimore, and the Ku Klux Klan. Of course the Air Force has a terrific advantage over us. They can parade an impressive bunch of colonels who will state that the situation is well in hand. It's hard to oppose this, and the only thing on our side is when we can win support of academic people and the public. We would welcome anybody checking our sources, because we are very careful about documentation."

"What about reports from Communist countries?" I asked.

"It's very hard to get information from them, of course. But back in 1952 when Major Keyhoe was working very closely with the people in the Air Force project, they were feeding information to him which he used in his early books. He was shown Air Force intelligence reports of sightings in Russia. And occasionally since then, I recall one case a few years ago, where CBS reported from Moscow that there were sightings around there. You occasionally get reports from eastern European countries. In fact, a year or two ago there was a Yugoslavian reporter who went around all over his country interviewing people. He was astonished, because everywhere he went, he found people who had seen them."

"Do you think the official position stems from the fear that people might panic?"

"This was very strongly suggested to people in 1952, and it commonly occurs in all writings on the subject. The idea keeps popping up that people would panic if the truth were known. I don't think people would be that panicky. They've learned to live with the H-bomb, and I think the Government constantly underrates the public about what they can take. We've had over the years, as you can imagine, thousands of letters. In fact, we have a file problem. Far and away the largest percentage of people express intense curiosity. Very few, very rarely, does anyone express fear. The only fear we have encountered is shown by people who did not take the subject seriously enough, were uninformed about it, and were suddenly confronted with it."

"Any reports in the last few days, for instance?" This would be the last week in October, 1965.

"Yes, but they're fragmentary. It takes time for them to get in. I was talking to our subcommittee member in Indianapolis yesterday, and he said that in the last two days there was a case where the State Police were following a UFO around in their car till the wee hours of

163

the morning, trying to catch up with it. And another case, in Marion, Indiana, where a UFO moved over radio station WMRI, and at that moment, nobody could hear the station. Another case of an electromagnetic effect, of which we get many. We got similar reports from Los Angeles by telephone that in the past week there have been many sightings, including one that we call a 'satellite object.' This is a large, reddish, elongated object, often cigar shaped, flying across the sky, and then smaller points of light coming out of it, and moving along independently."

"I've heard a couple of reports up in Connecticut recently—quite recently. Do you have any detail on those?"

"Unfortunately," Hall said, "both of them, after preliminary investigation, appeared to be very shaky cases. One was a photograph taken by a staff photographer of a newspaper. We got the pictures for analysis, and the 35-mm sprockets and the identification of the film was cut off, and until we get an explanation for that, we can't take them too seriously. And the other one was a report of a UFO descending toward a hillside. Some reporters climbed up the mountain, and they found a burned spot there on top of the hill. But our Connecticut subcommittee members report that that was nothing but the remains of a campfire. So again, there's no real evidence. We can't be too careful of how we check these things out. Nothing will weaken our case more than an irresponsible report. There are enough responsible ones without fooling around with the weak cases. Connecticut has had its share, though, of responsible cases. One I recall in '62 or '63, where a state representative saw a UFO around Hartford. This was a triangular-shaped object, it sped by in broad daylight, quite shiny and metallic."

"Could that have been a delta-wing jet?" I asked.

"No, it was shaped more like a Mercury capsule. And a conical object has been observed quite a bit recently, particularly over Virginia, and occasionally other states for the past year. And this is something pretty new in the history of UFO reports."

"What about the apparent capacity to change shape? That seems to come up once in awhile," I asked.

"This," said Hall, "we don't accept as established. I think it's simply a shifting of lighting pattern. At least this seems to be more reasonable. These things often have glows around them, and haze or vapor, and these would very easily alter the appearance of one. And also a disk-shaped object viewed from different angles would tend to create the illusion of different shapes, or changing shapes."

"Now what about that vapor trail that was evident in the picture I investigated up near Pittsburgh?"

"Yes. That wasn't vapor really, that was something detected by the film that was not seen by the eye. We don't know, but if the pictures are authentic, as they appear to be—and we checked them out very thoroughly—we checked them out especially because of the age of the person who took them, a young boy. We're always cautious in such cases, but this one checked out so well, we got such good, strong character statements about him that there seems to be no doubt about him. Granted that the picture is authentic, this would seem to be some kind of a clue to the propulsion which we have some of our technical people looking into right now."

"What about the comparison of some of the sightings with sound, and those with no sound?" I asked.

"Sound appears to be heard only at very close range. And our experience with reports is that seldom has there been a very noisy UFO, one that attracted attention to itself by its noise. Although I believe there are a few exceptions to that. Usually, when sound is reported, it's a very faint hum or buzz. Or whining sound. In fact, it's often been compared to the sound of a generator."

"How about animals? The effect on animals. I've run into several reports of this."

"Yes. Ever since the very early sightings in the United States—I recall back in July, 1947, soon after the first one reported in the postwar period in this country, in Portland, Oregon. There was a policeman walking along near a flock of pigeons on the ground. And the pigeons became very alarmed and agitated, and started flapping around, and he looked up and saw this disk-shaped object passing overhead. Ever since then, there have been sporadic reports of this. But again, in this past year, which I think is really a reflection of our ability to get more information, there have been numerous reports of dogs and livestock and cats and birds reacting in the presence of UFOs. This is reported in all parts of the country. As you know, in the Exeter, New Hampshire, case, this was reported very clearly. We've been getting so much more support lately, that the reports are more expert and technical and more detailed. All these people joining in to support us in places like Cape Kennedy and in the universities. Fact, we received a letter from a City Manager in a Los Angeles suburb which has a population of 90-some thousand, and he wants to form an affiliate for us out there. He strongly endorsed the need for more public information we had mentioned in one of our recent bulletins. But this is very interesting when a city official is willing to stick his neck out and form an affiliate."

"I've noticed," I said, "that your general attitude and that of Ray Fowler, up in New England, and the Pittsburgh NICAP group, seem to be an effort to try to *disprove* a case first, rather than trying to prove it. What about this?"

"This is very important," Hall said. "There's no question at all that the large majority of things that are reported as UFOs are *not*. They are stars or planets or planes, or something of this nature. But the Air Force carries it on from there, and claims that therefore *nobody* has seen anything out of the ordinary. But—the more people do contribute false reports for the record, the harder it makes our job to prove that there are good observers seeing something unusual."

"Have there been any slip-ups by the Air Force which indicate that they are holding back information?"

"I think there have been, in various regulations and statements on the subject. They put out annually, I guess, or at certain intervals, a thing called *The Inspector General's Brief*. It goes to all base commanders. And in one issue, they had a little headline: 'UFOs are serious business.' And the story was that all air base UFO officers should be equipped with all sorts of equipment, including Geiger counters and cameras and sample-collecting kit, and all this sort of thing. This would seem to imply that they were taking UFOs very seriously. This was not a classified document. Somebody happened to come across it and got a copy for us. Similarly, their own regulations spill the beans about their real attitude about the subject. The regulation is now labeled 'for official use only,' and they're trying not to give it out any more than they have to. This regulation states quite clearly that the only cases that will be publicly given out will be those which will have a conventional explanation. Anything unexplained is simply not to be released to the public. And a little interesting sidelight on that is that we cited this regulation in our bulletin, referring to Paragraph Number 9. Since then, they shifted that to another paragraph number—juggling the paragraphs around a little bit. I don't know whether that was deliberate or not, but it looks funny. I see no reason why they suddenly juggled the paragraphs."

"Has there been any direct pressure put on NICAP by the Air Force or Government?"

"None whatsoever," said Hall. "I think that since we've kicked up the biggest storm about this subject, if anybody were to be approached by the Government, certainly it would be us. And nobody has ever suggested that we have been doing anything wrong or harmful. And on the contrary, we've had trickled-down reports from government authorities that they approved of what we were doing. I've noticed that the Air Force often assigns people to the UFO subject who know little about it or its history. And they often make very seriously embarrassing statements to the public—gross errors which certainly weaken the Air Force position."

"You feel the close-range sightings are increasing?"

"The reports at very close range have been building up, especially in the past year. It is my firm conviction that if presently existing scientific equipment were brought to bear on these things, we'd have all the proof anyone would need. But it's not being done."

I knew personally a responsible official in the Federal Aviation Agency, and I dropped by his office in Washington late that afternoon. I felt that if I could get an informal picture of the FAA's attitude, it might help in making further appraisal, even though I was certain there was not much I could learn officially. A consultation with several men at the Agency, who preferred not to be named, produced very little. From the descriptions of the objects and their flight patterns, the people at the FAA admitted that the UFOs were grossly violating safety and identification regulations for any kind of craft whatever, if the descriptions from the witnesses were believable. Some of the men there granted that they were puzzled and baffled by the whole situation. One, a former Air Force pilot, said that he had heard many reports from his fellow pilots about UFOs, and that they had been just as baffled as anyone else. A secretary in the office said that she had just received a letter from Gettysburg, Pennsylvania, where people were reporting sightings several times a week. And as in Exeter, dozens of cars brought people nightly to try to see the objects. Officially, all the FAA people could say was that the subject was an Air Force responsibility, and that all information was supposed to be turned over to them for appraisal. No new light was shed on the subject.

Two new developments were shaping up, however, which were important because they would enable me to extend the time I could devote to researching the project. Both *Look* Magazine and Irving Gitlin, former producer of the carefully documented NBC-TV *White Papers* and *The Dupont Show of the Week* documentaries had read the original *Saturday Review* column I had done, and both *Look* and Gitlin were interested in the possibility of both a longer article and a documentary film. Since I had written and directed several films for Gitlin and NBC-TV, we were no strangers. We arranged to get together in Connecticut on the next evening, Friday, October 29, so that he could listen to the tapes and appraise the story for a possible film.

We both listened to portions of the tapes for over three hours. Gitlin agreed that so much testimony could not be faked or invented, and made a decision to begin the initial planning for a one-hour special documentary on the UFO mystery.

Meanwhile, several people called from Exeter to report that an unusual case had broken in the Boston and New Hampshire papers involving a highly respected couple who had encountered a UFO at close quarters back in 1961, and who had been so traumatically shattered by the experience that they had had to undergo hypnoanalysis by one of the highest-ranking medical psychiatrists in Boston in order to repair the damage they had suffered.

I had heard of this case from the Exeter police but had not followed it up because I was confining my research strictly to recent cases. Although I was resolved to keep to this plan, I felt it was necessary to explore a development resulting from this case, which was that the couple had decided to speak at a meeting at the Pearce Memorial Unitarian-Universalist Church in Dover, New Hampshire, on November 7, breaking a four-year silence they had observed because they did not want publicity or ridicule that might accrue from the exposure of their story. However, since the New England press had broken it, they wanted to correct any misconceptions arising from the sensationalized newspaper accounts, and agreed to speak on invitation from the church.

But I was to learn later of an interesting angle of that invitation. Lt. Alan Brandt, a public information officer at the Pease Air Force Base, was a member of the church, and had helped arrange the meeting. Perhaps this was significant. I learned by phone that it was just possible that the Air Force was unofficially permitting a story to leak out as a test reaction on the part of a public meeting. But this was pure speculation. I was interested in the meeting for another reason: With the interest in UFOs as high as it was in the area, what kind of turnout could such a meeting expect? Dover was about 15 miles north of Exeter, but there had been many reports of sightings from there also and nearby Portsmouth had its share. A large turnout would be some evidence of how much regional interest there was in the phenomenon.

These two factors prompted me to cover the meeting: possible Air Force connection with it, and an indirect Gallup-type poll as to general public interest. Further, Mr. and Mrs. Barney Hill, the couple who were speaking, had evidently experienced a severe reaction from their sighting, even though it had occurred four years earlier. The case involved hypnoanalytic therapy and could not be explored fully without far more research time than I had available at the moment, but the results of that therapy had brought out some amazing speculations. Under separate hypnosis, I learned, both husband and wife penetrated a period of amnesia which had lasted for two hours following the UFO landing next to their car. Under hypnosis, they related that they had been taken aboard the strange craft, assured that they would not be harmed, given a physical examination by a group of humanoid creatures, and released with the assurance that they would have no conscious memory whatever of the experience. The sessions were taped by the psychiatrist, then funneled slowly back to the conscious minds of the couple as the therapy progressed. The technique was successful in eliminating the dreams and nightmares both husband and wife had suffered following the experience. But neither Mr. nor Mrs. Hill made any claim as to the validity of what they had related to the psychiatrist under hypnosis. They had told close friends only that this was what had come out on the tapes, accounting for two hours which had mysteriously disappeared from an evening in their lives.

The story had broken in the papers, four years after the event, through a meeting of the Hills with technical people interested in the UFO portion of the story. The Hills had spoken at this session at the request of Walter Webb, a member of the staff of the Hayden Planetarium in Boston. It was the first time the couple had mentioned the episode to any but their closest friends. They were acutely sensitive to adverse publicity because Barney Hill, a leader in the New Hampshire NAACP, was a Negro; his wife Betty, a social worker for the state of New Hampshire, was white. Representing a mixed marriage, they knew that involvement with a sensational story like this could have damaging results because of the prejudices of some sections of the population. Both Hills were extremely intelligent, and highly regarded. Barney Hill had received citations and awards for his community work from both the Governor of New Hampshire and Sargeant Shriver. Betty Hill was a dedicated social worker, whom the Exeter police said was unflagging in her work to help the poor. The psychiatrist involved was an outstanding medical man, known throughout the world for his accomplishments in the neuropsychiatric field.

It was a complex, bizarre story. However, because it was four years old, I resolved to confine myself to the church meeting and to the exploring of any possible Air Force interest in it, official or unofficial.

CHAPTER XII

I arrived back in New Hampshire on Sunday, October 31, late in the afternoon. In order to be based in a slightly different location, I registered at Lamie's Motor Inn, an attractive motel in Hampton, just a few miles from Exeter. Prior to the Hill meeting at the church in Dover, a week away, I planned to tie up the loose ends left from my previous research.

The Exeter police reported some minor sightings in my absence, but none very interesting. In a follow-up call to Mrs. Gazda, Muscarello's mother, I learned that she and some friends had seen more of the objects, hovering over a field along Route 101-C. There seemed to be three of them, at low altitude, with varicolored lights, the general overall color being orange. I tried hard to persuade her that she might have seen ordinary aircraft, but she refused to be budged from her story because she insisted that the things remained stationary over the field, and that no sound whatever came from them. I showed her the print of the picture from Pennsylvania, but she could not say positively that the shape was the same as the ones she had seen. "Perhaps I might have looked at them from a different angle," she said, referring to earlier sightings. "And the ones I saw when you were away were cigar-shaped, which would rule out the disk shape you have in the picture. However, I will say that the sketch my son drew after the sighting he made with the two police officers *did* look like this. Almost *exactly*."

Mrs. Lillian Pearce, on Warner Lane, however, agreed that the Pennsylvania picture did look like some of the objects she and her neighbors had seen, although she had seen other shapes, too. "Unless, of course, the changing lights make the difference," she said.

While I was talking with Mrs. Pearce about the picture, a group of youngsters from the neighborhood there must have been five or six of them—came bursting in in great excitement saying that they had just seen a huge red object glide slowly across the trees at the end of the road, and disappear below them. They were excited, and I felt that this was no prank. On the other hand, they were all talking so excitedly at once, that I had trouble getting a clear description. They urged me to come out on the chance that it would reappear again, and taking my tape recorder, I walked down to the end of the road.

There was nothing in sight, but I made them go through what had happened a few minutes before, carefully listening to their inflections and tone of voice. They were still talking all at once, but the substance of what they were saying was that a couple of dogs had started howling, they looked up and the object, almost as big as the moon, moved slowly from left to right above them. It was mostly orange, but there were red lights around the rim, flashing off and on. They had it in view for almost five minutes, they said.

I was ready to charge this off to mass hysteria and imagination when I overheard one youngster, about twelve, say to her friend, "You know something, I really wish we could move away from here. It's just too scary with these things around all the time." She was not saying it for my benefit, and was so sincere and almost plaintive that I could not rule the incident out entirely. When a neighboring housewife, standing in her front door down at the end of the street, confirmed the youngsters' story, I was inclined to consider it at least a possibility.

On the following morning, November 1, I followed up half a dozen leads by phone; they were interesting mainly because they indicated the high frequency of sightings in the area.

At noon, I stopped by the power plant on Drinkwater Road in Exeter, and spoke to a couple of the engineers for the Exeter and Hampton Electric Company. They had heard many stories about UFOs but had not been aware that so many people were reporting them above or near power lines. They were intrigued with the idea, though, and planned to investigate it. They said that high-voltage power lines do create an electromagnetic field, and that if the objects had any kind of affinity for electromagnetic fields, the power lines would be an obvious attraction. There had been no unusual voltage losses reported on the meters, but, they added, it would be possible for an object to enter an electromagnetic field without affecting the voltage.

The question as to whether the power lines could create the image of a UFO was brought up, but since the phenomena had frequently appeared far from the lines, and since most descriptions indicated the UFOs as a structured craft, this theory was highly unlikely. Most descriptions also were contrary to St. Elmo's fire, sun dogs or other known phenomena.

I made a mental note to check more thoroughly with the electric power companies later. At the moment, I planned to begin what I had wanted to find the time to do since I started the research: make a random check, with mostly cold-turkey interviews, in a circle around Exeter. This would, I felt, preclude any rehearsal of descriptions. I had done this, in a sense, when I dropped by Bessie's Lunch in Fremont, but I had learned ahead of time that there had been a concentration of sighting near the place, and consequently it could not be considered a purely random check.

Before going out on this new survey, I went to see Bob Kimball, who was with his brother George in their living room on Grove Street. George Kimball had been an Air Force pilot. One key to the whole mystery, to me at least, was the sighting Kimball and I had made. Although it was so brief and at such a high altitude, our own sighting made more believable what others were reporting. The tendency for Kimball and me was to alternately believe and disbelieve what we heard about UFOs. To believe that hovering machines stopped in midair, came directly at cars and people, hurtled off into space at lightning speeds, was difficult even though you didn't doubt the character of the people involved. But *not* to believe such overwhelming, continuous, and repetitive testimony was equally hard.

Bob Kimball, his brother and I rehashed the sighting again in detail.

173

"I had the binoculars," said Bob, "and I looked at it with the glasses. It was still an orange ball, or a disk on end. I couldn't tell which. By the time I could hand them to you, both the plane and the object were gone."

I said, "The plane was too small to be a B-47 or -52, but it was a jet, so it had to be a fighter. No private plane could move at that speed."

"We can assume that," said Kimball. "There's no question it was a jet fighter."

"And the fighter looked as if he were in hot pursuit, trying to close in on the object. But he was making no headway."

George Kimball spoke. "Assume the plane was going six hundred miles an hour, and they're in sight to you for one hundred miles—horizon to horizon, say, at an altitude of five thousand to eight thousand feet, which would give you a wider horizon than normal. That's fifty miles to your left, and fifty miles to your right. You would have fourteen seconds of visibility."

"The speed was probably less than that," Bob Kimball said. "The B-47s and B-52s fly over here at about one hundred twenty knots. This plane was going much faster than that. He was moving. He was low. I was surprised to see a jet fighter that low at night. Much faster than a jet usually moves at that altitude in that area. He was moving out."

We continued discussing it at length, checking George Kimball for details which his Air Force experience might clarify. At the end of the talk, the situation remained the same. We had seen something unexplainable in ordinary terms.

The first stop in the partially random survey was a grocery store called Puggio's, on Front Street, a mile or so out from the center of Exeter. The proprietor had not seen any UFOs himself, but he told me that three or four weeks before, the entire neighborhood was up in arms about a strange object which crossed the sky. He did not leave the store to go out and look himself, but he said, "The people from across the street were out gazing up there. Some people came out with field glasses, and they were all excited about it. Two or three funny things

174

moving up and down in the sky, they said. They all said it wasn't Echo or a satellite."

I walked across the street, knocked on the door of a house, and a woman told me: "I was out several nights looking. The one I saw was not quite the size of a full moon. It was bright and round, between a yellow and a natural color. Before that it was high, and I thought it was a star. Then it moved down fast and got bigger. Then it moved sideways, stopped, moved again. I don't know what it was."

I drove out toward Kensington, spotted an elementary school, and went inside to find a teacher. At least the report—positive or negative—would be articulate. I found one in Mrs. Esther Prescott, who taught the 5th and 6th grades. She was gracious enough to let me interrupt her class because she thought it was important that this subject be explored thoroughly.

"Our daughter," she said, "is a junior at the University of New Hampshire, and her experience was so frightening that somebody has got to find out what these things are. She came home one night almost hysterical. This was two or three weeks before anyone around here had reported anything like this. She told us, and there were some other young people in the house, and they laughed at her. So my husband and I, just to calm her down, told her that we'd go out with her and look ourselves. She was so upset, I can't describe it to you. But by the time we drove to where she had seen it, nothing was there. Then later, when the police officers from Exeter reported a description of almost exactly what she had seen, she was so relieved, I can't tell you how relieved she was. And she is a very lucid, calm person. Her father and I didn't doubt her in the least, because we know what kind of a girl she is. She said she had never seen anything like it before, that it was literally as big as a house, and it had a red glow. And not a bit of noise. Not a bit. This took place directly over what we call Round Hill. It was a genuinely frightening experience."

She mentioned several other people, including the two librarians who had sighted the objects later.

So far, the random survey was bringing amazing results. I had no reason to doubt either the store owner, the woman or the schoolteacher, each of whom had been

175

called on without warning or preparation. I drove farther south from Kensington, spotted a large farm machinery sales and repair agency, and went in to talk to several of the men there. Each of four men knew people who had seen the objects, but had not seen any themselves.

I drove eastward toward the ocean and stopped at a small motel called Johnson's Motel. One of the men in the farm machinery agency had heard that there had been sightings over there. Although this would not strictly be part of a random sample, I wanted to find out if the lead was valid. In a sense, it was. Mrs. Johnson, a motherly woman who ran the homespun motel, had not seen a UFO herself, but some three weeks before, her three grandchildren had run in screaming to tell her that a huge object had come down low in the field right outside the motel. "They screamed that it was an airplane, but it wasn't making any noise. I told them I'd be out later, but like a darn fool, I waited too long. By that time it was gone. They said, Nanny, it's way down low, and it's got all funny lights on it. Well, I still wouldn't have thought too much of it, except another person and his wife saw the same thing right near here, and were nearly scared out of their wits. My daughter lives in Amesbury, and a fellow who works with her husband also saw the same thing that night."

I got the name of this man—an Albert Doughty in Amesbury—and called him on the phone. Mr. Doughty told me with considerable emphasis that he had had quite an experience. He was driving from Seabrook toward Prescott Farms about three weeks previously, at 9 or 9:30 P.M., with his wife at the wheel. "When I first saw it, it was all lit up, and it was high. I told my wife, that's not a plane, stop the car. It was all lit up all over, and there were red and green lights going around it. And it was stopped still in the sky. We went on for awhile, then stopped again. We watched it for quite a time, and then it started to move. Then right near the shopping center, the darn thing just started to zoom right toward our car. Right directly at us. Very, very fast. Right toward us. And it scared the holy hell out of my wife. She said, For God's sakes, Albert, get home as fast as you can. It seemed to come right down

176

straight, and it was so big. And my wife actually almost went into a panic. All she was interested in was getting home."

"What did it look like when it got closer?" I asked.

"Well," Mr. Doughty said, "I was so darned scared and so was my wife, that to tell you the truth, I don't really know. In fact I don't know how close it really got. Then when I learned that some other people had seen these things, I said to my wife, Thank God we're not going out of our minds. You know, you really wouldn't believe these things unless you saw them yourself. I'm convinced now that everybody can't be wrong, can they?"

I thanked Mr. Doughty for his information, drove to Route 1, and stopped at a grocery store. For the first time, no one I spoke with there had seen any sort of object, nor did they know of any leads. Statistically, though, the survey was ahead of the game, and it continued that way in the evening when, at the lounge in Lamie's Motor Inn, I conducted a more comfortable survey. I spoke with eleven guests and employees. Of the eleven, three had seen and described with reasonable accuracy a sighting following the general pattern. Eight others knew personally people who had encountered the phenomenon in some form or other.

On the morning of November 2, I finally got around to the Hampton Coast Guard station to see about the incident involving the two young men who had been brought to the station in a state of shock by the police. Francis Bajowski, chief of the installation, could not release the names of the men involved, however, because of regulations. But he agreed that if the Air Force base in Portsmouth would allow it, he would do so, and also have the man who had been on duty that night tell me informally what had happened when the two youths had come into the station. All other statements, the Chief said, would have to come from the Coast Guard information office in Boston. Throughout our talk, the Chief was cordial, but somewhat evasive. I tried to reach Lieutenant Brandt to get permission for the Chief to release the names, but he was off duty that day. Meanwhile, I stopped at seven stores, gas stations, and restaurants in the Hampton-Exeter area. Five out of the seven gave me direct leads to friends who had seen the objects.

In midafternoon, I went to Officer Bertrand's house to get his reaction to a story the Pentagon had released to the local papers about his and Officer Hunt's sighting. It was such a garbled distortion of facts that I could not understand how the Pentagon could release it. Later, an officer at the Pease Air Force Base told me he was "shocked at the Pentagon's stupidity."

With a Washington, D.C., dateline of October 27, 1965, the news story read:

The Pentagon believes that, after intensive investigation, it has come up with a natural explanation of the UFO sightings in Exeter, New Hampshire, on September 3.

A spokesman said the several reports stemmed from "multiple objects in the area," by which they mean a high-altitude Strategic Air Command exercise out of Westover, Mass., was going on at the time in the area.

A second important factor was what is called a "weather inversion" wherein a layer of cold air is trapped between warm layers.

The Pentagon spokesman said this natural phenomena causes stars and planets to dance and twinkle.

The spokesman said "We believe what the people saw that night was stars and planets in unusual formations."

I was confident that no one, including the Air Force, had investigated this sighting in greater detail than I had. What's more, the release was a direct slam at both Bertrand and Hunt and their capacity to distinguish between "stars and planets" and an enormous, silent craft which had brought Bertrand almost to the point of pulling his gun. I had spent part of two nights patrolling with Bertrand and Hunt, and had come to respect them and their jobs. For the Pentagon to ascribe their sighting to either "high-altitude exercises" or "stars and planets in unusual formations" was patently absurd. If anything, it could only lead eventually to the embarrassment of the Pentagon.

Bertrand was very calm about it. "If they want to turn out ridiculous statements like that," he said, "that's their business. I know what I saw. They don't. And of course I can't accept what they say there. I know for sure it had nothing to do with the weather. I know for sure this was a *craft,* and it was not any plane in existence. I know for sure it was not more than a hundred feet off the ground. I'm not saying it's something from outer space. I'm saying I don't know what it was, and from this newspaper story they've released, I know damn well they don't either. I know it didn't have any wings, and I know it wasn't a helicopter. Or no balloon, or anything of that sort. It's absolutely stupid of them to release something like that."

For the first time since I had met Bertrand, I saw him grow irritated. "I'm not getting paid for all this, and I'm not trying to make up a big thing. And I saw an unknown craft of some sort. It was no helicopter. I was near enough to hear the choppers, if it had been one. It had brilliant lights on it, that you just don't see on aircraft, plus it had no wings whatever. You couldn't see any tail section. In fact, the first reaction I got was that it was a huge, red fireball. But then I could immediately see that it wasn't. It was a huge, compact round thing with lights going back and forth. When Dave got there, it was a little farther away, but we sure as hell both checked each other out. Maybe if I stood in the field and watched it, I could have made out the image better. But all I could think of was getting the hell out of that field with the kid, because of being afraid of being burned. Do they think I would run from a star or a planet? Or a chopper or a balloon or an airplane? As I told you, an aircraft did go by later, far away and overhead. It was miles away—but I could still make out the wings and the running lights plainly. And there was no fog, no heavy air. Some nights there's a fog, and being near the seacoast, you get a heavy atmosphere. This was a crystal clear night. No humidity. Real dry. I just know that what the Pentagon says in that news story is not true. I don't care. They can believe what they want. I know it's a craft of some kind. If the Air Force wants to come and tell me they have an aircraft with no wings on it, and brilliant red lights, that can stop, hover, turn on a dime, and move without a damn bit of sound at one-hundred-foot altitude, I'm willing to believe it. And I'll go along with it, because that is what Dave and I did see. I'm not saying it's anything from outer space, but they don't seem to be able to. They make it look worse by printing things like this. They make it look like they're trying to cover the thing up. Now all of a sudden they seem to discover that they had these 'high-altitude exercises' from Westover Field. But it was a month, nearly two months, before they came up with this explanation. Of course, they must be doing this for the general public. They must know that they can't fool Dave and me. But I've heard people say: 'Well, it's all solved now. We can relax.' But *you* know from the people you've talked to, *I* know from what I saw, that they really *can't* relax."

From this moment on, Bertrand, Dave Hunt and I would have trouble believing anything the Pentagon released on the UFO subject. I had to admire Bertrand for not blowing his top completely.

Bertrand asked me if I had made any more headway in connection with the power-transmission line theory. I told him of the coincidences I had found near Pittsburgh, showed him the Lucci picture, and told him how this object had been hovering directly over the wires out there in Pennsylvania. In turn, he was reminded of a case he had been called out on several weeks after his own experience, which he had forgotten to pass along. The police desk had received a call from a woman named Sloane, on the Epping Road, who reported a bright red object which had lit up her home, her bedroom, and the surrounding fields. It was so bright that it had awakened her. Bertrand and Hunt had been dispatched to investigate, but by the time they got to the house the object had disappeared. They noticed, however, that Mrs. Sloane's house was right next to the high-power wires where they crossed the road near the Brentwood line. The thing had been hovering directly over the lines.

I drove out to the Sloane house, but no one was at home. The transmission lines, I noted, were not more than 50 feet from the house. The neighbors across the street, Mrs. Ruth Williams and her son Galen, were at home, however. Galen had spotted a glowing red object on Route 88 several weeks before, but had not seen any near his home. The object near the legendary Route 88 had moved up, down, back and forth over a group of trees about 100 yards away. He and a friend completely ruled out an airplane, and when they arrived in Hampton, they immediately phoned the Pease Air Force Base in Portsmouth. The officer in charge, in a rare expansive moment, told him that someone had sighted a similar thing in Dover, just about the same time.

Mrs. Williams, although she had not seen any object herself, had a full report on Mrs. Sloane's sighting. She had told Mrs. Williams about it the next morning: a huge red disk which had illuminated Mrs. Williams' house as well as her own. Mrs. Sloane had said that she was going to phone at the time, but decided to call the police instead because of the lateness of the hour.

I continued with the random survey, getting some hearsay, some direct accounts, from people who cannot be named, most of whom are military personnel.

—A coastguardsman from New Hampshire told me that although his station would never release any official information, he was on watch one night when an enormous reddish-orange disk moved slowly up the beach, not more than 15 feet above it. He confessed that he was so shocked by the sight that he went into the radio shack and closed the door.

—From an Air Force pilot I learned that pilots had been ordered to shoot at any UFO they came across in an effort to bring it down. But he said that they were apparently invulnerable, and that they were capable of outmaneuvering any aircraft the Air Force had. He said that he simply ignored the orders to fire on such objects, since he felt personally it would be better not to alienate them.

—A military radar operator reported that a UFO came directly toward the base, was clocked both visually and on the radarscope. It seemed as if it were brazenly going to land at the base. But instead of landing, it hovered over the base. The officer-of-the-day was notified, and he put a telescope on the object. As he watched, it suddenly accelerated to a speed of over 800 miles an hour, as clocked on the radarscope. It disappeared within a minute.

—A brilliant orange object landed directly off the edge of one of the runways at the Pease Air Force Base, illuminating a wide area where many of the Air Force officers and their families lived, according to a member of a high-ranking officer's family. Some wives reported that the light was so bright that they thought it was morning; one actually started to get dressed until she realized it was still the middle of the night. Phone calls swamped the switchboard at the air base, and eventually the base was cut off by the commander from outside communication. The fire unit of the base was dispatched to the end of the runway as the object took off and disappeared at an unclocked speed.

—I was given several more reports about the constant scrambling of jet fighters after the strange objects; when radar sightings had been made in concert with visual sightings.

—Constant radar reports were being made at the Portsmouth Navy Base. In one instance, an object hovered over a water tower at the base before taking off at incredibly fast speed. It was checked both visually and by radar.

—One highly qualified officer at the Pease Air Force Base told me that he had been skeptical about UFOs before he had been assigned to the command at Portsmouth. He was no longer skeptical at all. At least 15 pilots at the base felt the same way.

—An Air Force refueling officer told me that a refueling operation was broken off abruptly when an enormous UFO appeared directly off the wing of a KC-97 tanker, confirmed visually by the crew and by instrument by a radar tower.

—An Air Force pilot claimed that the most sophisticated jets and weaponry were no match at all to the speed and maneuverability of the objects.

—Two additional officers of the air base told me that they were shocked and dismayed by the Pentagon report issued about the Bertrand and Hunt case in Exeter. They said it was so unbelievable in the light of what local authorities knew, that it could make the Pentagon a laughingstock. They said in no uncertain terms that the report was severely damaging to the Air Force.

Although none of the personnel supplying this information can be identified, for their own protection, these reports are no less real than any of the other information I put directly on the tapes. In fact, in view of the position of these people, the stories reinforced the thesis that UFOs not only existed, but were beyond the capacity of the military to deal with them. This impotence, of course, might be the underlying reason why the Government was carrying out its ostrichlike program of nonrecognition. The public has a naïve and childlike faith in the military, and anything admittedly beyond its control might shatter this faith forever.

CHAPTER XIII

By Wednesday, November 3, I realized that I was coming to a full impasse in the research. The scuttlebutt, the rumors, and the off-the-record remarks of the military had convinced me of the impact of the mystery, but the evidence was repetitive and did not indicate a conclusion.

Several new frustrations developed that day. One was that I learned I would not be able to see young Muscarello for several weeks, when he would return to Exeter on leave from his boot training at the Great Lakes Naval Training Center. The other was that although the Air Force had granted permission for the Coast Guard at Hampton to release the names of the two young men who had had such a harrowing experience, it was impossible to find out immediately their whereabouts, because they were summer workers at an ocean-front restaurant which had closed for the season. I was able to get at least some of the details from the Coast Guard station regarding the case, which was most interesting because of the low altitude of the object, and the total shock the principals had experienced.

The Coast Guard log, of course, was laconic and in the customary officialese language:

At 0400 on 2 August, 1965, Walter Shipman and Chris J. Kalogeropoulos, both working at Connie's Cozy Kitchen, Salisbury Beach, Massachusetts, reported an Unidentified Flying Object to the Hampton Beach Police, who brought them to the Coast Guard Station, where a UFO report was made.

(Anthony Warren, the coastguardsman on duty at that time, told me they were cold sober, something he established immediately, because he would have recommended their arrest otherwise.)

Police Sgt. Farnsworth, according to Warren, came by with the two men, but both were so shaken that they refused to get out of their car. They were finally persuaded to come into the station, where they reported that the object moved in from the ocean, directly toward their car. They thought at first it was a helicopter or a jet in trouble, but eliminated that explanation because there was no sound, and it moved up, down and sideways as it followed their car. They increased their speed, but still it followed them. Finally, they made a U-turn, and the object did likewise.

Warren had them fill out a form in detail, went over the road where the sighting took place, but was unable to see anything. "When I opened the door of their car," said Warren, "the first thing I checked was whether they were drunk or not. They definitely were not. I didn't want to get involved in reporting any story from crackpots. I asked them how big it was, but they were so upset they couldn't say exactly. All they could say was that it was *big!* After that, I wrote down what they saw, and sent it on to Pease.".

With all the investigation I had done, I suddenly realized that I had never studied the original location of Bertrand's and Hunt's sighting on Route 150, to see if there had been any high-tension power lines nearby. While it would not prove anything if there were, it might add another piece of evidence to the theory that the objects at least seemed to utilize some kind of electromagnetic force from or be attracted to the power which surges through this network of wires which makes up the Northeast Grid.

On the way, I noticed an appliance store on Route 1 near Hampton, and since a cable was loose on my tape recorder, I decided to see if it could be repaired. At the Downer Appliance Company, I ran into a Phillip McKnight, who went to work on the ailing cable. At the same time, I asked him if he had run into any reports of UFOs and he said he knew of several. As a Boy Scoutmaster, he knew families of his troop members who had clearly observed the objects, some at close range. He told me that Mrs. Parker Blodgett, of Shaw Hill, had encountered a particularly vivid sighting near her home. He was impressed with this, because Mrs. Blodgett was an able and prominent citizen, and president of the New Hampshire PTA. This interested me, because Shaw Hill was the area where young Ron Smith, his mother, and aunt had encountered UFOs twice at close range.

I talked with Mrs. Blodgett in the living room of her restored pre-Revolutionary farmhouse that commanded a sweeping view of the countryside.

"It was September 21, and it was after midnight," she said. This was approximately the date Ron Smith had indicated he had seen an object in this same area, although he could not remember the exact date. "I was going to bed, between one-thirty and two A.M. And I turned off the lights in the living room here—they face on the southeast. And I suddenly saw this very bright, blinding ball of light up over the trees there, about one hundred yards away. It was deeper red, almost, on the top, in sort of a semicircle. At the bottom was an extremely bright glowing light. It was just sort of hovering there over the trees."

"How big did it look?" I asked.

"It covered an area from the chimney of that house there, to the tree here in the yard," she said. This, I noticed, would make it enormous. The area spanned almost a hundred feet, as far as I could estimate.

"It was above the trees when I first saw it," she said.

"How far above them?"

"Not very far. Just above them. I would say it was above the pine trees you see in the distance, rather than over my house here. It was a little farther off. It was just hovering, and I was thinking I should call somebody and get them up and let them see this. Because they're going to think I'm crazy in the morning. Then— it started to spin real fast, and went zoom. And it was out of sight."

"It spun?" I had had other reports of this, and wanted to get a clearer description.

"It spun," Mrs. Blodgett said, "just a circular motion, then it went zoom. And it was gone within a second."

"How did it spin?"

"It just gave a spinning motion."

"Can you tell me a little more about the color?" I asked.

"It was a reddish color. Reddish to an orange, a red glow. But it did have a lighter, a light glow underneath it. Which I thought might be due to the fact that it was slightly hazy that night."

"Hear any sound?"

"No sound *at all.*"

"Did the lights make any pattern?"

"I saw no pattern of lights, as it's been reported. There was a twinkling around the edge, but no pattern."

"You're familiar with running lights on airplanes?"

"Oh, yes. Of course. They go over here every night. It wasn't like that at all."

"Was this the only one you've sighted?"

"This is the only one I have sighted. A friend of mine claims he saw it. And there was an Air Force plane following close behind the thing. So they must be well aware of it. Some officers have stopped by here inquiring, as a matter of fact. But they give us nothing to go on. The thing that bothers me is that these things should not look like they're out of science fiction—but they actually do. It's all so fantastic. Really, it is."

"Are there any high-tension power lines near here?" I asked.

"What are they, exactly?" she said.

"They're the high poles or steel towers that carry electrical power. Not the ordinary poles that go along the road. These usually go across country, with a wide path cut through the trees around them."

"Now that you mention it," she said, "I think there are. Right down the road here."

I went out and looked and about a quarter of a mile away, I saw familiar multiple poles and heavy strands of wire.

From Shaw Hill it is only a short drive to Route 150, and to the spot where Muscarello, Bertrand and Hunt watched the object hover above them in the field. I parked my car but I could not see any high-tension wires from that point. I decided to go to the house directly across from the spot, and was greeted by Jeanne Fiset, a student at the University of New Hampshire, who commuted to classes from her home. Miss Fiset learned the next day about the incident that had taken place only a few yards from her house, having slept through all the confusion and excitement.

"You were sleeping when the police cars came out here?" I asked.

"Yes."

"Did you hear anything at all?"

"No, I did not. Not that night. The following night I did, though."

"What happened then?"

"The following night we began seeing all these cars across the road, and we thought maybe the flying object was going to come back, because so many people were gathered out there looking for it. I guess it was about nine o'clock when all the cars started coming. And we had heard that this boy, Muscarello, was planning to come back. But neither my father, mother, nor I saw anything. And I don't think anyone else did, either. The following week, the boy talked to us and told us what he had seen. And how it scared him."

"Was he convincing?" I asked.

"Yes, he was very convincing. He said he was not going to leave the area until he had seen another one. He wanted to prove to everyone that he had seen something. He was coming out here every night, he said, with either his friends or his mother. And he did. He asked us if it was all right to come and knock on our door, no matter what time it was, if he saw it again. He wanted us to see it, too. We said that would be all right. And a couple of weeks after that first night, it was about one-thirty in the morning, I heard this knock on the door. It sounded as if someone was trying to tear the house down. My mother and I went to the door, and the boy was there and said he had seen it again. He had a friend with him, and the friend had seen it, too. My mother and I looked in the sky, and at first, we didn't see anything. Then, all of a sudden, coming across the sky, we saw this red object, it was about the size of a ball. It was smaller than the moon, but not as small as a star. The boy said, That's it, I know it is, because just a few minutes before, he had seen it flying low. A plane was apparently chasing it."

"Did you see the plane?"

"Yes. And we could hear it, too."

"You could see the running lights?"

"Yes. They were flashing."

"The object was ahead of the plane?"

"Yes."

"About how far ahead was it?"

"It's hard to tell. Say the object was way down the field across the road, and the plane was up by the house here. This object, the first object, not the plane, went down by the trees across the road, behind the house, came out from behind it, and just plain stopped in the air. Then it came back from the same direction. Now, a plane just doesn't do that. Also, did they tell you about the animals in the neighborhood? Everybody told us that the dogs in the neighborhood really kicked up that first night, and especially the horses across the road began making all kinds of noises."

"I heard about that," I said.

At this point, Miss Fiset's father arrived home, and I talked with him about the night of the original sighting.

"I heard a lot," he said, "but I didn't check it out at that time."

"What did you hear?" I asked.

"My dog was whining. And he seemed very scared. So I got up to see what was the trouble. Then I heard the horses, all the way across the road. And they were whinnying away, they were *really* acting up. I got up and I spotted the police cars sitting outside there in the darkness. I couldn't figure out what it was. I could see the lights flashing on and off, the dome light of the cars.

And my wife got up, and she looked out too. I thought it must be just a minor accident or something, so I went back to bed."

I was not able to talk to Norman Muscarello until several weeks later, when he came back to Exeter on leave from the Navy. But the interview with him was strangely anticlimactic. The recorded tapes of Officer Bertrand, Officer Hunt, his mother, Officer Toland, Miss Fiset, so surrounded the incident in detail that Muscarello's story was simply a total but necessary confirmation of everything which had happened on that predawn morning of September 3. It coincided almost exactly with the description given by officers Bertrand and Hunt. He demonstrated how he had dropped down on the shoulder of the road to keep away from the object when it came toward him. When the Look photographer, Jim Kareles, asked him, "Why did you do that?" he replied: "Wouldn't you?" The interview with him completed the cycle of the original incident at Exeter, which had set into motion such a long and arduous period of research. Most interesting was the lack of any basic distortion in the many accounts of that incident.

After leaving the Fiset house, I walked once more across the Carl Dining field, and down the slope, as Bertrand and Muscarello had done. I reached the far end of the field and looked toward Hampton. I was almost shocked to see what I had been looking for: a long line of high poles and wires of the high-power transmission lines of the Exeter and Hampton Electric Company. They had been hidden by the trees when I first looked for them. They added another piece of evidence to the power-line theory.

Before the scheduled meeting at the church in Dover on Sunday, November 7, I had time to return to New York and arrange for the start of the documentary film with Irving Gitlin, and also to see Look Magazine about arranging for their photographer and senior editor to make plans for the picture story to accompany the article.

At home in Connecticut I found a letter bearing the

return address of A. Reid Bunker, Sr., of Plaistow, New Hampshire. I immediately recognized the name of one of the people recommended as a witness by Mr. Healey, of Bessie's Lunch. I had called him during the latter part of October, but far from getting any kind of clear report of an observation, he would scarcely admit that he had seen anything. I was disappointed at the time, mainly because he had been recommended so highly as a witness. I opened the letter and read it:

DEAR MR. FULLER,

When you called the other night (October 24) I thought that it might be one of my fellow workers—I get a lot of ribbing about seeing flying saucers, etc.—I hope you understand. I will try to put down on paper what my wife and I saw—hoping it might help you in your investigation.

We were *under the high-power lines* [the italics are mine] at Fremont, N.H. (Route 107). And we were there about an hour or so, when at 10:45 P.M. we saw an object approach from the northwest going to the southeast. It had red lights mostly, and sort of green and white lights. The lights *did not* flash on and off. It was completely silent, and was within a quarter of a mile of us. It was at treetop level, and gave the impression of a long graceful bounce instead of a straight flight like a plane. Now, if this was a saucer-type object, and was revolving or tipping back and forth, we might have seen the lights on the other side of the object, thus giving the impression that it was bouncing very slightly in flight. We watched it for about half a minute, then it went behind the trees toward the southeast.

About five minutes later, two men on another road came over to where we were, and asked us what we saw—they had seen the same thing and were quite excited about it. Hope this helps.

Sincerely,
A. REID BUNKER, SR.

The letter was interesting as a reflection of the reluctance of many witnesses to discuss the subject at the risk of being ridiculed by their friends, plus the mention of the ubiquitous high-tension power lines.

Also in the mail was an editorial Conrad Quimby had written for the Derry *News*, which demonstrated the impatience many people in New Hampshire were feeling about the attitude of the Government and the Air Force.

Its headline was: UFO PHENOMENON: TIME TO HEAR FROM THE WHITE HOUSE. It had appeared in the issue of October 28. The editorial began:

> Several weeks ago, we became interested in the story of several people in and around Exeter who said they had been approached at night by a huge object which was glowing red, and tilted as it moved toward and away from them. The source of this UFO sighting was so close to Derry that we decided to send a reporter over to see what he could find out. . . .
> It's been speculated by some, such as the National Investigations Committee on Aerial Phenomena, that the President and the Pentagon are fearful of public reaction to official reports that might reveal a whole new concept of interplanetary life. . . .
> If the White House is holding information about UFOs because it fears that the public might go haywire, we find the observation about as wild as some of the more lunatic UFO stories. We believe that the public can take just about any kind of explanation, even one which might tend to make the White House look like a teller of Halloween tales. . . . It seems to this paper that the White House is acting like a fretful old spinster in not parting with its version of what lies behind the UFO phenomenon.

I could only agree with Quimby's thesis. Regardless of the initial shock, the public had shown its capacity in many disasters to react and recover with resiliency. The people who had encountered low-level UFO sightings unquestionably registered initial shock, but most recovered quickly and spent hours trying to see them again. In other words, hysteria shifted quickly to interest and fascination. The truth cannot be kept under cover indefinitely, and the situation could be worse if the public were unprepared for a sudden announcement. What in the history of human beings could possibly be worse than the hydrogen bomb and the threat of nuclear war? What evidence had UFOs shown that they were hostile, assuming of course that they were in such plentiful existence as the reports all over the world seemed to indicate?

In the same mail was more news, sent along by Gordon Evans, which was most illuminating. It was a reprint of the Proceedings of the First Annual Rocky

Mountain Bioengineering Symposium, *held at the United States Air Force Academy* in May of 1964. The symposium was sponsored by the USAF Academy itself, along with the Committee on Electrical Techniques in Medicine and Biology of the Institute of Electrical and Electronic Engineers. It included a paper presented by a highly respected scientist, Frank B. Salisbury, of the Department of Botany and Plant Pathology, Colorado State University. His subject was "Exobiology"—in plainer terms, the study of life beyond the earth. His opening remarks, and other comments, struck me as being extremely apt in the light of the research which had been completed in and around Exeter:

> The existence of this symposium testifies to the possibility that man shall in the relatively near future discover or fail to discover some form of extraterrestrial life in the solar system. The purpose of my discussion is to present briefly some of the current arguments for and against the existence of extraterrestrial life in the solar system.
> It is quite amazing how rapidly this topic has expanded in recent years, and how it has moved from the realm of science fiction into a field of thought dignified by the impressive title "exobiology"!

The paper went on to discuss the possibilities of this form of life, citing in detail some unanswered questions about Mars, meteorites, and other solar system phenomena. The material was carefully documented. And in one section, the scientist turned his attention to UFOs:

> To complete our list of evidences in favor of extraterrestrial life, we should cite the testimony of various witnesses who claim to have experienced or seen a visitation by an extraterrestial intelligent being. Many of these accounts fall into the realm of religion, and because of their nature, they cannot be objectively studied by the methods of science. A number of others, however, involve non-religious accounts of sightings of unidentified aerial phenomena, including flying objects which might conceivably be interpreted as extraterrestrial spaceships. Since 1947, a few thousand of these sightings have been carefully recorded and placed in the files of various organizations, and thousands and perhaps hundreds of thousands more have occurred but have not been reported. Many of these are easy to shrug off as misinterpreted natural phenomena (meteorites, ball lightning, the planet Venus, etc.) . . .

The ones which are not so easy to dismiss as natural phenomena or as unreliable witnesses might some day prove to be psychological phenomena. This is the faith of many investigators. At this point, however, we have no proof of this, since most of the phenomena are certainly not explained by our present concepts of psychology. In many cases, the most parsimonious explanation remains that of the extraterrestrial spaceship.

It is my conviction that the accounts should be eagerly studied by the exobiologist. As evidence for exobiology, the unidentified aerial phenomena are probably no more borderline than some of the other evidence already mentioned above.

The paper states that the number and quality of the sightings are much higher than is imagined by most people who have not made a special study of the question. It points out that many of the witnesses are scientists, engineers, and other highly competent observers, and mentions the numerous simultaneous sightings on radar, from aircraft, and visually from the ground.

Salisbury also pointed out that a number of photographs have been obtained, accompanied by the witnessing of the object simultaneously by a large number of reliable people, essential to corroborating the taking of the picture. The Salisbury paper continues:

At present, we seem either to be afraid of the topic or to feel that it is unworthy of scientific comment. . . . Certainly fear has no place in the search for truth, and if the unknowns relating to the topic are someday solved, then we will have made considerable scientific progress.

I couldn't help noting that while the Air Force was busy pretending to the public that UFOs were nonexistent, the Air Force Academy was sponsoring a symposium that was deadly and scientifically serious about UFOs and their possible effect on "exobiology."

In another statement made by Salisbury, he says:

I must admit that any favorable mention of the flying saucers by a scientist amounts to extreme heresy and places the one making the statement in danger of excommunication by the scientific theocrasy. Nevertheless, in recent years I have investigated the story of the unidentified flying object (UFO), and I am no longer able to dismiss the idea lightly.

I had to agree that this thought was fast becoming my firm position.

CHAPTER XIV

The Pearce Memorial Unitarian-Universalist Church in Dover is a gaunt and Gothic structure, struggling against the erosion of years, weather, and parishioner indifference. A new, younger group has given the parish fresh life lately, and its regular Sunday evening series of provocative discussions and lectures was beginning to build new interest in the church. Attendance at these meetings had averaged slightly above 50 people on Sunday evenings, and although the hall was able to hold some 400, this small attendance was a respectable figure for a new program in the developmental stage.

I felt that the size of the audience on the night of November 7 would reflect local interest in the UFO subject. Mr. and Mrs. Hill, who were to talk about their traumatic experience with a UFO some four years previously, were anxious to counteract some of the sensationalism of the New England press. If the church hall were nearly filled, it would indicate that the recent frequency of the sightings had impressed a considerable portion of the population. If there were a small attendance, it might mean that the sightings I had recorded were more limited in the area than I thought.

The weather was miserable. The raw, cold rain and a cutting New Hampshire wind might encourage people to stay by their firesides instead of beating their way to a drafty auditorium. But although the meeting was scheduled for 7:30, the audience began arriving over an hour in advance. By 7 o'clock the auditorium was filled, and by 15 minutes after the hour, literally hundreds of people were being turned away. A loudspeaker was hastily improvised for the basement, where part of the overflow gathered. People were standing against the back wall up to the limit of fire regulations. It was a totally unprecedented crowd, far beyond the expectations of the church committee who had planned the event. Some people had driven from towns 40 miles distant, only to be turned away. Church members found they were unable to gain entrance to their own church. My earlier guess had been that there would be a large crowd, but I had changed this estimate when the heavy rain began in the early afternoon and continued without letup.

I was also surprised to see that Lt. Alan Brandt, the Public Information Officer at Pease AFB, was on the speaker's platform in his Air Force uniform. It indicated that there was at least tacit Air Force approval of his being a speaker at the meeting, but whether or not it suggested that the Air Force was ready to leak out UFO news at a meeting like this, or test public reaction, no one could tell. Lieutenant Brandt's introductory speech was certainly vague and unilluminating. He merely reviewed the Air Force policy on UFOs as expressed in its own handbook, without any further elaboration. He did indicate that the Air Force took UFO sightings seriously and that anyone sighting them should report them to the Pease Air Force Base immediately.

The Hills spoke very circumspectly of their experience. They pointed out emphatically that although their hypnotic therapy had revealed to them on tape recordings that they were taken aboard the strange craft and given a physical examination by intelligent humanoid beings, they could not testify that this was the truth. They *could* testify to their conscious sighting of the UFO as it came down near their car, but beyond that neither the Hills nor the psychiatrist could fully explain the mystery of the two hours of amnesia which followed, aside from the astonishing information revealed under regressive hypnosis.

The crowd packed into the church sat spellbound as the Hills related their experience. The couple had left Canada, driving south toward Portsmouth, and stopped at a restaurant in Colebrook, New Hampshire, on the Canadian border. "When Betty and I left Colebrook," Mr. Hill said, "we never remembered the exact time until we were regressed back under hypnosis. Here, I had looked at a clock on the wall, and the time was five minutes after ten at night. We drove down Route 3, and when we arrived at Groveton, Betty called my attention to a light that was moving in the sky. And I looked at it, and actually to me it was nothing unusual except that we were fortunate enough to see a satellite. It had no doubt gone off its course, and you could see that it was going along the curvature of the earth. It was quite a distance out, meaning that it looked like a star.

"So, this is exciting in itself, and we had 7 x 50 binoculars with us, which we always take with us on vacation. And I stopped the car, so that we could both get a look at the object. Suddenly, Betty said, Barney, if you call that a star or a satellite, you are being ridiculous. Just look at it. So with the naked eye, without taking the binoculars, I could see that it was not a distant thing far out there, but now more like a plane. I said, Betty, we obviously made a mistake. That's a commercial plane on its way to Canada. It was traveling from the south, going north. And I was facing west, meaning I was facing toward Vermont. So I took the binoculars and started looking, and then I was completely amazed. Because instead of continuing on the northerly pattern, it turned toward the west, toward the direction of Vermont, completing the turn and then coming in toward us. Then I noticed a winking sort of light pattern, not at all like a conventional aircraft. And although I was amazed, I told Betty that it was probably a Piper Cub or some other light plane, and that it wasn't anything to be concerned about.

"We got into the car, and started driving south on Route 3. Betty continued to look out and she said, Well, Barney, if it is whatever you're calling it, I don't know why. Because it's still out there, and still following us. I would slow down occasionally, and would look out and see that it was still there. And I felt a little uncomfortable about the whole thing. I thought that probably some hunters or fishermen had a light plane, and could see us on the highway, and were following us.

"So when we reached Cannon Mountain, if you're facing

south, Route 3 goes to the left of it. And this object went around the western side of the mountain. So that when we passed Cannon Mountain, there's a figurehead, referred to as the Old Man of the Mountain. The object now hovered around and was now facing us on the highway, still some distance away. I was completely baffled by this, and I was hoping a car would pass us one way or another, because there was some comfort thinking I could stop someone and ask if they saw the same thing."

Mr. Hill then described the actual encounter. The object settled down, about 200 feet in the air. He began walking toward it, peering through the binoculars. It looked to both him and his wife like a huge pancake. Around the base was a band of light, and through the binoculars he saw a row of structural windows. What's more, he could actually discern figures inside the craft, and he ran back to the car, jumped in, and started to drive off.

Then the craft rose up, circled the car, and went out of sight over the roof. Both the Hills heard a strange, electronic beeping sound and began to feel a strange tingling sensation. It was at this point that their memory was blocked completely for a two-hour period of total amnesia.

The Hills refused to discuss the details of their experience as recalled on the tapes under hypnosis. They did not regain consciousness until they had driven some 30 miles to the south. The professional help they sought was instrumental in relieving them of the traumatic neuroses resulting from the experience, but they both insisted that they were making no claims beyond the conscious recollection of the incident.

"We just don't know the answer," Mr. Hill concluded. "We sought the best professional psychiatric help possible, and this is the answer we got."

So intense was the interest of the audience, that the question-and-answer period following the talk lasted for over an hour. Several in the audience revealed their own experiences with UFOs.

After the session, I joined the Hills and Walter Webb, of the astronomy staff of the Hayden Planetarium in Boston, for a cup of coffee. Webb had been instrumental in arranging professional help for the Hills, and was extremely interested in the UFO aspect of the case because of the stature and reliability of the couple. Webb pointed out that in spite of the strangeness of the information revealed under hypnosis, he and several other scientists were taking the case very seriously. The Hills, he said, had shown great restraint in keeping the incident away from the glare of publicity for over four years, and both husband and wife ranked far above average in intelligence. Although the case remained a mystery, it was still under serious study.

Monday, November 8, was spent mainly with Gereon Zimmermann, a senior editor of *Look,* and Jim Kareles, staff photographer of the magazine, as we made the rounds of several of the key witnesses to review their stories and photograph them for the picture story to accompany the article. I was relieved to have others spot-check the interviews. We covered Mrs. Hale, Mrs. Gazda, the entire community in the area of the Pearce home, the police, Ron Smith, Bessie's Lunch, the Jalbert place by the power lines in Fremont, and Chief Bolduc and his family in the same neighborhood. In reviewing their sightings with them, it was interesting to note that the descriptions remained basically the same as when they had given them to me a few weeks previously.

At the Bolduc house, Jesse Bolduc had joined the ranks of the observers since the time I had first talked to him. He confessed that he no longer laughed at his wife, and admitted that he had to eat his own words.

At the Jalbert home, the entire family reported continued sightings, and both Joseph Jalbert and his mother recounted a most interesting observation which had happened since I had first met them.

Joseph had recently noticed a reddish, cigar-shaped object in the sky, high over the power lines. It hovered there motionless for several minutes—exactly how many he did not know because he was so absorbed with watching it. After a considerable length of time, a reddish-orange disk emerged apparently from inside the object, and began a slow, erratic descent down toward the power lines. As it reached a point within a quarter mile of them, it leveled off, then moved over the wires until it reached a point several hundred feet away. It then descended slowly until it was only a few feet above the lines. Then a silvery, pipelike object came down from the base of the disk and actually touched the lines, remaining there for a minute or so.

The protrusion then slowly retracted into the body of the object, and it took off at considerable speed—exactly how fast, Joseph could not estimate—then rejoined the reddish cigar-shaped object and disappeared inside it.

Joseph's mother had not seen this but had observed a similar occurrence some 20 miles away, near Manchester. The only difference in their descriptions was that the protrusion extending down from the object she observed was reddish rather than silver colored. Joseph was very reluctant to bring this sighting up. His younger brother had prodded him into telling about it, and when Zimmermann, Kareles and I asked him why he was so hesitant, he told us that the whole thing looked too scary and he didn't like to talk about it. "It's the first time I've ever seen one of these things touch anything," he said, "and it happened so near to me that I really tried to put it out of my mind."

By Tuesday, November 9, I was ready to close out the research and begin the long job of trying to correlate all the tapes and notes. Several more reports of sightings were brought to our attention that morning, but most proved to be repetitive, and I could see no reason for extensive interviews. One, however, I looked into thoroughly because it involved an alleged landing outside a house in Exeter in a heavily populated area.

Mr. and Mrs. Joseph Mazalewski lived at 2 McKinley Street in Exeter, in one of a group of modest houses separated, in some cases, by vacant lots. They occupied the first floor of the house, and both of them worked during the day, coming home at noontime for lunch.

I caught them at noon on November 9. They were each in their sixties; both pleasant and cordial. At approximately 2:30 in the morning, sometime in September of 1965—neither could recall the exact date—Mrs. Mazalewski was awakened by a brilliant light illuminating her first-floor bedroom. At the same time, she heard a loud humming noise which startled her. Her husband, asleep in another room, was not aware of it at this time. She sat up and was able to see out the window from her bed. A large cluster of different-colored lights approximately 20 feet away from her bedroom window were blinking in an indefinite pattern.

"I watched for fifteen minutes," she said. "I sat on my bed and kept watching it. I said to myself, what the heck is that? And it kind of scared me, you know. I kept hearing this noise. It scared me."

"Could you imitate this noise?" I asked her.

"I really don't know if I could," she said. She tried, making a sound similar to the humming of an electric generator. "It was right flat on the ground," she went on. "In back of that tree."

She pointed to a small tree, now leafless, about 15 feet from her window.

"Flat on the ground?"

"Yes, right on the ground, as far as I could see. And those lights kept blinking and blinking."

"Could you make out any shape?" I asked.

"No, the lights were too bright," she said. "They looked almost like Christmas tree lights, you know?"

"What was your reaction to it? How did you feel?"

"I was wondering what it was. It really scared me. I sat here, just watching and watching. I didn't even think to wake my husband up in the next room at first. Then when I finally did get so scared I couldn't stand it anymore, I called in to him. I said, Gee, Joey, there's something out there in that field. There's all bright lights out there."

Joseph Mazalewski spoke up. "I was already putting my pants and my shirt and my slippers on. I wanted to go out in the field, to see it close. She said to me, No you ain't going out there!"

I turned to Mrs. Mazalewski. "Why wouldn't you let him go out?"

" 'Cause I didn't have any idea what it was out there. And I was scared. I didn't want something out there pulling him into something."

"Did she really stop you?" I said to her husband.

"She sure did," he said. "She wouldn't give me my slippers. I started toward the door, and she stood in front of it. She said, You're not going out there!"

"I had the funniest feeling through me," said Mrs. Mazalewski. "It gives you the funniest feeling. It was an *awful* noise."

"The lights kept blinking all the time?"

"Yes. And that noise kept going all the time."

"Flat on the ground? Not vertical?" Mrs. Mazalewski was so intense and upset about recalling the incident that she had trouble articulating.

"This was flat on the ground," she insisted.

"You sure you couldn't make out the shape of the object behind the bright lights?"

"No, I really couldn't make out what was behind them."

"Did the sound stop suddenly?"

"Yes, it did. And when I looked out again, it was completely gone."

"I went out the next morning," Mr. Mazalewski said, "and I couldn't notice anything unusual in the field. It must have just been floating right above the grass."

"Anybody else in the neighborhood see it?" I asked.

"Nobody that I know of," said Mrs. Mazalewski. "A lot of people around here keep talking about seeing these things, but I don't know if anybody saw anything this exact time."

Mrs. Mazalewski had obviously undergone a traumatic experience. Unfortunately, her description was too vague to be of much help, but the low-altitude report was of interest because it represented the second one in two days.

I met the *Look* Magazine men back at the motor inn in Hampton for dinner. It was a cold, sparkling clear night, with a brilliant hunter's moon, and the huge fireplace in the dining room was a welcome sight. We met at about 5:30, and as I was leaving my room, I noticed that the electric lights flickered, faltered for a few seconds, and then came on brightly again. I thought nothing of it, went on into the dining room where Zimmermann and Kareles were waiting for me in a booth. We ordered martinis and prepared to relax.

As the waitress brought the drinks, she had a broad smile on her face. She had been helpful in the past in supplying the names of people she had heard about who had sighted objects, and was interested in the story as it developed.

"I suppose this is all your fault," she said, putting the martinis down on the table.

"What is all our fault?" I asked.

"You mean you haven't heard about it?" she asked.

"Heard about what?" Zimmermann asked.

"The blackout. The power failure. All over the east."

"You're kidding," I said. The lights in Hampton were blazing brightly. I did recall, though, the flicker as I had left my room.

"It just came in over the radio in the kitchen," she said. "New York, Albany, Boston, Providence, all of Massachusetts, are absolutely black. Not a light burning. This is no joke, I mean it."

This seemed so incredible that we hardly took it seriously. I got up, went back to the room, and turned on the television set.

I was startled to see the news staff of NBC-TV broadcasting in faint candlelight. The picture was fuzzy and barely discernible. The commentary, of course, confirmed all that the waitress had told us, and more. I still found it hard to believe. And, of course, the first thing which crossed my mind was the long series of UFO sightings involving the power lines, such as Joseph Jalbert's report the evening before. I forgot completely about dinner.

When Jim Kareles came back into the room, I was already poring through the 203 pages of transcript of the tape recordings. The words "power lines" or "transmission lines" appeared on an alarming number of pages. I began making a notation in the margin of the transcripts wherever a reference like this was made. Jim Kareles helped me correlate the information. There were 73 mentions in various locations by various people. These included either the actual use of the words, or references to locations near where the power lines ran.

I sat glued to the television set, waiting for some word as to the cause of the unprecedented failure. The news commentators were as confused as everybody else. No one seemed to have any idea of the cause, and never in history had there been a power blackout of such extent. I tried to phone my home in Connecticut, but was told by the operator that the only calls she could put through were those that were a matter of life or death.

The Portsmouth-Exeter area, we learned, was one of

the few pockets of light in the entire Northeast. I found small comfort in that, because I thought of the millions of people in the large cities who must certainly be trapped in cold, dark subways or jammed, stuffy elevators.

I waited in vain throughout the evening and early morning hours for more news but no announcement came which gave even a clue to the mystery. I ran through the transcripts again, still noting the phrases and descriptions referring to the power lines. Suddenly, the major emphasis of the entire UFO research—the power lines—was now becoming the focal point of a new mystery—no less mysterious than the UFO phenomenon I had been dealing with for weeks.

The country was moving, it seemed, from one Space Age ghost story into another.

Or were they both the same?

CHAPTER XV

The blackout caused by the failure of the Northeast Power Grid created one of the biggest mysteries in the history of modern civilization. Eighty thousand square miles and 36,000,000 people—one-fifth of the nation's population—were suddenly plunged into inexplicable darkness.

Massachusetts, New Hampshire, Rhode Island, Connecticut, Vermont, New York, New Jersey, Pennsylvania and parts of Canada were totally or partially affected by the failure. The President ordered a sweeping investigation. Nearly 800,000 persons—equal to the entire population of Washington, D.C.—were trapped for hours in elevator shafts, subway cars, or commuter trains. Airline pilots circled vainly to find a way to land at darkened airports.

The miracle was that panic and darkness failed to leave a massive death toll. Only a few accidents were reported, and these might have happened with or without a blackout.

By November 11, *The New York Times* was reporting that the Northeast was slowly struggling back toward normal, but that the cause of the blackout was still unknown. Authorities frankly admitted that there was no assurance whatever that the incredible blackout could not occur again, without warning.

There was a curious lack of physical damage: The utility companies looked for something to repair, but there was nothing. Only a few generators were out of action as a result of the power failure, not a cause. What's more, the utilities were able to restore service with the exact same equipment that was in use at the time of the blackout. What happened that night was not only far from normal; it was mystifying.

If there had been a mechanical flaw, a fire, a breakdown, a short circuit, a toppling transmission tower, the cause would have been quickly and easily detected. Mechanically, however, the system as a whole was in perfect repair before and after the failure.

William W. Kobelt, of Wallkill, New York, is one of the thousands of line patrol observers who, according to *The New York Times*, went into action to try to discover the trouble. He is typical of all the others. He flew over the lines of the Central Hudson Gas and Electric Corporation at daybreak after the blackout. Cruising close to treetop level, he checked wires, insulators, cross arms and structures of the high-power transmission lines. He looked for trees, branches which might have fallen over the wires. "We looked for trouble—but couldn't find any at all," he said.

Robert Ginna, Chairman of the Rochester Gas and Electric Corporation, said that his utility had been receiving 200,000 kilowatts under an agreement with the New York State Power authority, which operates the hydroelectric plants at Niagara Falls. "Suddenly, we didn't have it," he said. "We don't know what happened to the 200,000 kilowatts. It just wasn't there."

Edward L. Hoffman, assistant to the chief system electrical engineer of Niagara Mohawk, told *The New York Times* that it was true that some generators dropped out of phase, but that this was "secondary to the main cause of the failure."

Early in the blackout, it was announced that a line break near Niagara Falls had caused the trouble. A fast check immediately ruled that theory out.

At 10 P.M., it was announced that the crux of the difficulty lay at a remote-controlled substation on the Power Authority's transmission lines at Clay, New York, a town 10 miles north of Syracuse. The high-tension 345,-000-volt power lines stretching over Clay are part of the authority's "superhighway" of power distribution, running into Niagara Falls, east to Utica and south to New York City.

Niagara Mohawk repairmen who drove out to Clay found the substation in apparently perfect order. There were no signs of mechanical failure, fire or destruction. Another report sent FBI investigators and State Police to the desolate Montezuma Marshes outside of Syracuse, but they found nothing out of order there, according to *The Times*.

Something else happened outside Syracuse, however, which was noted briefly in the press and then immediately dropped without follow-up comment. Weldon Ross, a private pilot and instructor, was approaching Hancock Field at Syracuse for a landing. It was at almost the exact moment of the blackout. As he looked below him, just over the power lines near the Clay substation, a huge red ball of brilliant intensity appeared. It was about 100 feet in diameter, Ross told the New York *Journal-American*. He calculated that the fireball was at the point where the New York Power Authority's two 345,000-volt power lines at the Clay substation pass over the New York Central's tracks between Lake Oneida and Hancock Field. With Ross was a student pilot who verified the statement. At precisely the same moment, Robert C. Walsh, Deputy Commissioner for the Federal Aviation Agency in the Syracuse area, reported that he saw the same phenomenon just a few miles south of Hancock Field. A total of five persons reported the sighting. Although the Federal Power Commission immediately said they would investigate, no further word has been given publicly since.

Pilot Ross's sighting took place at 5:15 P.M., at the

moment when the blackout occurred in the Syracuse area. At 5:25 P.M., a schoolteacher in Holliston, Massachusetts, watched through binoculars with her husband an intense white object in the sky moving slowly toward the horizon. At the same time, David Hague, a seventeen-year-old from Holliston reported an identical object, moving toward the southwest.

In New York City, simultaneously with the blackout, two women declared in two separate statements that they sighted unusual objects in the sky.

In the statement of Mrs. Gerry Falk, she says: "Between five and five-five P.M., November ninth, I was driving along Mt. Prospect Avenue, West Orange, New Jersey. As I reached the corner of Mt. Prospect Avenue and Eagle Rock Avenue, I noticed a red streak in the sky. I stopped for a light and saw it again. I tried to get the attention of the driver in the next car, but was unable to do so. It is a heavily wooded area and hilly, and as I reached the crest of a hill, I saw it again.

"It was shaped rather like a half-moon, with two tips facing up. It was pale red, not like a flame, and there appeared to be something at the tip. It was very high in the air. At first I thought it was a sky-writer, but then I saw it was different from anything I had ever seen. The sun was going down to the right. This was on the left. It continued going up."

Mrs. Sol Kaplan, of Central Park West, New York City, was watching television in her bedroom, which faces the Hudson River to the west. Her TV set went off and the lights went out. "I looked out the window," she states, "and there were a number of planes in the sky, more than usual. As I kept looking, I saw a big circular dome—it was not flying, but going up and down and sideways. It was silvery-looking, no lights like an airplane. I was looking through binoculars."

Life photographer Arthur Rickerby took a strikingly dramatic picture of the New York skyline just after the blackout. In the western sky, a brilliant, silvery object appears that has not in any satisfactory way been explained, after it appeared in the November 19, 1965 issue of *Time*. Although some claim it is Venus, photographer Rickerby is inclined to disagree.

In Philadelphia, several witnesses in many parts of the

city reported seeing a "curious cloud, shaped like an up-ended coin with a handle" in an otherwise cloudless sky, according to Ruth Montgomery, Hearst columnist. They later discovered it was seen at almost the exact moment that the power failure occurred. Philadelphia itself was unaffected by the blackout.

Walter Voelker, a research engineer, told Miss Montgomery: "The most curious aspect was that by the time my wife and I saw the 'cloud' and could stop the car in traffic for a better look, it had shifted to the other side of the sky. We saw it in three different locations. Later, we learned of others who had had similar experiences in sighting it." Several sightings of a similar description were made in and around Bloomfield, Connecticut, at approximately the same time that the blackout struck.

According to NICAP, at 4:30 P.M. on the day of the blackout, pilot Jerry Whittaker and passenger George Croniger saw two shiny objects above them, chased by two jet planes. One UFO put on a "burst of speed" to outdistance them. Other UFO reports at the time of the blackout came from Holyoke and Amherst, Massachusetts, Woonsocket, Rhode Island, and Newark, New Jersey.

In spite of the lengthy report issued by the FCC, the Great Blackout has still not been adequately explained. Ostensibly, backup Relay #Q-29 at the Sir Adam Beck generating station, Queenston, Ontario, was eventually pinpointed as the source of the massive failure. But further investigation, hardly noted in the press, showed that nothing in the relay was broken when it was removed for inspection. In fact, it went back into operation normally when power was restored. The line it was protecting was totally undamaged. "Why did everything go beserk?" *Life* Magazine asks in an article about the blackout. "Tests on the wayward sensing device have thus far been to no avail." A later statement by Arthur J. Harris, a supervising engineer of the Ontario Hydroelectric Commission, indicated that the cause was still a mystery. "Although the blackout has been traced to the tripping of a circuit breaker at the Sir Adam Beck No. 2 plant, it is practically impossible to pinpoint the initial cause." As late as January 4, 1966, *The New York Times* in a follow-up story indicated a series of questions regarding the prevention of future blackouts. The news item says:

"These questions more or less are related to the cause, *still not fully understood*, of last November's blackout." The italics are ours.

The Great Northeast Blackout was a mystery, but not any more puzzling than what followed on its heels. On November 16, a series of power blackouts hit many parts of Britain. Dozens of sections of London were darkened, and telephone operators in Folkestone, on the south coast, worked by candlelight.

On November 26, NICAP was advised that power failures in St. Paul, Minnesota, were reported by the Northern States Power Company simultaneous with the appearance of objects overhead giving off blue and white flashes just off Highway 61. Fifteen minutes later, just north of the original sighting, a resident on Hogt Avenue reported a "blue-glowing" UFO as all house lights and appliances in the area went dead. A motorist also reported that his car lights and radio went out.

The power company announced that it was unable to determine the cause of that blackout.

By December 2, sections of two states and Mexico were plunged into darkness after a widespread power failure in the Southwest. Juarez, Mexico, was hit, as well as El Paso, Texas, and Las Cruces and Alamogordo, New Mexico. Authorities were unable to explain the cause of the trouble.

A few days later, on December 4, portions of east Texas were knocked out electrically, with 40,000 houses losing power. It was the third major blackout since the Northeast Grid failed.

By December 26, the mystery was growing deeper. The entire city of Buenos Aires, and towns as far as 50 miles away, were plunged into darkness by a power failure, with hundreds trapped in subways beneath Buenos Aires' streets. The cause was thought to be a single generator.

On the same date, four major cities of south and central Finland were hit by a loss of electrical power attributed to a single insulator.

Going back to 1962, an interesting fact was revealed by Eileen Shanahan of *The New York Times*. "Still not widely known in the eastern United States," she wrote under a November 21, 1965, dateline, "is that the North-

208

east power blackout was not the first wide-area power failure experienced in recent years. *There was one covering an area four times as large* [our italics] as the New York-New England blackout, and a less extensive one last January. Both were in the Midwest and involved such major cities as Omaha and Des Moines.

"Although the 1962 wide-area failure in the Midwest was well known to power experts before the Commission's survey was completed last year, the National Power Survey [published about a year before by the Federal Power Commission] made no significant mention of it, while recommending an enlargement of the kind of interdependence that made Tuesday's blackout so extensive. The Commission has offered no explanation for the omission."

Further evidence tabulated by NICAP on electrical interference of UFOs in the past enhances the possibility that there may be some relationship between the phenomenon and the wide-area power blackouts:

—On September 3, 1965, a glowing disk-shaped object hovered at low altitude over Cuernavaca, Mexico, as the lights of the town went out. It was witnessed by many, including Governor Emilie Riva Palacie, Mayor Valentin Lopez Gonzalez, and a military zone chief, General Rafael Enrique Vega.

—On August 17, 1959, the automatic keys at a power station turned off as a round-shaped UFO passed overhead, following a trunk power line. As the object disappeared, the keys went on again automatically, and service returned to normal.

—On August 3, 1958, parts of Rome, Italy, were darkened as a luminous UFO passed overhead.

—In 1957, lights went out at Nogi Mirim, Brazil, as three UFOs passed overhead. Also in 1957, a UFO hovered over Tamaroa, Illinois, as the electrical power failed.

One news story on January 13, 1966, is particularly interesting because it received little attention in the press aside from the Portsmouth, New Hampshire, *Herald* of that date, even though it was an AP release, with an Andover, Maine, dateline:

The Telstar communications satellite tracking station was

blacked out by a power failure which hit a 75-mile area in western Franklin County.

Electrical power failed at 4:30 P.M. Wednesday and was restored at 11:20 P.M.

A spokesman for the Central Maine Power Co. blamed the failure on "an apparent equipment failure which somehow corrected itself."

Noteworthy are two things: 1) The power failure involved a space satellite, and 2) in this age of science and engineering, the equipment "somehow corrected itself." Coupled with the stories of the numerous other blackouts, this is strange indeed that the engineers could not figure out how it went out—and how the failure was remedied.

On the following day, an AP story datelined Augusta, Maine, stated that Chairman Frederick N. Allen of the Public Utility Commission indicated that there was no negligence by the two power companies involved. The Central Maine Power Company said that the blackout was caused by the failure of a big transformer in its Rumford substation.

CMP Vice-President Harold F. Schnurle went on to say that it had not been determined why the transformer failed or why it restored itself to service nearly seven hours later.

The relationship of the Unidentified Flying Objects to the power failures is entirely circumstantial, of course. Both UFOs and the Great Blackout still remain unsolved. But stranger yet is the incapacity of modern science to come up with any kind of real answer to either question. More baffling still is the attitude of the large bulk of the scientific fraternity in presumably laughing off a phenomenon testified to by hundreds of technicians, other scientists, airline pilots, military personnel, local and state police and articulate and reliable citizens.

In addition to NICAP, another organization is probing hard into the phenomenon, maintaining strict objectivity, and committed to the premise that the UFO phenomenon, whether it consists of physical fact or rumor, is important enough to warrant objective investigation. Under the direction of Mr. and Mrs. L. J. Lorenzen, the Aerial Phenomena Research Organization (known as APRO), Tucson, Arizona, includes in its membership Dr.

James A. Harder, Associate Professor of the College of Engineering, University of California; Professor Charles A. Maney, Emeritus Professor of Physics and Mathematics, Defiance College; Dr. Robert Mellor, Assistant Professor of Botany at the University of Arizona; Dr. R. Leo Sprinkle, Assistant Professor of Psychology, University of Wyoming; Dr. Frank B. Salisbury, Professor of Plant Physiology, Colorado State University; and many others of high standing in the academic community. Research Director of APRO is Alvin E. Brown, Staff Scientist and member of the Research Laboratory, Lockheed Missiles and Space Company.

When more scientists become able and willing to investigate the subject without prejudice, some progress might be expected that has been lacking to date.

I started on this story as a friendly skeptic. I ended the research with a conviction that it is no longer a laughing matter, and that it is vital and important for the mystery to be solved one way or the other.

In the hands of the Air Force and the Secretary of the Air Force office in the Pentagon, the investigation can almost be considered a farce. The statements made by the Office of Information of the Secretary of the Air Force are often inaccurate, unfounded, and demonstrate a lack of objective investigation that even a reporter would hesitate to utilize in assembling a hasty news story. The embarrassment of the officers at the Pease Air Force Base regarding the Pentagon explanation of the Bertrand-Hunt-Muscarello incident on September 3, 1965, was genuine. Any well-informed officer at the base knew that "stars and planets in unusual formations" or "high-altitude exercises" could not possibly explain a huge, silent craft hovering at rooftop level, lighting up the entire area, especially when one of the witnesses was both a police officer and an Air Force veteran, and the other a police officer of excellent reputation on the Exeter force.

The Pentagon explanation was released to the local press on October 27. To the general public in the vicinity of Exeter, a final evaluation had been made, and the case was closed. Officers Bertrand and Hunt were, in the eyes of the local community, grossly incompetent, incredibly poor observers, or simply unadorned liars.

But in the third week in November, a month after the

Pentagon explanation, officers Bertrand and Hunt jointly received an undated letter from Wright-Patterson Air Force Base, and signed by Major Hector Quintanilla, Chief of the Project Blue Book. It read:

MR. EUGENE BERTRAND, JR.
MR. DAVID R. HUNT
Exeter Police Department
Exeter, New Hampshire

GENTLEMEN,

The sighting of various unidentified objects by you and Mr. Norman Muscarello was investigated by officials from Pease Air Force Base, New Hampshire, and their report has been forwarded to our office at Wright-Patterson Air Force Base. This sighting at Exeter, New Hampshire, on the night of 2 September has been given considerable publicity through various news releases and in magazine articles similar to that from the "Saturday Review" of 2 October, 1965. A portion of this article is attached for your information. This information was released by the National Investigations Committee on Aerial Phenomena, a private organization which has no connection with the government. As a result of these articles, the Air Force has received inquiry as to the cause of this report.

Our investigation and evaluation of the sighting indicates a possible association with an 8th Air Force Operation, "Big Blast." In addition to aircraft from this operation, there were five B-47 type aircraft flying in the area during this period. Before a final evaluation of your sighting can be made, it is essential for us to know if either of you witnessed any aircraft in the area during this time period either independently or in connection with the objects observed. Since there were many aircraft in the area, at that time, and there were no reports of unidentified objects from personnel engaged in this air operation, we might then assume that the objects observed between midnight and 2 A.M. might be associated with this military air operation. If, however, these aircraft were noted by either of you, then this would tend to eliminate this air operation as a plausible explanation for the objects observed.

Sincerely,
HECTOR QUINTANILLA, JR., *Major, USAF*
Chief, Project Blue Book
1 atch.
Article "Saturday Review"

Curiously, the letter was not only undated, but the large brown envelope in which it was mailed bore no postmark whatever. The Air Force labels bear the legend POSTAGE AND FEES PAID—DEPARTMENT OF AIR FORCE, so that cancellation is unnecessary.

The letter referred to the sighting as September 2, when of course it took place on September 3. It also indicated that the high-altitude exercises were conducted from midnight until 2 A.M., while the police officers encountered the close-range object at approximately 3 A.M. But most ironical was the indication that the case was still in process of "final evaluation," while the Pentagon had already released its own "final evaluation" over a month before the letter arrived.

Officers Bertrand and Hunt replied to the Air Force with this letter on December 2, 1965:

HECTOR QUINTANILLA, JR., *Major, USAF*
Chief, Project Blue Book
Wright Patterson AFB
Dayton, Ohio

DEAR SIR:

We were very glad to get your letter during the third week in November, because as you might imagine we have been the subject of considerable ridicule since the Pentagon released its "final evaluation" of our sighting of September 3, 1965. In other words, both Ptl. Hunt and myself saw this object at close range, checked it out with each other, confirmed and reconfirmed the fact that this was not any kind of conventional aircraft, that it was at an altitude of not more than a couple of hundred feet, and went to considerable trouble to confirm that the weather was clear, there was no wind, no chance of weather inversion, and that what we were seeing was no illusion or military or civilian craft. We entered this in a complete official police report as a supplement to the blotter of the morning of September 3 (not September 2, as your letter indicates). Since our job depends on accuracy and an ability to tell the difference between fact and fiction, we were naturally disturbed by the Pentagon report which attributed the sighting to "multiple high altitude objects" in the area and "weather inversion." What is a little difficult to understand is the fact that your letter (undated) arrived considerably after the Pentagon release. Since your letter says that you are still in the process of making a final evaluation, it seems that there is an inconsistency here. Ordinarily, this wouldn't be too important except for the fact that in a situation like this we are naturally very reluctant to be considered irresponsible in our official report to the police station.

Since one of us (Ptl. Bertrand) was in the Air Force for four years engaged in refueling operations with all kinds of military aircraft, it was impossible to mistake what we saw for any kind of military operation, regardless of altitude. It was also definitely not a helicopter or balloon. Immediately after the object disappeared, we did see what probably was a B-47 at high altitude, but it bore no relation at all to the object we saw.

Another fact is that the time of our observation was nearly an hour after 2 A.M., which would eliminate the 8th Air Force operation Big Blast, since as you say this took place between midnight and 2 A.M. Norman Muscarello, who first reported this object before we went to the site, saw it somewhere in the vicinity of 2 A.M., but nearly an hour had passed before he got into the police station, and we went out to the location with him.

We would both appreciate it very much if you would help us eliminate the possible conclusion that some people have made in that we might have a) made up the story, or b) were incompetent observers. Anything you could do along this line would be very much appreciated, and I'm sure you can understand the position we're in.

We appreciate the problems the Air Force must have with a lot of irresponsible reports on this subject, and don't want to cause you any unnecessary trouble. On the other hand, we think you probably understand our position.

Thanks very much for your interest.

Sincerely,
PTL. EUGENE BERTRAND
PTL. DAVID HUNT

Nearly a full month went by, but the officers received no reply whatever from Wright-Patterson. Finally, on December 28, the officers wrote again:

HECTOR QUINTANILLA, JR., *Major, USAF*
Wright Patterson AFB
Dayton, Ohio

DEAR SIR:
Since we have not heard from you since our letter to

you of December 2, we are writing this to request some kind of answer, since we are still upset about what happened after the Pentagon released its news saying that we have just seen stars or planets, or high altitude air exercises.

As we mentioned in our letter to you, it could not have been the operation "Big Blast" you mention, since the time of our sighting was nearly an hour after that exercise, and it may not even have been the same date, since you refer to our sighting as September 2. Our sighting was on September 3. In addition, as we mentioned, we are both familiar with all the B-47s and B-52s and helicopters and jet fighters which are going over this place all the time. On top of that Ptl. Bertrand had four years of refueling experience in the Air Force, and knows regular aircraft of all kinds. It is important to remember that this craft we saw was not more than 100 feet in the air, and it was absolutely silent, with no rush of air from jets or chopper blades whatever. And it did not have any wings or tail. It lit up the entire field, and two nearby houses turned completely red. It stopped, hovered, and turned on a dime.

What bothers us most is that many people are thinking that we were either lying or not intelligent enough to tell the difference between what we saw and something ordinary. Three other people saw this same thing on September 3, and two of them appeared to be in shock from it. This was absolutely not a case of mistaken identity.

We both feel that it's very important for our jobs and our reputations to get some kind of letter from you to say that the story put out by the Pentagon was not true; it could not possibly be, because we were the people who saw this; not the Pentagon.

Can you please let us hear from you as soon as possible.

Sincerely,

PTL. EUGENE BERTRAND
PTL. DAVID HUNT

By mid-January, the patrolmen had received no reply. On January 19, 1966, I went to the Pentagon to call on Lt. Col. Matson Jacks, press information officer in the Department of the Air Force, to see if there was some further information available about the case and to try to learn first hand the general attitude of the Air Force beyond its statements of policy.

Colonel Jacks was congenial but not very communicative. He restated the Air Force policy routinely, tapping a pack of Belair cigarettes on his desk and looking nonmilitary in a brown civilian suit.

"We don't attack people who say they saw these things," he said. "We don't really question what a person thinks he saw. We don't quarrel with it. We issue our reports resulting from our investigations, and our conclusions are that UFOs are no threat to national security, and that they are nothing advanced beyond known phenomena. If there's anything to it beyond that, I'd like to be among the first to know."

I asked him if he would like to review the tape recordings of the people I had interviewed in the Exeter area, but he wasn't interested. "I told a neighbor of mine, someone who is supposed to have seen one of these things," he said. "And I said: 'If you want to believe in UFOs, have fun. Enjoy it. God bless you.'"

For statistical information, the colonel brought to his desk Mrs. Sarah Hunt, who handles this in the Community Relations Division of the Office of Information. She would, the colonel explained, have more exact information on the Exeter police case.

When she arrived, I asked her the exact status of the case. "That is one of the few which have been classified as being unidentified," she said. She explained the apparent discrepancy between the Wright-Patterson inquiry, the early, incorrect Pentagon release, the wrong date and time in Major Quintanilla's letter, and the lack of a date on the same letter as a combination of inexperienced secretarial help and the setting up of a new filing system. "You very seldom find these reports jibe as to date and time," the colonel added. When I pointed out that the police officers in Exeter seemed to be rather upset about this, both the colonel and Mrs. Hunt expressed their regrets.

I went to the Community Relations Division on another floor with Mrs. Hunt to arrange for getting more details on the Exeter case. On the way, I indicated to her that the Pentagon's stories and releases simply didn't add up, and that I had trouble believing them. Lt. Col. John F. Spaulding, in charge of the division, told me that he was sure the Exeter case was a case of mistaken identity, but admitted that he had not investigated it personally. I asked him if he were keeping an open mind about the case.

"Are you saying that I'm lying about this?" he asked, with a sudden archness.

"Not at all," I said. "I'm just wondering how you are able to be so certain on the basis of secondhand reports."

The colonel didn't take to this too cheerfully. He drew himself up and said, "Sir, you are talking to an officer in the United States Air Force!"

Then he melodramatically walked off and out of sight. Later, when I said to Mrs. Hunt that it looked as if I had upset the colonel, she told me that he had had a lot of problems on his mind during the day, and wasn't feeling in too good a mood.

In spite of his mood, Colonel Spaulding later sent along copies of many of the records the Air Force had on hand of the Exeter case. Among the points which provided new information were:

—In his signed statement to the Air Force investigators, Patrolman Bertrand said: "At one time [the lights] came so close, I fell on the ground and started to draw my gun." He also noted that the lights were always in line at about a 60-degree angle, and when the object moved, the lower lights were always forward of the others.

—In the official Air Force report of the investigation by the Administrative Services Officer of the Pease Air Force Base to Wright-Patterson, dated September 15, 1965, the following information was included: *Identifying Information on Observer*: (1) Civilian. Norman Muscarello. Age, 18. 205½ Front Street, Exeter, N. H. Unemployed (will join Navy on 18 Sept '65) Appears to be reliable. (2) Civilian. Eugene F. Bertrand, Jr. Age, 30. Exeter Police Department. Patrolman. Reliable. (3) Civilian. David R. Hunt. Age, 28. Exeter Police Department. Patrolman. Reliable.

—In the same official report, a statement by Major

David H. Griffin.* Base Disaster Control Officer, Command pilot. *"At this time have been unable to arrive at a probable cause of this sighting. The three observers seem to be stable, reliable persons, especially the two patrolmen.* I viewed the area of the sighting and found nothing in the area that could be the probable cause. Pease AFB had 5 B-47 aircraft flying in the area during this period *but do not believe they had any connection with the sighting."* (Our italics)

The difference between this report of the actual investigating officer at Pease AFB, and the one officially released by the Pentagon to the local press on October 27 is marked and startling.

When I left Exeter, the sightings were still continuing, seemingly without letup. In the early months of 1966, as many as two or three reports a week were being received by police in the vicinity of the town, one of which induced a dyed-in-the-wool skeptic to run to the police station with a full account of a UFO viewed by at least seven people on February 15, 1966.

The publication of the *Look* article, under the title "Outer Space Ghost Story" brought a wave of reaction from all over the country. Letters poured in from obviously intelligent and reliable people who had never before been willing to reveal sightings of UFOs of their own. I was invited to appear on many major network television and radio shows, that had previously steered away from the subject. Even the Voice of America recorded a 40-minute interview with me on the Exeter incident. In all these interviews, I pointed out that Exeter was only one location of many, that the story was growing more intense daily everywhere in the world. On Christmas Eve, before the *Look* piece had appeared, I was interviewed by U Thant's Chef de Cabinet on the research I had completed for the article. Since then, the UN has expressed serious interest in the phenomenon.

* The Exeter police recalled the name of the investigating officer as Major Thomas Griffin. Both men are at the base.

On the discussion program *The Open Mind,* moderated by Dr. Eric Goldman, on leave from Princeton University to act as academic adviser to President Johnson, I met with Dr. Menzel, head of the Harvard University observatory, Dr. Hyneck of Northwestern, Dr. Sprinkle of the University of Wyoming and Dr. Salisbury of Colorado State University. Only Dr. Menzel precluded the possibility that UFOs could be a reality, but his reasoning was so resistant to new evidence that had developed that we engaged in a rather sharp exchange of words on the air. His answer to the Exeter case was that the policemen involved were "hysterical subjects," but he could not even recall their names on the air, had never met them, had not investigated the case personally at all. His answer to the Beaver Falls, Pennsylvania, photograph was that it "appeared to be a double exposure"—yet he did not know the name of the photographer, knew nothing about the circumstances under which the picture was taken, had not examined the negatives, nor talked with any of the photographers who had done so. I was surprised and startled that a man of Dr. Menzel's standing could make such flat, unsubstantiated statements publicly. It seemed to symbolize the resistance of part of the scientific fraternity to approach the subject with an open mind.

*   *   *

On February 9, 1966, the day after the *Look* article appeared on the newsstands, the Pentagon finally wrote a letter of apology to Patrolmen Bertrand and Hunt:

DEPARTMENT OF THE AIR FORCE
Washington

OFFICE OF THE SECRETARY   *February 9, 1966*

GENTLEMEN:

Based on additional information you submitted to our UFO investigation office at Wright-Patterson Air Force Base, Ohio, we have been unable to identify the object you observed on September 3, 1965. In 19 years of investigating over 10,000 reports of unidentified flying objects, the evidence has proved almost conclusively that reported aerial phenomena have been objects either created or set aloft by man, generated by atmospheric conditions, or caused by celestial bodies or the residue of meteoric activity.

Thank you for reporting your observation to the Air Force and for your subsequent cooperation regarding the report. I regret any inconvenience you may have suffered as a result.

Sincerely,
[s] JOHN P. SPAULDING
LT. COL., USAF
Chief, Civil Branch
Community Relations Division
Office of Information.

MR. EUGENE BERTRAND, JR.
MR. DAVID R. HUNT
EXETER POLICE DEPARTMENT
EXETER, NEW HAMPSHIRE

In thinking back over the research, the highlights that stand out on those points detailed in this book that are almost irrefutable:

—Dozens of intelligent, reliable people reported UFO sightings, many reluctantly because of the fear of ridicule.

—Most of these reports were widely separated, and the people concerned were not involved in any collusion.

—Most of the sightings were similar in description, in spite of minor variations which can be expected, and should be expected, from varied viewpoints.

—Police and military were reporting the same type of phenomenon as the ordinary layman.

—The constant relationship of UFOs to the high-tension power lines of the Northeast Grid was inescapable.

—The constant reports of the effect of UFOs on animals pointed up the possibility that human error was unlikely in these cases.

—The reports of electromagnetic effects on lights, ignition, radios and television indicated a similar conclusion.

—Photographs checked by experts, with full character investigation of the photographer, added further evidence that psychic aberrations, mass hypnosis or hysteria or mistaken identity could be ruled out.

—The verified cases of genuine shock and hysteria indicated further that the low-level, near-landing reports were valid.

—Radar reports and scrambling jets chasing the objects indicated that the Air Force was not only cognizant of the objects, but appeared to be impotent to do anything about them.

—Federal Aviation Agency regulations minimized the possibility that the craft were developmental weapons of the United States, since such craft would not be permitted to operate at such low altitudes in populated areas, causing shock and hysteria to the population.

—Secret foreign craft would be unlikely because such actions in the violation of air space would have long since brought about an international incident, just as the single case of the U-2 over Russia had done.

The most logical, but still unprovable explanation is that the Unidentified Flying Objects are interplanetary spaceships under intelligent control. NICAP and others have been supporting this hypothesis for years. Its credibility, however, has suffered by the support of the crackpot fringe. In spite of this, the hypothesis remains stronger than any other theory advanced.

The biggest remaining question is the apparent attitude of government and scientific authorities who have shown no indication of setting up a full-scale project either to prove or disprove the existence of UFOs. Or if they have, the ostensible paternalistic protection of the public is not consistent with democratic principles. The reaction of those who have experienced close encounters with UFOs in the Exeter area has been one of shock, followed by intense curiosity rather than sustained panic. An unprepared public is far more likely to panic than an informed one. Truth isn't likely to remain hidden forever.

In the light of recent developments, the situation has reached a point where it appears to be the duty and responsibility of the Government either to reveal what it knows, or to order a scientific investigation on a major scale and report the findings immediately to the public at large.

BERKLEY BOOKS ON THE OCCULT

THE EDGE OF THE UNKNOWN   (S1626—75¢)
  Sir Arthur Conan Doyle

SENSE AND NONSENSE OF PROPHECY
  Eileen J. Garrett   (S1636—75¢)

WINGED PHAROAH   (N1646—95¢)
  Joan Grant

THEY FORESAW THE FUTURE   (Z1833—$1.25)
  Justine Glass

INCIDENT AT EXETER   (Z2539—$1.25)
  John G. Fuller

THE SECRETS OF NUMBERS   (N2532—95¢)
  Vera Johnson & Thomas Wommack

Send for a *free* list of all our books in print

These books are available at your local newsstand, or send
price indicated plus 25¢ per copy to cover mailing costs to
Berkley Publishing Corporation, 200 Madison Avenue, New
York, N.Y. 10016

50